CATHERINE BATESON

Lisette's Paris Notebook

ALLEN&UNWIN

SYDNEY · MELBOURNE · AUCKLAND · LONDON

This project has been assisted by the Australian Government through the Australia Council, its arts funding and advisory body.

Australian Government

Australia Council for the Arts

First published by Allen & Unwin in 2017

Allen & Unwin
83 Alexander Street
Crows Nest NSW 2065
Australia
Phone: (61 2) 8425 0100
Email: info@allenandunwin.com
Web: www.allenandunwin.com

Allen & Unwin – UK
Ormond House, 26–27 Boswell Street,
London WC1N 3JZ, UK
Phone: +44 (0) 20 8785 5995
Email: info@murdochbooks.co.uk
Web: www.murdochbooks.co.uk

A Cataloguing-in-Publication entry is available from the National Library of Australia: www.trove.nla.gov.au. A catalogue record for this book is available from the British Library.

ISBN (AUS) 978 1 76029 363 5
ISBN (UK) 978 1 74336 956 2

Cover and text design by Debra Billson
Cover images by Hanna Bobrova, Anna Kozlenko/123RF, and Nancy White/Shutterstock
Internal images by DeAssuncao_Creation/Shutterstock, moloko88 and Anna Kozlenko/123RF, and Nancy White/Shutterstock
Set in 11.5/16 pt Adobe Garamond Pro by Midland Typesetters, Australia
Printed in Australia by McPherson's Printing Group

10 9 8 7 6 5 4 3 2 1

MIX
Paper from responsible sources
FSC www.fsc.org **FSC® C001695**

The paper in this book is FSC® certified. FSC® promotes environmentally responsible, socially beneficial and economically viable management of the world's forests.

For Helen – her summer book, at last!

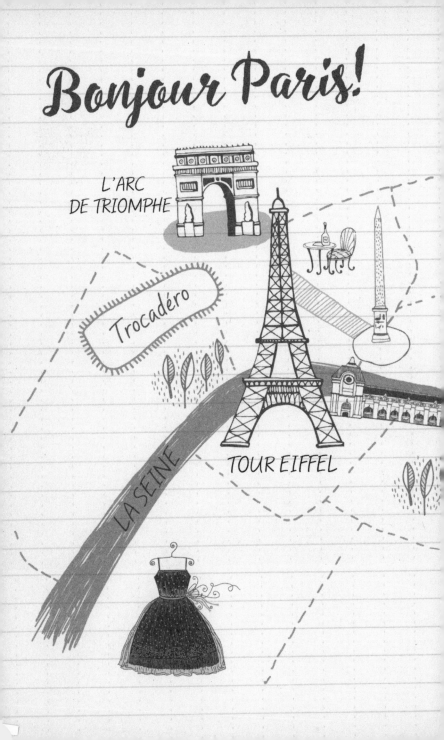

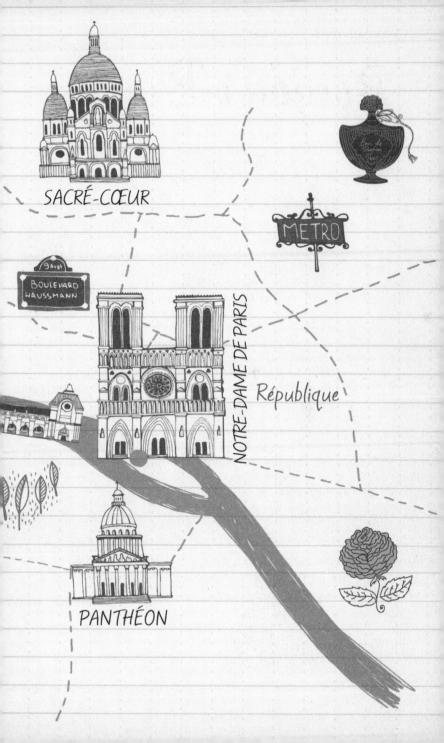

SACRÉ-CŒUR

METRO

BOULEVARD HAUSSMANN

NOTRE-DAME DE PARIS

République

PANTHÉON

Chapter

1

What do you wear to Paris? Ami and I discussed it for hours but I still couldn't think of anything suitable. Ami said a trench coat with nothing underneath but your best underwear. That was only if some boy was meeting you at the airport, I said.

By the time I landed in Paris, the anger that had burned with wildfire intensity during the first leg of the journey was a pile of hot ashes somewhere between my heart and my stomach, right around where my Vivienne-circa-1970s-inspired tartan kilt strained against the airline food, popping open the smallest safety pin. Anger was replaced by the equally uncomfortable emotion of fear.

Would I be able to understand anything? How did the airport train work? Where was my apartment? What the hell was I doing in Paris?

But I knew what the hell I was doing in Paris and that sailed me through the passport check, the baggage claim and on to the RER platform without faltering. It carried me right past the suburbs, which were like ugly suburbs anywhere, to the correct station, up the stairs lugging my suitcase and out into Paris proper. Paris and Notre-Dame!

'Oh my God!' I said, and then corrected myself, 'Oh mon Dieu!'

Until that moment I had not believed in Paris. It was a city that existed in movies, *Vogue* magazines, my French teacher's memories and my mother's imagination. I'd read about it, I'd seen it once removed, I'd even talked about it in French conversation classes. I took three steadying breaths, shouldered my backpack and grasped my suitcase handle more firmly. This was *my* city for the summer. This was where I would conquer my fears and remake myself. I'd arrived a caterpillar – okay, a caterpillar in plaid and safety pins – but I would transform into a butterfly. I hoped.

I walked across the bridges (the Seine! a barge decked out as a tourist boat! pale stone and orange shutters!) and past a square, nervously checking my map as I went, and wishing I'd allowed myself some data coverage. Google Maps – I missed it already! Some of the smaller streets just weren't on my flimsy piece of paper. My sense of direction, which worked in the Southern Hemisphere, had gone on strike in Europe. (Europe!) My suitcase bumped and wobbled over the cobblestones. (Cobblestones!)

I found my street, which was really an alley, purely by accident, and by that time my suitcase wheels were complaining. I walked past the back doors of cafes and restaurants and the kitchen staff, idly smoking, checked me out. I tugged at my tartan skirt. Probably should have put that zip in: the safety pins didn't feel secure enough for Paris. *Paris!* My heart did a little extra thump just for that word. Soon I'd be sipping café au lait at the front of one of those cafes, I promised myself, not skulking past the dishies on their smoke-o.

Further along the street a young woman scooped up water from the gutter to wash her face. She had such bad bed hair that it was matted in thick dreads at the back. I tried not to stare at her. I gripped my suitcase tightly and strode past her and her bundle of belongings. She was only slightly older than me and living in a doorway. That wasn't the Paris of old movies.

My building, however, was and seeing it in real life lifted my heart again. It was six storeys high and each window was decorated with its own box of flowers. On the ground floor was the shop, La Librairie Occulte, owned by Madame Christophe, my mother's clairvoyant and my landlady – concierge? – for the summer.

I peered through the window. It was just like any bookshop catering for weirdo mystics. There were salt lamps, crystals and piles of incense. All the signs were in French, although some boasted a small English translation for the tourists. In a corner of the room there was a woman working on a laptop. I pushed open the door, setting chimes ringing, and squeezed between the bookcases and display cabinets. Sweat had begun to bead on my forehead and I knew the stale airline food smell clung to my clothes. I'd left Melbourne in tartan-and-tights-weather and arrived in Paris on an early summer day.

3

'Bonjour, Madame,' I said in my best French accent. 'I'm Lise.' Back home, I'd been Lisi despite being christened Lisette by my romantic Francophile mother. In Paris I'd be Lise, silent 'e' and more sophisticated. It was my bon voyage present to myself.

'I have expected you,' the woman said. She shut the laptop and lifted the smallest dog in the world from her lap and tucked it under one arm. When she stood up I could see that she was wearing a charcoal grey sleeveless shift, more Chanel than clairvoyant, and a scarf that changed from ruby red to dark purple, depending on where the light caught it. She came from behind the desk to air kiss each of my cheeks and I could smell expensive perfume, rather than incense. She was perfectly balanced on stilettos and even the wrinkles on her face were designer.

'You must take after your father,' she said, holding me at arm's length. 'Your mother is quite round, yes? With curls? Your father is tall and fair, yes?'

Up until only a while ago I would not have been able to answer that question. For years my mother had acted almost as though I'd been immaculately conceived – but now my backpack contained four photos of my father and yes, I was definitely his daughter. I nodded.

'Welcome to Paris, Lisette.'

'Actually, I'm called Lise.'

'In Paris you will be Lisette. This is Napoléon. Come, I will show you the apartment.'

I didn't have time to even pat the dog before Madame

4

Christophe popped him in his basket, clipped out a back door and then smartly up five floors of steps. I dragged my suitcase behind her, panting, until we reached the very top. Madame Christophe flung the door open. 'Voilà!'

I'd expected some kind of kitchen and a balcony with a proper table and two chairs. There would be a view of the Eiffel Tower, the Sacré-Cœur or something else iconic. I didn't even have a balcony. I stood in the smallest 'apartment' in the world. It was effectively one room with a kind of kitchen annexe. I pushed past the bed and opened one of the windows. The air was still and hot. I looked up and down the narrow street. If I stood on tiptoe I could just glimpse the Seine. That was something.

'I will leave you to make yourself comfortable,' Madame Christophe said sternly. 'The bathroom is on the landing. Practically an ensuite. You will share it with no one as everyone is in the South.' She turned on her heel and clipped back down the stairs.

Apart from an ugly chest of drawers and the bed, the apartment was empty, which was a good thing in one way as there wasn't room for anything else. Where was the antique four-poster bed, the heavy wardrobe I'd imagined filling, and the washbasin stand?

I unpacked my suitcase and slid it under the bed. Apart from my 1970s Westwood tartan phase, I'd also embraced a kind of grungy seventies aesthetic based on op-shopping, upcycling and some of my own sewing. When I had first agreed to go to Paris, Mum had been really excited. She'd studied the latest issues of French *Vogue*, sketched designs and looked at fabric samples. She is the seamstress, I just sew. She'd wanted a whole upmarket hippy look – wafty cream silks, pale linen wide-legged trousers as far from my old fisherman's trousers as oysters are from battered flake.

'But everyone wears that kind of stuff,' I'd said, stabbing my finger at a perfectly beautiful maxi dress that was, the caption told us, 'mousseline de soie incrustée de dentelle', which translates as unbelievably expensive.

'Hardly,' Mum said, 'not at that price!'

'You know what I mean.'

'I'm not offering French lace, Lisette. Just something more . . . elegant and grown-up?'

I was all dress-ups – I could hardly escape fashion, living with a seamstress, but I'd wanted my own spin on it. In the end, I'd let her help me make a maxi skirt. I'd imagined a fabric with a sugar-skull pattern but we'd negotiated on tissue-thin gauzy stuff instead, subtly patterned with tiny skulls. It was almost too cool but Mum talked me into it. She also insisted on lining the skirt to just below my knees. I felt like a proper adult when I swished into my next French class to show it off.

'Isn't it perfect?' I asked Madame Desnois.

'You will feel alien,' she prophesised. 'It is more London than Paris. The French are more chic than' – she searched for an adequate word – 'punk.'

'This is high-class punk,' I explained, 'this is punk couture.'

Now, leaning out the window into the heat, I wondered if I shouldn't have made just one white or cream top. Why hadn't

I packed sandals? It was just too hard to think of summer in the Melbourne winter and I hadn't wanted to listen to Mum's advice at that point. My French boy would buy me clothes. He'd dress me up to meet his parents who'd live in the country somewhere smelling of lavender. His parents would be charmed by my skull theme and his father would pour me a vin ordinaire and teach me to roll my 'r's the way Madame Desnois wanted.

I tested the bed. My feet stuck over the edge. The pillow was a long sausage that squished flat as soon as my head touched it. I'll just close my eyes for a few minutes, I promised myself. Just five minutes.

I stayed there, drifting in and out of consciousness, the sounds from the street wafting up through the window, until someone called up the stairwell, 'Lisette! Lisette! À table!'

'Some French girl,' I thought sleepily. 'There's another girl up here. That's nice.' Then I woke up properly and remembered that Lisette was me, I was Lisette.

I followed the smell of coffee to a small room that was Madame Christophe's living room. A round table in one corner had been set for two. The plunger coffee was strong and served with long-life milk. The baguette had some kind of good, nutty cheese balanced on top of ham, a smear of mustard and a decent slather of butter. I wasn't hungry but hunger wasn't necessary. I ate my portion and crusty crumbs flew over the lace tablecloth. Madame Christophe sipped her coffee and looked away. I could hear myself chewing.

'You must walk,' she said when I'd finished.

'Walk?' I was still exhausted and my stomach was full. The dog was asleep in his basket and I wanted to curl up, just like him. My eyes felt scratchy with invisible grit. I'd been awake for nearly twenty hours straight if you didn't count cat naps. Couldn't walking wait?

'Walk,' she repeated. 'You must walk until dinnertime, then you come back and eat, if you can, and go to bed. It is necessary to defeat the jet lag.'

'I'm tired now,' I said, but Madame Christophe ignored me and cleared away the crockery.

I trudged back up all the flights of stairs to get my backpack and camera and then all the way back down.

'You are not taking that?' Madame Christophe eyed my canvas backpack.

'Why not?'

'It is like a tourist.'

'Don't French girls carry backpacks?'

'Of course not. We have the handbag, the clutch or the pochette. And there are thieves.'

'A thief couldn't get into this,' I said, pointing out the buckles.

'But they do. They have the knives.' Madame Christophe mimed a knife slicing the canvas straps.

'It's all I've got,' I said. 'I'll be fine.'

'You do not carry anything valuable?' Madame Christophe said. 'You have not your passport?'

'Of course not.'

She shrugged in a resigned way and then pushed me out

into the street. It was only after the door had closed that I remembered I had left my map behind. I could easily have gone back in, but Madame Christophe was watching me from near the tarot display. I stuck my head in the air, shouldered my backpack and set off walking in what I hoped was a good direction.

Everything was old. Everywhere I looked was another old building. It wasn't even as though they were monuments, they were just buildings. I tried to memorise which way I'd gone but the streets curved and twisted and, at one point, I went down an alley and ended up back where I'd just been. Within fifteen minutes I had no idea which direction I'd started out from. I sat for a while in a square opposite an impressive building. It was the Hôtel de Ville – the Town Hall of Paris! – but I couldn't stop myself from yawning.

'Eavesdrop,' Madame Desnois had advised. 'Wherever you are, listen to the people. Of course, there are not so many French in Paris in summer, but you will still hear the language.'

I tried to eavesdrop, but it was too hard. The couple closest to me, both eating ice-creams, were definitely not French. There was an American woman with a couple of kids nagging her for McDonalds. An intense conversation between an older couple was in French – I caught isolated words – but it was too fast and private for me to follow. I sat there until I was in danger of falling asleep in the sun and then I started walking again.

Old buildings and old streets were great, but there were rules for walking in Paris that I didn't know yet. You couldn't stop and gawp or people ran into you. You certainly couldn't take photos or people muttered at you under their breath. You didn't stare at the beggar with the cats on leads or he would hold out his hand for change you didn't yet have. You certainly didn't stop where the woman knelt on the pavement as though praying, her hands holding a small paper begging cup. Who could do that? On the dirty footpath? It was all utterly – and wonderfully – overwhelming.

Then I found the BHV, a huge department store with five levels of shopping, French style. Dogs shopping along with their owners! I tried to pat one and was snarled at by both it and its mistress.

'There are rules of etiquette,' I remembered Madame Desnois telling me anxiously. 'Lisette, I don't think you quite understand how formal the French can be.'

Apparently you needed an introduction before you patted someone's dog. How was I going to survive twelve weeks without anyone, not even the dogs, talking to me? I started with the clothes. They were expensive, but so chic and French. Even though I was definitely not chic, in my cobbled-together kilt, maybe I would be by the time I left Paris? These clothes floated from their hangers, elegantly declaiming their desirability. Well, I'm here now, I thought, so I explored each floor of the BHV as though I was desperate for beach towels, new shoes, baby clothes, picture frames and even DIY tools, which I discovered in the basement. Despite the snarling dogs, the supercilious shop assistants and the other shoppers who ignored me, the store was a cocoon. I wasn't jostled and no one begged for money. I'd have time to get used to the real Paris, I thought, when I was less tired, more confident and not wearing heavy Docs.

By the time I left the store it was late afternoon, although still very light. I walked out onto a different street and had no idea where I was. I should have taken photos with my phone of my directions, like Hansel and Gretel leaving crumbs in the fairytale. Around me was a surge of Parisians, all the women wearing high heels and scarves, all the men in designer crumpled linen and polished, beautiful shoes. I ended up on a larger street, near a group of food shops. Dinner. My stomach growled.

It would have to be classic for my first night in Paris. My first night in Paris, I repeated to myself, cheering up instantly. Goat's cheese – I could say that to the shopkeeper and I did when he finally turned to me. Who knew there would be so many different kinds? I gave up trying to understand what he was saying and just pointed to a pretty pyramid, and then another wrapped in a grape leaf. I bought a supermarket baguette – it would do until I found a proper bakery – and I tried to ignore the mouth-watering smell of the rotisserie chicken. I wouldn't be able to eat a whole one and I couldn't remember how to say free-range in French.

Surprisingly, there was a carousel on the street, right next to a metro station – and a map. I couldn't find my street on it. My feet were aching and I wanted a shower more than anything else in the world.

'Excuse me, honey.' A woman approached, holding

something out. 'This might be more detailed.' Her words were molasses-slow, in contrast to the low, rapid speech around us. She carried an impressive handbag firmly tucked under one arm. It was a bigger version of the anti-theft one Mum had tried to foist onto me before I left. Even if I hadn't heard her voice I would have known she was American from her flat shoes, which, no matter how much they tried to look otherwise with cute straps and colourful soles, were just fancy runners.

'I can't read a map worth a dime,' she said, 'but if you turn it around and around, sometimes you get lucky. You know what I mean?'

Together we turned the map until we found my street and then she pulled out a purple pen and outlined my route. 'You take it,' she said. 'They're free and my husband's collected half a dozen already. I just skip monument to monument myself – you memorise a few and they'll take you all the way home. Metro stations are useful, too – hell, they *are* monuments over here.'

Her name was Ginger, she said, and she offered me a hot chocolate. I was about to refuse when I caught something in her eyes, behind the purple-framed spectacles, that reminded me of how lost I felt.

'I'd love that,' I said, 'if you have the time.'

'I've got time,' she said firmly. 'I've got all the time in the world. Todd's in back-to-back meetings until dinner and dinner's an age away. They all eat so late over here. I guess that's European but I'm ready to eat an alligator by the time we finally sit down.'

We found a cafe and sat, rather doubtfully, side by side. The chairs were all lined up to face the street.

'I'm not used to this,' I whispered to her. 'In Melbourne, even outside, the chairs are arranged so you can talk.'

'It is so you can watch the people,' the waiter, who had snuck up behind us, informed me haughtily. 'In Paris we watch the people, the life, the fashions. In Melbourne, perhaps not so much?'

'I don't think he was real fond of your outfit,' Ginger said when he'd whisked away with our order. 'It's a little out there.'

'It's not that bad,' I said, pulling at the skirt to align the safety pins. 'But I know what you mean.'

'At least you speak some French,' she said comfortingly. 'That will definitely help.'

I wasn't so sure. Even though I had ordered in French, our waiter had replied in English. It was only my first day – I clung to that thought.

'You're so brave,' Ginger told me as we said goodbye, 'when I was your age I was doodling wedding dresses in the margins of my college books.'

'But you're here now.'

'Sure. That's what counts,' she said, but she didn't sound terribly certain. 'You have – what do they say? Bonne chance, you hear!'

I followed the purple line all the way back to Madame Christophe's and was about to knock on the closed shop door, but she popped out as if she'd been waiting, still in stilettos, scarf and fresh lipstick.

Chapter

2

*Paris is the centre of haute couture and all things stylish.
That's why Mum insisted on me learning French, the language
of Chanel. My great-grandmother owned a Chanel jacket.
It was called 'The Jacket', and she wore it on every grand
occasion for as long as she could fit into it. Even now
The Jacket, which hangs in my mother's studio like the
piece of art it is, smells faintly of Greatma's perfume.
Already Paris makes me feel gawky, as though I
were thirteen again, copying the Year Ten girls.*

'I did not have a chance to give you the door code. And you have no sense of direction, so you were lost,' Madame Christophe said, with some satisfaction, I thought.

It wasn't a question but I answered anyway. 'I met a woman, we had hot chocolate together and she gave me a map.' I flourished it as proof.

'An American. They have no memory, but large collections

of maps. And before this American with her collection, what did you do? No, don't tell me. You went to a shop. That is what you did. Your first afternoon in Paris and you shopped.'

'I bought some goat's cheese.' I proffered the bag. 'One is like a little pyramid. The other's wrapped in a vine leaf. So pretty!'

'That you would have bought on the way home. No one buys chèvre on the way out. You found the BHV.'

'After walking for ages.' Why did she have to sound so condemnatory?

'Notre-Dame is across the Seine. There is also the Tuileries if you walk far enough. The Jardin des Plantes. But no, you visited a shop? Never mind. We remedy all tomorrow. For now you had better eat your chèvre and then sleep.'

I wanted to set up wi-fi on my laptop but apparently one couldn't do that in the evening. Perhaps it interfered with Madame Christophe's digestion? She would let me know how to log in at breakfast. She had already informed my mother of my safe arrival so I need not be anxious about that. Perhaps I should study my map and plan some instructive days in Paris, rather than wasting my time at the BHV? Clearly I would have to skip monument to monument to satisfy Madame Christophe.

I trudged upstairs to the bed that was too short for me. My first day was over. Mostly successful, I allowed myself, ticking off the pluses on my fingers: I had managed the airport and the RER, I'd found my apartment and met my . . . met Madame Christophe. I had become completely lost but the afternoon had been salvaged by meeting Ginger and managing my first cafe, Parisian style. I'd eaten baguette and goat's cheese for dinner. I hadn't needed to talk to Mum. I'd even squeezed myself into the miniscule shower in my 'practically an ensuite' and washed my hair. Not bad.

The next morning it was clear that not everyone had left Paris for the summer. It was six-thirty and I could hear the discrete sounds of people leaving their apartments. I was in Paris, the City of Love, and I would show Madame Christophe that I wasn't at all interested in shopping. (Although I had seen some very cute earrings.)

I was expected – or permitted? – to breakfast with Madame Christophe each day. It was an agreement Mum and Madame Christophe had come to – partly, I was sure, so that Mum could keep a virtual eye on me. When I sauntered down, wearing a black T-shirt with braces, tartan shorts, knee-high socks and my Docs, I found the table set for an intimate petite déjeuner of croissants – surprise, surprise. Napoléon was already at Madame Christophe's feet, looking up at the pastry while trying to maintain a certain emperor-like dignity.

'I am organising you,' Madame said, pouring coffee into my cup. 'A friend of mine runs French classes for the art students and I have managed to convince her to put you in her class. It is a rare privilege.'

'No need to do that,' I said. 'I'll improve as I go along. It'll be easy – I'll just talk French to everyone. We could, too?'

Madame Christophe gave me a long, pitying look. 'I need to practise my English,' she said. 'Also, your mother does not want you shopping. You are here to learn things.'

'Madame Christophe, I don't mean to offend you, but I am not a child. I am old enough to make my own decisions about what I do.' Why did everyone think I needed every single thing decided for me?

But Madame Christophe had moved on and was reading the paper as she delicately dunked her croissant in a big milky bowl of coffee. Disgusting. Then she tore off the end and fed it to Napoléon. He growled at me. He was siding with his mistress.

Madame Christophe said something softly in French but Napoléon bared his teeth, which although small were sharp, despite an apparent diet of croissant.

'Napoléon, this is our guest,' she said severely, although I felt her tone was directed at me, rather than her absurd dog. Madame Christophe seemed to expect me to say something to him.

'Good morning, Napoléon,' I said. 'It's a big name for such a small dog.'

'He was a small man, Napoléon Bonaparte. He was not, of course, French.'

I bit the inside of my cheek to prevent myself spluttering croissant across the table. Was she implying that Bonaparte would have been taller if he'd been French? And if he wasn't French, what was he?

There was an awkward pause while I swallowed laughter and pastry.

'I had no idea,' I said conversationally, 'that he was short. Or that he wasn't French. I didn't do history.'

This, unfortunately, captured her full attention. 'What do you mean, you did not "do" history? What is this "do"? Of course *you* do not do history. History, it is made, not done. Do you mean you did not study history? *That* is an outrage.'

'Oh, we did Australian history in primary school.'

'Australian history. That would not have taken so long,' she said and disappeared my country with a snap of her fingers. 'You should have studied the history of Europe. Europe shapes the world.'

'What about China?' I asked. 'China's important.'

China was dismissed with an eloquent shrug. I reminded myself to tell Ami. She would have something to say about that!

'It is excellent that you are to study French with my friend. You will find her knowledge and opinions extend beyond language. She is a woman of decision and elegance – her shoes! Oh là là! You will benefit. It will cost only ten euros for a lesson and you will attend twice a week. I will show you on the plan where to go.'

'I'm not at all sure about attending French lessons.'

'Your mother agrees with me. Ten euros is nothing compared to the education you will gain. An opportunity resembling this does not often happen.'

Ten euros a lesson – twenty euros a week. What was Mum thinking? I had to Skype her!

I told Madame Christophe firmly that I had to arrange internet access as soon as possible. I also ate a second croissant, avoiding Madame's lifted eyebrow.

The wi-fi was easier to set up than negotiating a French mobile SIM card, which took forever. It was late in the afternoon by the time I got on to Mum.

'It's fantastic,' she said. 'Darling Sylvie has been able to organise—'

'I know, right? At the cost of twenty euros a week, Mum! Do you know how much that adds up to by the end of my stay?'

'It's such a great opportunity, Lisi – you simply can't walk away from that. Also, it's a way to meet other kids. What I would have done at your age to learn French in Paris, Lisi!'

'It's not in my budget,' I said flatly. 'I want to go out too. I want to be able to eat an ice-cream in the Tuileries and there's no point in meeting people if I can't afford to go clubbing with them.'

'Lisi, you don't even like clubbing!'

'Well, whatever. The thing is, Mum, I'm making my own decisions now.'

'Lisi, I thought learning French in Paris was your dream?'

There was the problem. Mum had summed it up with unusual clarity. *She* thought this was *my* dream. If it had been left up to me, I wouldn't have even taken a gap year. I would have gone to uni with Ami and hung out in the cafes and bars. But it was useless telling Mum that. It was useless arguing against her. She was too persuasive. She had it firmly fixed in her head that a gap year was essential and three months in Paris would set me up for the years of study ahead. In the end, I'd taken up her idea of coming to Paris as much to find myself, away from her, as to discover Paris. Sure, I could justify it by saying I was here for the art – an opportunity to see the real things before studying Arts (if that was what I was going to do). If I'd been driven by any real ambition, I could have stood up to Mum. But I didn't have a clear picture of my future self. Who was I? Who could I become? I was far less interested in the labyrinths of the Louvre than I was in the secrets of my own heart. I loved being able to speak French, sure. It had great show-off cred – but was it my actual heart-felt, close-held *dream*?

'I'll transfer the money tomorrow,' Mum said, and I could hear the resignation in her voice. 'It can be my little gift.'

'It's not about the money,' I said. I'd started with the wrong argument and I'd lost. It was going to end up like everything else – I'd resist, briefly, then surrender and the lines between what I wanted and what Mum wanted would blur as though they were drawn in charcoal, not permanent ink.

'Then what is it?'

I sighed. I needed a clearer outline of myself, but even this far from home I was all shade and shadow. If I argued with Mum she just became sad, hardly ever angry. Her sadness made my edges collapse.

'It's just that I don't like having something like this foisted on me.'

'But darling, travel means taking up opportunities. I thought we'd agreed on that. This is clearly an opportunity.'

We'd agreed? I couldn't argue anymore. 'According to an

American woman I met, travel is skipping from monument to monument.'

'I'm sure you'll have time to do that too. The lessons are only twice a week. You'll have them with a bunch of art students. It's very generous of Sylvie to organise them. I do hope you sounded grateful, Lisi, and didn't display that sulky teenage side.'

'Mum! You're treating me like a kid!'

'Sorry,' she said, 'I think the connection is a little problematic. I can't really hear you. I'll put the money in your account and you make the most of this, Lisi, okay? I'm trusting you to do that. I can't wait to hear all about it. Love you. Love you so much, darling.'

'Love you, too,' I replied automatically. It was interesting that the Skype connection was clear enough for her to deliver a mini lecture, but too dodgy for her to hear my side of the argument.

I got up and looked out the window. The small street was cobblestoned. I could see half a dozen people wandering past and as many dogs. There were two couples, leaning into each other as they walked. I supposed I could find out more about the lessons. Who were these art students? Maybe it wasn't such a bad idea. Art students were bound to be interesting, if a bit hipster. Suddenly it didn't sound so pedestrian to be taking French lessons in Paris.

I could see myself at uni the following year, dipping a croissant in my latte and saying, 'Of course, I was in Paris, learning French and living with this mad clairvoyant my mother had met over the internet. Madame had the smallest dog in the world called Napoléon, because he was a short man and not French.'

'Wow!' my audience would exclaim. 'That must have been so awesome.'

The story would be better with a French romantic interest. He'd have that kind of hair that droops into one eye. I clearly wasn't going to meet a French boy at French class, but the other students would have friends and they'd be French artists. We'd all go clubbing or whatever you did in France – probably something more philosophical. He'd call me Lise from the start, but maybe Lisette when he was being romantic. We'd drink absinthe. Actually, I probably wouldn't. I don't drink anything green. But I could pretend.

To be honest, I hadn't had a great deal of success with Australian boyfriends – but that was to be expected at my school. The hot boys were interested in two things only: sport and sex. The physics nerds couldn't look at girls without stuttering. Then there'd been Ben. He'd managed whole sentences. Not that it mattered in the end.

If a French boyfriend presented himself, I'd certainly say yes to opportunity!

Chapter 3

STILETTOS

I don't wear them. Neither does my mother. Although she does wear their younger sister, kitten heels. High heels were originally invented so the wealthy could rise above the mud and crap (literally) that flowed down the city streets. Then in the 1950s, a Frenchman revisited that idea, but gave it his own sadistic twist by narrowing the heel to the stiletto as we know it; capable of performing a lobotomy at a pinch. I wear flat shoes. I like to pretend I'm firmly grounded and anchored to the world.

The French lessons were on Tuesday and Thursday mornings at ten-thirty and lasted for two hours, Madame Christophe told me, or until her friend Fabienne, Madame Fontaine, decided to stop. She was generous with her time. Until Tuesday, Madame Christophe recommended I improve my mind.

'The Louvre?' I asked, unfolding my map.

'Definitely before the Americans arrive for the summer. But perhaps first the more intimate Musée d'Orsay or Musée de l'Orangerie.' Of course, she added, if I preferred to shop, and she could quite understand that I needed some good clothes, there were many beautiful boutiques in the arrondissement, but really I'd be better off waiting for the sales. That's what Parisians did. The sales would begin at the end of the month and last for six weeks. I would have plenty of time to choose my purchases before the end of my Paris stay.

Clearly I was never going to convince her that I wasn't a confirmed shopper.

With this advice, my interview was over and Madame Christophe sallied forth with Napoléon for his morning walk after reiterating that I was to provide my own lunch and dinner, implying that the breakfast deal should make me feel special. It was a rare arrangement.

I trudged back up the stairs to chart my route. I was going to work this city out. Ten minutes later I was doing exactly that. Along the Seine, past the bookstalls I'd seen in photos – most of which, admittedly were shut up and locked. Every so often I stopped and pinched myself. I was walking along the Seine! I was in Paris! I took a billion photos.

I wasn't sure what kind of drugs Madame Christophe had been taking with her breakfast, but to call the Musée d'Orsay 'intimate' was like saying a Great Dane was a tad larger than Napoléon – the dog, that is. The place was huge and jam-packed with famous art. What else had I expected? Except this was famous famous. I'd turn a corner and there would be another painting I recognised from a reproduction – Van Gogh, Degas, Rodin. I couldn't take it all in.

After about two hours of walking, the paintings began to blur. I was arted-out. It was clear that others felt the same – there were people sitting on bench seats, dazed expressions plastered on their faces. Couples were okay – they could hold each other's hand or kiss. I wished that I were part of a couple. I contemplated that as I sat beside some girls who were checking their phones and talking in both French and, perhaps, Italian at the same time. The three of them wore wedges – no wonder they were sitting down!

Why don't I have a boyfriend? An essay in one hundred words by Lisette Addams.

I don't have a boyfriend because Sally, my mum, was ditched by my father before I was even born and hasn't trusted heterosexual men ever since. Also, she doesn't go out much, so snogging opportunities were strictly limited in our house. Who wants to make out to the sound of your mum's sewing machine? Plus, she's on a lifelong quest for perfection and no member of the male gender is ever going to cut it. Then there's me – I wasn't brought up to know about football, camping holidays or other team sports. I can set a table for four courses, recognise a fish knife, a Chanel and a bias cut. Ami, my best friend, calls my home The House of Estrogen. I'd say those are major hurdles when it comes to the opposite sex.

Despite that I did have a boyfriend briefly but it ended when we tried to have sex. I still don't want to talk about it.

I improved my mind for two days. It was extremely tiring. Every piece of art was so big, so important. I couldn't understand how anyone could be an artist in Paris. Everyone had already painted, sculpted or printed everything you could think of – *and* they were all famous for it. If I were an artist in Paris I'd be suicidal. I told Madame Christophe this over croissants on the morning of my first French lesson.

'It is true,' she nodded, 'it is all in the past,' and she sighed and fed Napoléon – who I'd won over with croissant tidbits to the point that he now sat between us. 'We have made haute couture our contemporary art. You should see *that* exhibition – it will be superb!'

'A fashion exhibition? I'd love to see that!'

'There is still time. It is at the Hôtel de Ville. I was waiting for you to see the billboards. You must walk with your eyes closed!'

'I do not,' I said, 'but Madame, I have only been in Paris three full days.'

She may have sensed the fact that I was cranky – she was a clairvoyant after all – because she patted my hand and smiled. 'We will see it together,' she said. 'I have two hours this evening.'

'Thank you.' I could hardly believe the pat and the smile. Were we becoming friends?

'It is nothing,' she said and stood up, ready to take Napoléon for his morning promenade. 'Enjoy your class.'

It might have been nothing to Madame Christophe, but I was fed up with visiting museums and galleries by myself. The first time had been a bit of a novelty. I'd enjoyed pretending to be a serious international art student. By the time I'd got to the Centre Georges Pompidou the previous afternoon, I'd longed for someone to nudge or exclaim to, and envied the tourists taking each other's photos in front of Marc Chagall's *The Wedding*.

I practically skipped along the route to my French class. It was in the basement of the ugliest building I'd seen in Paris. The receptionist took my money and my name and gestured me languidly towards some stairs. In honour of the occasion – and in anticipation of the friendship material – I was wearing my skull maxi skirt. I paused to smooth it down, took a deep breath and pushed the door open. Half a dozen or so students, most a little older than me, glanced up before returning to their conversations. English was the dominant language. I plonked down in a spare seat between a guy and a very cool-looking girl.

'Bonjour,' the guy said, 'you are English?'

'Australian.'

'Ah, unusual. I am Anders.' He held out his hand.

'Lise,' I said, shaking it firmly.

'You are an artist?'

'Not really,' I said and was saved from saying more by the entrance of our teacher. Fabienne was around my mother's age but her lace shirt revealed a black bra and she wore it with matador pants and impossibly high red stilettos. She exuded confidence and launched into French without any preamble.

I was at least three sentences behind, and grappling to catch up, by the time she said something I did understand. 'We have a new student today. Please welcome Lisette to class.'

'Actually, it's Lise.' I spelled it out in the French alphabet, aware that my face was as red as Madame Fabienne Fontaine's high heels.

'Australians shorten everything,' she announced to the class, making a cutting motion with her fingers. 'Nothing can be allowed its full size. The French, we lengthen everything.'

The guy called Anders raised his eyebrows and said, sounding out the words with deliberate care, 'So that is why French men are supposed to be such good lovers?'

'Very funny, Anders.'

'Excuse me, Fabienne, but I don't understand.' The girl sitting next to me looked worried.

'Anders was making a joke,' an American girl next to her said and she whispered something that caused Goldie to clap one hand to her bright lipstick and laugh.

After this strange introduction, things proceeded more normally. Fabienne asked each of us in turn what we had done on the weekend and we all answered in our different levels of French. She wrote what we had said on the board, sometimes changing the construction we'd clumsily put together so it was more grammatical.

That was all familiar to me. What was completely different was that Fabienne offered her opinion on every activity – and she had strong and always correct attitudes to everything.

The American announced that she had gone to see some

experimental dance troupe who did a 'mathematics dance' and Fabienne's finely plucked eyebrows rose to her hairline.

'Mathematics dance? Please explain more, Mackenzie. Naturally this sounds like a joke to me.'

Mackenzie waved her graceful arms around trying to describe the way the dance had been performed. Anyone could tell she was frustrated by her lack of French vocabulary. She managed to convey that the dancers performed in a kind of grid, but the only person who really understood was Anders, who had seen the same performance.

'The dance,' he explained, 'was experimental and meant to be both expressive and not always beautiful.'

'Why create something that is deliberately not beautiful, particularly in the medium of dance?' Fabienne asked and promptly answered her own question. 'Of course, young artists feel the need to go against the tradition of beauty and the classic. They think they are creating something new simply because it lacks beauty, but in reality all they have done is reveal their own failure to understand the complexity of the classic and build on it.' She didn't stop there, however, and went on to explain this problem with contemporary dance prevented her from ever seeing a performance. I wasn't sure how much of her rant Mackenzie had even understood, but Fabienne's tone made it clear she was dismissing Mackenzie's weekend activities.

Mackenzie was perplexed. 'It was just a dance. I didn't take it too seriously.'

This did not appease Fabienne. 'So you wasted your creative time on something not to be taken seriously?'

'It wasn't like that.' Anders stepped in. 'There was a group of us. One of the dancers is the new girlfriend of someone we know. It was more for that we went.'

After Fabienne had corrected some of what he had said and written it on the board, she returned to Mackenzie and asked her more about her weekend. If I had been Mackenzie I wouldn't have been able to put together a proper sentence after that attack, but Americans must be braver than that, although when her turn was over she seemed relieved.

I wasn't looking forward to being in the hot seat. When I admitted I was having a gap year between finishing school and starting university, Fabienne declared this concept non-existent in France, a ridiculous waste of time, and I would have been better served had I begun uni and applied for an exchange, which I surely would have got because my French was surprisingly not too bad, considering I was an Australian. Well, merci for that! I tried to explain gap years were common for Australians. It was a chance to travel before settling down to more years of study.

'Imbecilic,' Fabienne said with unshakeable certainty. 'As if you have really studied before university. Now in France, maybe. Le Bac is difficult. But in Australia? I don't think so.'

'So what else do you do with this year?' Anders was on another rescue mission.

I turned to him gratefully. 'I've worked,' I said, 'in hospitality, at a French restaurant, Le Voltaire. Now, I'm in Paris to – well, go on learning French, I guess, look at art, and because my mother wanted it.'

I had meant to say 'because my mother wanted me to experience the world more', or something like that, but the truth had slipped out.

'Your mother wanted it?' Fabienne repeated. 'She came with you?'

'No,' I said, 'sorry, I meant something else.'

'Your mother wanted to come to Paris and sent you instead?' she persisted.

'Not quite.'

'Your mother works?' Anders offered. 'So she sends you to travel for her – lucky for you!'

'She's a seamstress,' I said.

'Ah,' Goldie, the girl with bright lipstick, said, 'did she make your skirt?'

'I made it, with her help for the lining,' I said.

'Your mother is a seamstress.' Fabienne pulled the conversation back to order. 'That explains why she wants to be in Paris. There is no fashion in Australia. And the prices of European clothes there – shocking! You must all buy when the sales start – but you must not go to the Champs-Élysées or rue de Rivoli. The shopping there is no good.'

'What about Les Halles?' Anders asked with an odd smirk.

'Les Halles is a disaster,' Fabienne said with a theatrical shudder. 'You must certainly not shop there! You come to France for quality. You come to the famous sales for quality that is affordable. I buy shoes, of course.' She stuck out one high heel to show us, as if we hadn't already seen them.

After we'd admired her shoes, she returned her attention

to me and demanded to know what I'd done so far in Paris. I told her I'd seen a lot of art and listed the galleries I'd gone to.

She approved of this. 'Of course, in Australia, you learn about art from books,' she explained to the rest of the class. 'Oh yes, I was there. Briefly. Very clean toilets – and as far as I am concerned you can tear those art books up and use them in those toilets. You cannot learn about art like that. So you are right to see as many masterpieces as you can while you are here. But for contemporary art, Paris is no good. It is surprising, but Australia is much better. There is good contemporary art to see in Australia.'

I had studied the reproductions she so contemptuously dismissed and although I knew now they were nothing like the real thing she made me feel deeply sorry for myself – and my mother. Mum had bought art books and we'd studied them together, Mum pointing out details of each painting – how the colours in this one shimmered with light, and those in another were separated and flat. She'd told me stories about the artists until some of them were nearly as real to me as our neighbours.

'Perhaps,' I said, trying to sound calm and dignified while I seethed, 'it is that which allows us to create good contemporary art. It must be difficult to be an artist in Paris when you are surrounded by such magnificent examples of everything.' What was the word for suicide? I didn't know. 'I would want to murder myself,' I said and my words seemed a little too loud and more emphatic than I'd meant.

There was a moment of silence and then Anders clapped. 'Bravo!' he said. 'I feel like that here also. I work and work and work and still I question what it is I am working so long at, and why, when the others have done the same before me.' He turned to Fabienne and said, 'I think the Australian is sensitive.'

I wanted to tell them that my father had been an artist but the words stuck in my throat. I couldn't answer any questions about my father's art. I had only seen one painting. Instead, I studied Anders. He was a few years older than me but had an air of authority and was clearly not afraid of Fabienne. He matched her shrug for shrug. She flirted with him and I could see why. He was tall and muscular. An abstract, serpentine tattoo ran up his forearm. He wore a much-washed shirt with rolled-up sleeves as though he had come to the class straight from his studio. His ruddy blond hair was slightly longer at the front and slicked back. He was undeniably hot, and Fabienne with her pencil-thin eyebrows, look-at-me shirt and heels was definitely cougar material.

'So, Anders, you worked on the weekend?'

'I did, Fabienne. I worked. But I also went to a party and I drank a lot.'

She laughed. 'I think you always drink a lot, you Germans, when you party?'

Anders shrugged. 'It is the only way to escape the problems of the life of an artist that Lise talked about. We work, we see our work and then we drink.'

'But then you work again, the next morning.'

'For there is nothing else,' Anders said and his tone was serious, almost grim.

Fabienne nodded. 'We have a saying in Paris, "métro, boulot, dodo". It is clear, yes?'

'I do not get the boulot bit,' Anders said. 'That is what is missing for me.'

'And for you others, you agree?' Fabienne asked, which raised a flurry of questions as they hadn't understood the Parisian saying of metro, work and sleep.

The class went over time. I was longing to get out and eat something. My stomach rumbled embarrassingly during a quiet moment and Goldie laughed at me and then touched my hand and whispered 'me too', but in French, of course.

We couldn't leave until Fabienne had finished a small rant about books. Mackenzie mentioned that she was reading a writer called Françoise Sagan – a name familiar to me because my mother had read her books. Fabienne told Mackenzie that Sagan was a celebrity but not a good writer and Mackenzie would be better off reading Marcel Proust or Albert Camus. Proust might be beyond her level of French and what a pity to read him in any other language, but Camus was easy because even if you didn't understand the exact words you could still feel his passion. Mackenzie told Fabienne she read as a distraction. Fabienne indicated this kind of reading was not French. It belonged to the United States. Mackenzie said that she was from Canada, actually.

'But not, alas, French Canada.' Fabienne dismissed her and turned to me. 'In Australia, you study Camus?'

'No,' I said, 'or not at the school I went to.'

'That's a great pity. What philosophers did you study?'

34

'Philosophy wasn't an option at my school, actually.'

'Disaster! What did you study, if not literature and philosophy?'

I decided to take a lesson from Anders and shrugged. Fortunately it was one-thirty by then, so Fabienne slid off the desk and indicated that the class was over.

'I can speak now in English,' she said, 'and I want you all to say thank you for Lisette. She has saved our class. I am very grateful because it would have been a financial disaster to not have this in my life. And for you, the class survives.'

Everyone murmured thank you in English, German and French and smiled at me. For ten seconds I felt as though I was part of the group. The feeling disappeared when we all left the room and it was clear that Anders, Goldie and Mackenzie were going to have lunch together. They drifted to the exit chatting and I walked slowly behind them. I would have something to eat at a cafe, I thought – I'd seen a place that smelled as though it had good coffee. I would have lunch in a cafe and pretend I wanted to be alone.

Then Anders turned and said, as though it was the most natural thing in the world, 'And you, Lise, saviour of our class, you'll join us?'

I found myself smiling too widely to be cool but I didn't care. 'Yes, please!'

Anders made a space between him and Goldie where I slipped in and matched my steps to their pace. I had new friends. New friends in Paris, France.

Chapter 4

Fortuny draped, Valentino cut on a bias, Chanel was the suit, Vivienne is England on acid, speed and steroids. These are the things I know. Not philosophy. Not Camus. Hopeless!

I'd wanted it to be my best afternoon in Paris so far, and it was. How could it not have been, sitting on the edge of the Seine with the artists, chewing on crusty baguettes filled with soft cheese, grilled eggplant and capsicum while Anders ploughed through what he called a 'meat lover's delight', which had two kinds of preserved meat in it.

'That stuff will kill you,' Mackenzie told him and reeled off a bewildering series of facts about the small and large intestines while Anders ate on, unperturbed.

Most of the conversation was about art shows I hadn't seen, friends of theirs who all seemed to be staying in the same block of studios, or artists I wasn't familiar with – to the point of not being sure whether they were dead or alive.

At one point Goldie caught my eye and laughed. 'It's okay,' she said, 'don't look so worried. Mackenzie and Anders create proper art. Me, I make glass sculptures. My trials are more practical. Where in Paris can I get good glass rods? They worry about their philosophical approach. I worry about heating points and tools. You know, I am currently using an ancient butterknife I picked up in a flea market as the main tool for my work.'

'Pollock used a stick, towels, his own feet if he thought it would work,' Anders said.

'Jackson Pollock?' I knew who Jackson Pollock was. We'd done a school excursion to Canberra and seen *Blue Poles*. When I mentioned that, Anders and Mackenzie were interested. 'Was it angst-ridden?'

'Angsty?' I asked.

Anders nodded and leant in eagerly for my answer. I tried to remember the painting. If I'd known then that a handsome German guy was going to be quizzing me about it one day, I'd have paid more attention.

'It was big,' I said, nodding emphatically, as though big was a word that referred to more than mere size. 'Big and – strangely ordered.' I started to remember fragments of what my art teacher had said. 'You think the painting is chaos, but it isn't. I mean there's no focal point, but there's still order.'

'I think it is only the boys who go for Pollock,' Goldie said. 'My preference is Helen Frankenthaler.'

Mackenzie dismissed Helen Frankenthaler with an explosive, 'Phht! You would, Goldie. It's all those soft, limpid colours. Why don't you just worship Marie Laurencin and be done with it?'

'I like Marie Laurencin,' I said, surprised by my own voice. She was one of the painters I'd sought out in L'Orangerie. 'She did a portrait of Chanel. I bought two postcards. I'm going to send one to Mum.'

Goldie smiled at me. 'You and I gravitate to the female. Mackenzie is pioneering and Anders is, after all, deeply German. They like the angst.' She pronounced the word the way Anders had.

'We need the angst.' Anders laughed. 'Without the angst, the joy is hidden. Everything becomes the same and nothing is felt. Is this not so, Lise? Even for pretty girls who should know nothing but joy.'

Was he calling *me* pretty in that patronising way? I narrowed my eyes. 'Yeah, sure,' I said, 'I suffer when my French *Vogue* isn't delivered on the due date. That's my angst.'

'Touché,' Anders said.

'You'd better apologise,' Mackenzie told him severely, 'we frontiers people don't like being talked down to by Euro trash.'

Anders got to his feet, causing a flurry of disturbed pigeons, and gave me a short bow. 'I am sincerely sorry. It was a clumsy compliment.'

'You're forgiven.'

'Forgive, but don't forget,' Goldie advised. 'What's the time? I can hear my glass sirens calling, calling.'

'I have to go too. I've got a – an appointment. To see the haute couture exhibition.'

I chucked the last of my baguette at the pigeons, who descended with such feathery force that Mackenzie shielded her face.

Anders smirked. 'So you do get *Vogue* delivered?'

'Why else learn French? An Asian language would be far more useful in my part of the world.'

'But you will be at our next French lesson?'

'Of course.' I waved jauntily at everyone even though I was hours early for Madame Christophe. If I had stayed any longer, I'd have had to flirt and I was out of my league.

Instead, I found my way to a park. I dragged my camera out of my backpack and took photos of the statue, the pigeons and the hedges. The French lessons were worth it, I thought. I'd have to Skype Mum and apologise. I'd have to thank Madame Christophe, too. I liked Goldie, who reminded me of Ami. She was the only other girl I'd met who would have worn a mustard plaid skirt, short enough to reveal lacy stocking tops, with a purple T-shirt. I wondered what country she came from – somewhere exotic by her looks. Maybe the Philippines? Mackenzie was earnest and sweet and we both spoke the same language. Anders was another plus, and even though he was too hot to be single, he was clearly open to flirtation. If I was game.

When I was tired of sitting in the park, I explored the shops in the covered walkway that surrounded it. Over half of them were small galleries and I had to agree with Fabienne. I didn't see a single piece of art that I would have hung on my bedroom wall.

Madame Christophe was waiting for me outside the building even though I wasn't late. She was studying her shop window and motioned me over to join her.

'I do the window, but it is not quite correct, is it? It needs to attract the Americans.'

Madame Christophe had put a small sample of almost everything she sold in the window. It was cluttered. I had helped Mum do the windows of her studio, La Vie en Rose, and I'd grown up with less is more. Not that I always agreed.

'It's a bit distracted,' I said carefully.

Madame Christophe frowned at the window. 'Perhaps you are right. We search for inspiration at the haute couture.'

I wondered briefly how Chanel would feel about being the inspiration for a clairvoyant's shop window, but she'd been the daughter of a laundrywoman and had no father – Mum never tired of telling me the Chanel story – so she'd probably be cool with it.

We set off, accompanied by Napoléon, of course. Madame Christophe had dressed for the exhibition in her signature charcoal, contrasted today with an acid green silk scarf. The pochette that swung at Madame's hip was a slightly different shade of the same colour and both matched the tiny bows on her wedges. It was audacious, I felt, for someone who was so classically French, and sure enough, Madame Christophe saw me looking and patted her pochette with affection.

'Sometimes,' she whispered, 'it is important to disorganise the rules. Schiaparelli knew this.' Then she winked at me.

Madame Christophe winked at me!

'Now, we visit the haute couture and give it our full attention.'

When we reached the Hôtel de Ville she stood aside so I had to pay for us both, but I was still filled with gratitude for the comradely spirit of her wink. It was right, I felt, for the gawky Australian to pay for elegance. Just as it was right for Napoléon, whining a little, to be placed in *my* backpack.

'Otherwise he might be trampled down,' Madame Christophe said. 'Oof – the crowd!'

It *was* crowded and so different to the fashion exhibitions I'd seen with my mother at home where a handful of middle-aged women, gay men and the odd cluster of fashion students moved from exhibit to exhibit with quiet, intense deference.

Here, people shoved each other to get closer and examine the beadwork on a Chanel buckle or the embroidered sun on the Schiaparelli cloak in greater detail. I noticed that when Madame Christophe wanted to stand her ground in a front of a piece she simply jutted out her sharp elbows and held them there. I copied her and copped the frown of a well-dressed woman, but if I was going to be gawky I was going to use it to my advantage. I didn't shift and when she pressed against me Napoléon came to the rescue by growling. The woman backed off, muttering 'Pardon' in an insincere voice.

'Incroyable!' Madame Christophe led us from one spectacular display to the next. 'The embroidery, the beads, the work! Oh là là!'

She asked me to take a photo but I was stopped by someone

who gestured quite angrily to a sign either Madame had not seen or, more likely, ignored.

'A pity,' she said, 'we will need to buy the expensive catalogue. This is how they make the money.'

I was sure that Madame Christophe knew all about conservation and flashes, she was just saving face. 'We French are like cats,' Madame Desnois had told me. 'When we make a mistake we look haughty and rearrange ourselves.' Madame Christophe had just twitched her tail back into place. The thought made me smile but I hid it as I shifted Napoléon to ease my shoulder. He was just as French as his mistress and moved right back.

The clothes – that was hardly a word that did them justice – were so beautiful it almost hurt. There were times when I tuned out from what I was looking at and listened, instead, to the talk around me. Many of the Americans gave the gowns a desultory look and continued a conversation they may have started over coffee. They contrasted with the French men – I knew they were French because of their shoes – who studied the finer details of many of the garments, before moving on to a beckoning Vionnet or Valentino. I didn't think all the men were gay. Some had come with women who appeared to be their wives and they sounded appreciative and knowledgeable as both partners gestured to a particular cut, fastening or scattering of sequins.

I tried to imagine having a similar conversation with, say, Ben.

'Oh, look, chéri,' I'd say, 'the simplicity of Le Smoking transformed to a Hollywood extravagance, but I prefer this quieter number with its cut-away jacket.'

'But non, mon ange, Le Smoking is a vision of splendour!'

Of course, Ben had never called me his angel and I don't think he would even know what haute couture is. He did have a great collection of funny T-shirts that he'd ordered over the internet. It was hardly the same thing.

'I love Valentino,' a young blonde next to me said to her companion. 'His backs make me look like a present someone has to open.'

Did she own a Valentino? I wanted to nudge Madame Christophe but she was examining an evening gown with a weird bustle. The woman left a trail of perfume behind her as heady as hundred dollar notes.

'And then I told her,' another American said behind me, 'well, if she and Junior are going to be married in Venice they'd better understand there's been a global financial crisis and adjust their bridal register accordingly. We won't all be able to afford air tickets, hotels and Tiffany!'

The evening gowns made me think of Mum and I swallowed a wave of homesickness and concentrated on reading the labels instead. The words were expensively musical: *broderie de fils de soie mordorés et de fils métallique* and *incrustations de cannelé de soie mordoré, perles de verre, dentelle mécanique de soie, mousseline de soie* . . .

Everything was silk. I imagined the whispering and fluttering of fabric if all the robes were suddenly animated, moving around, their crystals and jewels glittering in the low light and the fragile lace catching on our robust backpack straps as they shimmered past.

'Lisette! Regard this Vionnet masterpiece. This has refreshed our spirits, yes? We can examine my window with a cold eye. Tomorrow morning we begin our work. Tonight I have a date.'

I could no more imagine how this opulence was going to transform Madame Christophe's window with its collection of tarot card packs, candles and healing potions from obscure monasteries, than I could imagine the brave man dating her. Nonetheless I stood in front of a Madeleine Vionnet with chain necklaces falling from the neckline. It was impossible not to love. The gown was tissue-thin apple green silk and descended to the ground in a graceful column. It was a poem to spring. I could imagine the wearer turning from a garret window, shrugging out of her furs and then, laughing slightly, allowing a man to slip it off over her pale shoulders. She'd have to warn him that the necklaces came away with the frock. Perhaps he would know, being French.

Madame Christophe raised her eyebrows at me and we moved on to a more contemporary costume fringed with so much distressed denim that Madame, Napoléon and I shuddered as one.

'The catalogue.' Madame Christophe handed me the French version. 'Your mother will be delighted.'

'My mother might prefer the English,' I said.

'No, you will read it together. It will be practice for you when you have returned home.'

Before I could protest she had marched up to the cashier and begun the transaction. It was only left to me to hand over my debit card.

I thought of saying to Anders, 'One has to learn French, if only to read the haute couture catalogue.' It was the kind of thing you could say wearing a silk gown or The Jacket. Perhaps I would have to shop the sales after all. Maybe flirting, fashion and French were all inextricably linked and to become proficient at any one of them I was going to have to embrace the other two. After all, I was the great-granddaughter of a woman who had owned The Jacket. It was probably in my DNA.

Chapter 5

STOCKINGS

Lace-topped stay-ups would make everything else I owned more French. They are definitely the missing item in my wardrobe. I don't care if it's shopping.

The next morning I was woken by an urgent knocking at my door. 'Lisette, it is time! This is the day I do not open so we do the window!' It was only eight a.m.

'We need something frivolous in the holiday mood,' Madame Christophe said, when I came downstairs, 'but also with an underneath wisdom to attract the rich Americans. They both like authority and they resent it. They are children. It needs to be chic so they are reassured I am the real French, but friendly so they feel the trust. It needs to speak to l'amour. Everyone wants to know about love.'

The materials with which we were to accomplish this small miracle included a basket, a parasol, a length of blue silk and a hunk of crystal. I thought back to my visual communications design class and Ms Lui talking about the client's vision.

'I get that you want a window design that's sexy, elegant, wise and inviting,' I said, 'and I'm sure we'll achieve that, but before we start, let's talk about what your job means to you.' I felt very bold saying this to Madame Christophe but it was obvious she had window-dressing problems.

'It is not a job,' she said dramatically, 'it is my life. I am called. And the work, it is always about love and loss. Or directions in which to go to improve. It is the human condition for people to want to see the future.'

'But the future – what does the future mean?'

Madame Christophe gave a shrug. 'It is – there is an English expression – a closed book. But for me the pages turn.'

'Okay. That's perfect. That's what we need.'

'A book? Holiday reading?'

'Not holiday reading and not just one book. We need two – one closed and one open. Both old.'

'I do not understand,' Madame Christophe said, but she bustled obediently into her apartment and returned with two books.

It took ages but when we'd finished, the window was Parisian-chic, mysterious and timeless. We went outside to admire it and Madame Christophe kissed me on both cheeks. 'It is superb. You clearly have some of your father's genes,' she announced. Naturally I had, I thought, but I had to agree that the window was well done. We'd swathed a wooden plinth with the piece of dark blue silk and placed on that the closed book, weighted down with the hunk of glittering crystal. The silk trailed across the floor and where it ended, we'd placed the open book on a music stand. Next to that was a tall gilt pillar candlestick, signifying revelation. A scattering of tarot cards led from one to the other. Madame Christophe's clairvoyant services sign was tucked in one corner of the window.

'Lise!'

I whirled around from the window to see Anders, dressed in jogging shorts and a T-shirt dark with sweat. He still looked good.

'Hi,' I said awkwardly.

'So, this is what you do?' He gestured to the display. 'You are a window arranger?'

'I was helping,' I said.

Madame Christophe gave a discreet cough. I remembered my manners and introduced them.

'Enchanted.' Anders bowed and he should have looked ridiculous but he somehow managed to look charming, I thought. Madame Christophe didn't seem so convinced. She gave a small, stiff nod.

'It's very professional,' Anders said. 'If you've finished here, Lise, maybe we should have breakfast together? I will shower quickly at the studio and meet you back here in ten minutes? I had no idea you were so close. This is fortunate!'

'Regrettably, Lisette breakfasts with me,' Madame Christophe said before I could say a word. 'It is our small ritual. Alas, you will have to meet with her another time.' She dismissed Anders with a wave.

Anders raised his eyebrows at me.

'I'm sure I could miss it this time,' I said, but Madame Christophe was already walking back into the shop.

'Never mind,' Anders said. 'I do not want to cause any disharmony. Another time, Lise.' He waved cheerfully and jogged off.

I followed Madame Christophe into her apartment, seething. She'd treated me like a child. Again. On the other hand, she'd also made me feel as though I was important to her. I didn't know what to do and, as if in sympathy, Napoléon jumped on my lap and licked my chin.

'I am sorry' – Madame Christophe appeared from the kitchenette carrying a plate – 'but this morning, to thank you for your help, I bought you pain au chocolat from the good bakery. I did not want you missing it. He is from the French class, the jogger?'

'Yes.' I was somewhat mollified by the chocolate croissant, which looked deliciously decadent.

'Germans, they are so fond of physical exercise. Bizarre.'

'But healthy,' I suggested, fending Napoléon away from my breakfast.

'Perhaps. Who really knows? I have heard of people who drop dead as they run. Why run when you can stroll? What do you see? Everything is a blur, a dangerous blur. What else does this young man do?'

'He's an artist.'

'I have never heard of a serious artist taking exercise. He will not be any good.'

Anders was dismissed from the morning's conversation but not from my mind. He'd said it was fortunate that I was staying so close to the artists' studios. Had he meant anything by that? Perhaps he was single, but how could I find out?

'You like the pain au chocolat?'

'It's delicious,' I said honestly. The pastry was flaky and the chocolate rich and Madame Christophe had kept it warm. 'It's the breakfast of royalty,' I told her, 'and far too good for Napoléon to share.'

'It is a children's treat.' Madame Christophe dismissed my pastry. 'He likes you, my little Napoléon. I knew he would. He has an eye. He can see past the outside.'

I nearly choked. It was clear that Madame Christophe was criticising my outfit of choice for the day – a green vintage corduroy tunic I'd teamed with a T-shirt celebrating an obscure boy band. I was planning to buy some stay-up lace-topped stockings to underpin the irony of this outfit, but under Madame Christophe's reprimanding gaze I doubted the irony was apparent.

I changed the subject. 'How was your date?'

'He bought me a very proper dinner that I enjoyed greatly but alas there was no . . . what to say? No electricity ran between us. I am not convinced by this dating through the internet.'

I had to swallow my coffee quickly to avoid spraying it over Napoléon and the tablecloth.

'You're internet dating?' It didn't seem possible. Not Madame Christophe with her stilettos, scarves and pochettes!

'Once or twice,' she said with dignity. 'If I can be an online clairvoyant and use the internet for income, I can also look to it for romance. I am a woman of a certain age, chérie. I have seen in my own future another man, but one cannot sit and wait for the destiny to serve him up. One must work with the destiny. How is it that I am expected to meet him otherwise?'

'I thought,' I said, carefully choosing my words, 'that you were quite . . . happy alone?'

'Of course. Who would not be? I have friends, a calling and Paris at my doorstep. Is there a need for anything more? I do ask myself this.' Madame Christophe paused to present Napoléon her breakfast plate and the dog jumped off my lap straight away. 'Perhaps I am a little greedy like this one,' she said as Napoléon inhaled the pastry flakes. 'But then I think, no, Sylvie, you are woman of charm and intelligence. You deserve companionship, of the correct type. Not marriage, you understand. I am done with that. I have not time or room in my life for a husband.'

I could quite understand that. It was hard to imagine a marriage surviving in such small apartments. I said as much but Madame Christophe was puzzled. 'In Australia we have big houses,' I explained. 'Men have a shed. Where they go. To do man things.'

'A shed? What are these things men do in a shed?'

'I don't know,' I confessed. 'I've never lived with a man.'

'Of course, your mother abandoned the idea completely after your birth. It is difficult with a child and a business.

Even young as she was, she had no time for a full-time lover. It is better that way for certain women.'

'I don't think she has time for a part-time lover now,' I said, my tongue tripping over the word. 'I mean, she doesn't go out much.'

Madame Christophe shrugged. 'One day soon she will have a special friend. I know this.'

I shook my head. 'No. She has friends, and some of them are men, but the men are not . . . interested in women,' I managed, thinking of Jamie and Craig, my mother's two gay friends. 'Maybe my father was her one true love?'

'Phht!' Madame Christophe dismissed that idea impatiently. 'No, I have seen it in her cards,' she continued, 'believe me. There is someone. He is a businessman. Clever, but not devious. He gives her happiness.'

'Maybe the cards are wrong?' I said.

'You should not be jealous.' Madame Christophe patted my hand. 'You have a life, yes? You are here! With the German asking you for breakfast. Not a wise choice.'

'I wouldn't mind,' I said, ignoring the remark about Anders. 'If Mum had a boyfriend, I wouldn't mind.'

'You shouldn't,' Madame Christophe said, 'but there is the human nature. You may feel usurped. It would be foolish, but there you are.'

'And what do you mean, not a wise choice?'

'Just remember what I say.' Madame Christophe rose. 'Come. Let us forget about love and turn our attention to the commerce. Is our window attracting attention? Follow me! We look from the window of Monsieur Berger. He has already left for the summer.'

I followed her up the stairs into an apartment larger than mine, but by no means palatial. Monsieur Berger had bought his cushions from the BHV, and had a thing for candles. Madame Christophe swept past all this as though she'd seen it before, and maybe she had. She pulled back the heavy drapes, opened the windows wide and leant unashamedly out.

Across the street in the opposite apartment, an Asian man read a book to his son. Above them, a woman watered her basil plant. There were geraniums in window boxes and washing hung out on the balconies. It was so different from home.

'Attention! Regard!'

In the street, a couple walked up to the new window. 'Honey, it's a spiritualist's shop and so French! Let's get our futures read. Shame they're not open. We can come back, though. Do you have a pen?'

'It works!' Madame Christophe whispered in my ear, still pinching my forearm.

We stood there for about an hour and watched people sauntering up the street. Some stopped and admired the window, some fossicked through their bags and noted down the shop times, while others ignored the window completely. When one couple chose to kiss for a long time in front of it, Madame Christophe huffed exasperatedly, then clapped loudly to get their attention and gestured them away.

'Well,' she said eventually, with satisfaction, 'I think

we make a good job. It is a success absolutely and we have finished before lunch even. So now I will turn to my international clients and, perhaps, have another look at the men for dating. And you, Lisette? Your plans?'

'I'll go walking, I guess,' I said, 'and take some more photos. The usual tourist thing.' I sounded too forlorn. 'I'm going to buy some stockings, stay-ups with lace tops.' If I'd expected Madame Christophe to be scandalised, I was disappointed.

'A good idea. The lingerie is perhaps more important than what is put over it.'

I couldn't help thinking this comment was directed at what *I* put over it. 'I'll take Napoléon if you like,' I offered. 'I love the way dogs are allowed to go shopping.'

Madame Christophe cocked her head to one side. 'Yes,' she said, eventually, 'this is a good idea. He will lend you some chic. Otherwise one does not know if you will be allowed to buy anything.'

'I don't look that bad,' I said. 'This is vintage, Madame Christophe. Vintage!'

'It is not Paris,' she said. 'It is not summer.'

That was true, and the very instant that Napoléon and I walked onto the street I knew exactly what she meant. It was hot, too hot for corduroy, but I was stubborn and would not go back to change. 'We'll be in air con soon,' I promised Napoléon as we set off for the BHV. In his company I felt like a local, even though I'd been in Paris for less than a week. Napoléon made all the difference. If the shop assistants in the BHV scorned my vintage look, they hid it well, complimenting me instead on my French accent. The bewildering array of stay-ups temporarily put Mum's fictional boyfriend out of my mind. Some of the stockings were so sheer I couldn't imagine sliding them up my legs without them snagging on my leg stubble. Just as I wondering how I'd ever manage the contortionist act necessary to shave my legs in my tiny shower, I heard my name being called for the second time that day.

'Lise! How good to run into you!' It was Mackenzie. 'Oh, you're buying stockings like Goldie's.'

'Sprung.'

'You'll rock 'em,' she said. 'I just don't think I've got that look. Anyway, where I live, I'd be able to wear them for five days of the year without freezing my butt off. This weather is glorious! Oh my goodness, you've got a dog! How Parisian are you? Are you both free for lunch? I've found the best falafels in Paris – enormous. I'm living on them.'

'I should tell Madame Christophe before she thinks I've kidnapped Napoléon and sold him to dog traders. Although she is a clairvoyant. She should know we're having lunch, right?'

'Your landlady is a clairvoyant? How exciting! And look at you, Lise, you're so vintage. I love it. I need to do something with my style. Well, let's face it, I need to get a style. I'm sure she'd expect you both to be out for lunch. In Paris it can take days to choose the right stockings. After we've eaten I'll walk you back and you can introduce me, yeah? I'll get her to read my cards.'

'You'd have to make an appointment,' I said, rather protectively. 'She's very busy. She has international clients.'

'She must be good,' Mackenzie said. 'I love that kind of stuff. I know none of it is true but it's so comforting to hear it.'

'What if it's bad?'

'They never tell the bad stuff,' Mackenzie said with utter certainty. 'Are you going to buy those? Look, here are some plaid ones. They're totally you.'

'Don't they have to tell the bad stuff too? I mean, who'd believe it if the future was always good?'

'It's some kind of code of practice.' Mackenzie ushered us to the cashier's desk where she counted out the euros to buy a crop top bra. 'Or maybe that's just Canadian. Maybe European clairvoyants are darker. That would make sense to me. All that angst Anders talks about. I know this bra isn't sexy, but at least it's new, right?'

'It's not really a bra,' I said, putting my stockings on the counter. 'It's a crop top.'

'I know. I should have got something padded. My boyfriend's coming over for a week.'

The cashier looked at me and shook her head ever so slightly.

'You bought that for your boyfriend?' I asked.

'I'm going to be the one wearing it!'

'Mackenzie, we can do better.'

'I shall refund the money?' the cashier said hopefully.

'You don't like it either?'

The cashier shook her head more definitely. 'Perhaps for

the gym? But for a boyfriend, you need the lingerie, not the crop top.'

'Okay, back to the drawing board. Do you mind, Lise? It's a bit early for lunch anyway, isn't it? And you're obviously better at this than I am.'

Shopping with Mackenzie reminded me of trips with Ami, except it was Paris, not Chadstone, and we didn't know each other well, although that was no barrier for Mackenzie. It seemed that she had already decided who I was and that we were going to be firm friends, two brash colonials together.

Chapter
6

All the art students at French class are doing exciting, wonderful things. They are all talented. What qualities have I got that are different from anyone else, any other girl on a gap year? What do I know?

Madame Christophe didn't seem at all surprised when Napoléon and I arrived back in the late afternoon with Mackenzie in tow. Indeed, when Mackenzie said she'd love a reading sometime, Madame Christophe set down the pack she'd been shuffling, apparently idly, when we walked in and told Mackenzie to take a seat.

'You can do it now? That's so great!'

'You have a question? Think of it as you cut the cards,' Madame Christophe instructed, 'three times to the left. I think this is a suitable pack for you. It is based on the medieval cards. They are severely luxurious. This suits a Canadian, I believe.'

Mackenzie cut the cards obediently and sat like a school-girl, all docile attention. I was pretty certain the question was something to do with the arrival of Ethan, the boyfriend, for whom a lacy bra and undies set had been purchased – the first matching lingerie Mackenzie had ever owned. That didn't surprise me: Mackenzie was all skinny jeans, Converse and T-shirts. The only girly thing about her was her breathless conversation.

When Madame Christophe revealed the cards, however, it was clear that Mackenzie had not asked about romance.

'So many work cards for a young woman.' Madame Christophe smiled and pointed them out, her red nail polish bright against the cards. 'See, here and here and again. You work hard for your success, Mackenzie.' Madame Christophe's accent made Mackenzie's name sound exotically foreign. 'This is good, of course, but here is a warning card. You must not abandon other things in your life. This will be bad for you and your health – your inside health, not the body. A young man is in your future. He comes from far away. He is impor-tant to you, perhaps more than you realise. I see a reunion.'

'That's Ethan,' Mackenzie squealed. 'Will it be okay?'

'You must make time for him,' Madame Christophe said sternly, 'and let him know your appreciation.'

Mackenzie nodded seriously. 'Do you mind if I take a photo of the cards with my phone?' she asked at the end. 'I need to remember this, Madame. I agree with everything you said but when I start painting, everything else just flies out of my head.'

'But of course,' Madame Christophe said, 'and take my card. I work internationally.' She waved any notion of payment away. 'For friendship,' she said graciously.

'Lise, you should get yours read.'

'No, no thanks,' I said, backing away. 'I might sometime. But not now.'

'When you are ready' – Madame Christophe gathered up the cards and tapped them into a neat pile before putting them away in a silk bag – 'I will be here. I have the perfect pack. Not the tarot, but oracle cards nonetheless. I keep them for you.'

That was almost sinister.

'Thank you,' I said, trying not to sound insincere. 'That's kind of you.'

'Walk me back to the studios?' Mackenzie asked. 'Unless you're busy?'

'No, I'd love to.'

'I can't believe you don't want Madame Christophe to read your cards,' she said as soon as we were outside the shop. 'She's amazing. I mean that. I was a little sceptical, I admit. But she knew. The cards knew.'

'They can't know anything. They're just inanimate objects,' I argued.

'Well, I knew I needed a better balance in my life,' she said. 'This has been a wake-up call. It's good that it's happened before Ethan arrived.'

'So what's Ethan like?' I asked.

'He's into changing the world,' Mackenzie said. 'So, you know, vegan, environmentalist. He's going to have some food problems here – lucky I found the falafels! He studied science and works for an environmental protection agency back home. He's committed. We want to get some land and have a sustainable lifestyle. One day, when we have money.'

'Wow! I'm impressed, Mackenzie. You've got it sorted. So will you keep – what is it that you do? Painting?'

Mackenzie shrugged. 'I'm painting here in Paris, but my ambitions are more conceptual – some earth structures. Public art, not private. They require sponsors and grants. In the meantime, it's great to have the opportunity to paint. It's all art.'

We turned the corner, heading down to the block of studios.

'Hey, isn't that Anders? Anders!'

'Hi Mackenzie, Lise,' he said. 'Been shopping?'

Mackenzie nodded. 'Lingerie. Lise saved me from certain disaster, helping me choose something boyfriend-suitable.'

'Ah,' Anders said, 'so, Lise, you are a shopping companion?'

Apparently the moment I landed in Paris my reputation had been sealed. I was a shopper. I rolled my eyes. 'A girl has to do what she does best,' I said.

'This is useful to know.' Anders grinned. 'I am stupid about this aspect of life and I have an important present to purchase. I will ask for your help.'

Being a known shopper might have its upside. 'Of course,' I said, 'I'd be delighted to bring my extensive experience to bear on your problem.'

'You sound like a politician,' Mackenzie said.

'Or a diplomat,' Anders added. 'So, back to work, Mackenzie?'

'Yes,' Mackenzie said. 'Lise's clairvoyant read my cards. I need to work before Ethan arrives so I can take lots of lovely time off with him. The open studio dates loom.'

Anders gave a theatrical shudder. 'Tell me about it,' he said. 'The print workroom is full of artists. To secure a position, I wake at dawn. You are fortunate, Lise – Paris in summer is holiday time.'

'I'm practising my French,' I said defensively, 'and I'm going to museums. Heaven forbid that I should get my degree only having seen reproductions that are fit for toilet paper.'

'Don't get your hackles up,' Mackenzie said, patting my shoulder, 'you're entitled to a holiday, I'm sure. Anders is just grumpy. He's listed for the first of the open days.'

'It's true,' Anders said gloomily. 'I'm off to buy myself a Berthillon ice-cream to cheer myself up. Want to join me?'

'I can't,' Mackenzie said. 'I simply must get back to work. Anyway, I'm full of falafel.'

'But the tourist?' Anders looked at me and smiled winningly.

'Yes,' I said, 'I'd love an ice-cream.'

We left Mackenzie and backtracked, crossing the Seine to the Île de la Cité.

'This is one of my favourite views,' Anders said, stopping in the middle of the bridge. 'I even love the tourist barges. There is something about rivers.'

We leant on the rails companionably. If only he wasn't quite so distractingly handsome, I thought, looking surreptitiously at his blue-grey eyes and ruddy face.

Anders broke the silence. 'What are you thinking of? It's a boy, I can tell. A boy back home?'

'No,' I lied. 'I was just thinking how perfect Paris is.'

'Ha! That is true. When we think of Paris, we look as though we are thinking of love.'

I hadn't been thinking of love, exactly, but I could hardly tell Anders I'd been thinking about how hot he was.

'I want to show you something,' I said, to change the subject. I took him to a shop window, down a cobblestone street near Berthillon. The shop was closed. It had been closed each time I'd seen it. In the window was a fox, preserved by taxidermy. There was no explanation as to what the shop sold.

'Bizarre,' Anders said. I could tell he was intrigued. 'I have never seen this, Lise. Very odd. Thank you for showing me.' I felt as though I had given him some kind of unexpected present.

There was a queue at Berthillon, but there always was. 'I am having salted caramel, chocolate and coffee,' Anders announced. 'It will not look pretty, perhaps, but it will be delicious.'

'I'm having grapefruit, lemon and blood orange sorbet.'

'Too healthy,' Anders said. 'That isn't an ice-cream. It's a breakfast.'

'It's refreshing,' I said.

The couple in front of us had their arms around each

other. She was slouched against him, leaning her head against his shoulder. They were comfortably intimate. For a moment, I wished that I could lean that way against Anders and have his strong arm around my waist. I stood up straighter. We were just friends. Or perhaps we weren't even friends. What did we know about each other? Would I ever meet someone I was totally comfortable with?

'So,' Anders said, after we'd bought our ice-cream, and sauntered back to sit near the water, 'tell me about yourself, Lisette. Tell me about your life in Australia with your seam-stress mother. It would be winter there now, yes?'

I nodded. 'But not like European winter,' I said, 'although Melbourne gets pretty cold.'

'There is snow?'

'Not in the city.' I laughed. 'Not unless you go to the mountains, and sometimes not even then.'

'You ski?'

I shook my head.

'Skate?'

'No, not even that,' I said. 'I have rollerbladed.'

'I ski,' Anders said, 'every winter. It is seriously beautiful. That rush. But also I cross-country ski. That is hard work – but the serenity! If you do not ski, what do you do in winter?'

I shrugged. 'I don't know. We read books. My mother and I light a fire and watch movies together some nights.'

'It sounds so exciting,' Anders said. 'Do you do everything with your mother? I daresay she gets out her sewing and you talk together like in an old-fashioned book?'

'Of course not! I have friends. We go out.' Was that strictly true? Ami and I stayed in mostly. We did sew. We watched *Doctor Who*, drank green tea and sometimes knitted. There was no way to make that sound exciting, even though I loved those nights.

'What's the club scene like?'

I was on safer ground. 'I don't like clubs,' I said, 'but we live near a couple of bars with live music. We go there.'

Anders nodded. 'And your mother goes with you?'

'No!' I was indignant.

'I thought perhaps you have a very young mother?'

'She's not that young,' I said. 'She wouldn't come out to see a band.'

'Does she resemble you, your little sewing mother?'

'Not really. She has dark, curly hair and she's shorter than I am. She's a great dressmaker.' I wondered if I even liked Anders, despite his cool tattoo and artful stubble. 'What about you? What do hipsters do in Germany?'

Anders snorted. 'What all the interesting people do. I go to clubs, but also music concerts – piano recitals. My friends and I party in the summer. We travel also. We hike on weekends sometimes. It is a good life. You should come to Germany, Lise. It is different to Paris.'

'I'd love to go everywhere,' I said, and realised that what I'd said was true. I'd never thought of it before, but since being in Paris, I knew that I wanted to travel to new places. Maybe I was more like my father than I realised? When he'd abandoned Mum, he just took off and never came back. Mum had always called that narcissistic, selfish and ego-driven. But was it? Could you also call it adventurous, curious and – well, let's face it, young?

'There are so many places to see,' Anders said, carefully wiping his fingers on his paper serviette. 'It must be hard for Australians to do that, so far away at the end of the world.'

'Asia is close,' I retorted, 'also New Zealand. They ski there!'

Anders laughed. 'You are very fierce, Lise. I like that.' He leant forward. He was going to kiss me! I tilted my head towards him and closed my eyes. Nothing happened. Anders dabbed at the top of my T-shirt with his serviette. 'But you are messy!'

'The sorbet is dripping.' How mortifying!

'Only so it can be closer to you.' Anders smiled, looking into my eyes so intensely that I had to blink. 'That was delicious,' he continued, standing up and stretching his arms above his head, so I could clearly see his biceps and the tendons on his forearms. 'Now, I shall go back to work. And you, Lise, what will you do?'

'I'm going to take some photographs,' I said, making up my mind suddenly. 'It's too nice a day not to keep walking.'

'You should buy one of those Lomo cameras,' Anders said. 'They are more interesting. I can tell you are an artist, Lise, the seamstress's daughter. You must do better than take ordinary photographs like anyone with their digital camera. You must capture a Paris that is entirely your own. I can take you to a shop that sells them, if you are interested?'

Was I an artist? I now owned one painting of my father's. I'd hung it defiantly on my bedroom wall the day it arrived in the post, two days before I left for Paris. My father's wife, who I could never call my stepmother because I had not met her, sent it via the lawyers. It was a dark, brooding landscape dominated by hills and clouds. 'That's Wales for you,' Mum had said, but other than that she'd made no comment although her eyes were still red from crying. Only two days before that we'd learnt of my father's death. I loved the moodiness of the painting, which reflected my own.

'They're those 35 mill cameras, right?' I wanted to stop thinking about my father.

'But not too serious. They are a fun thing.'

'I could take black-and-white photographs,' I said. 'That would be cool. My friend, Ami, she bought one of the La Sardina cameras. I'd like a fish-eye. That would be great.'

Even if I didn't always like him, Anders intrigued me, and, this time, at least, he was offering me an opportunity I hadn't thought of for myself.

'Here,' he said when we stepped inside the shop, 'this is where you buy a camera. Not a fashion photography camera, a camera for happy accidents. Isn't that so, Maurice?'

There were a bewildering variety of cameras on display. Anders, obviously not in a terrible hurry to return to work, stayed and chatted. It surprised him that I knew how to load film. That felt good! In the end, I did choose a fish-eye Lomo. It was exciting – why hadn't I thought of if myself?

'It's perfect for summer,' Maurice said, 'but don't use it in winter. You need light for these. When you are tired of seeing everything through a fish-eye, maybe you will return for a different one.'

'Perhaps I will,' I said. 'Thank you, Anders. I wouldn't have bought this without you.'

'It is always my pleasure to help someone discover their creativity,' he said with that oddly formal bow. 'I hope you will have much fun with it. What will you photograph first? The beautiful Seine?'

'No,' I said, 'everyone does that. I'm going back to that stuffed fox.'

'So macabre' – Anders was startled – 'especially for an Australian. Here, add your number to my phone. Then I can call you when *I* need shopping help.'

'I like macabre,' I said, taking the phone.

'Odd little Lise,' Anders murmured, and then, 'goodbye.' Instead of shaking my hand, he bent and kissed me on both cheeks, surprising me. Then he took my chin and looked at me again, shaking his head. 'A dead fox. You are an artist.' And he kissed me again, quickly on the mouth, before walking away.

The last kiss was so unexpected, I only registered the warm softness of his mouth. I hadn't even had time to enjoy it properly. But perhaps that was a good thing? Why had he kissed me? It was friendship. Definitely friendship. It wasn't a boyfriend kiss, I told myself sternly. It was interesting, too, that Anders had wanted my phone number. What did it mean? Anything? Nothing?

It was all too puzzling. I tried to put it out of my mind

while I walked back across the bridges. I decided I'd make cards out of the photographs. I'd send the fox card to Ami. She'd get a kick out of that. If she'd taken a gap year, too, we could have been doing this together. I needed to talk to her. I missed her life advice.

Chapter

7

When Mum was pregnant with me and her own mother hated her, she strutted out in fringed suede boots and a minidress that just stretched over the bump I was then. I've been doodling outfits I could wear that would be different from my usual style. I wanted fun chic, a mashup of vintage with some added Vogue elegance. I'm thinking sixties – a black baby-doll dress to wear with my new stockings. I'd embroider a lipstick kiss on the Peter Pan collar. I could wear it with my Docs. But not in Paris.

I didn't hear from Anders, but I wasn't surprised. He would be busy preparing for the open studio exhibition. I did find myself thinking of that light kiss more often than I should have, and looking forward to the next French class. In between classes I took a lot of photos and found a place close by that sold and developed black-and-white film. My first results delighted me. The fox looked almost real, the barges were straight out of a picture book and even the bookstores by the river looked like

nonchalantly out of a dress. It would have to be a dress. There were too many awkward fastenings on everything else. I'd need to be wearing good undies, too. Undies! They'd have to come off.

Was there a website that told inexperienced artist's models what to wear? I googled and discovered a site with lots of great advice – none of which I could take. No, I couldn't practise with friends first. No, I couldn't attend a life drawing class as an artist before modelling. And how on earth could I think about negative space as I changed from pose to pose? Clothing seemed like the least of my problems – but the only one I had a chance of fixing.

I studied the haute couture catalogue for inspiration. I could completely understand how one could shrug out of a Vionnet, or slither from a Fortuny. Okay, the necklace dress would have been tricky, but there were plenty of other dresses that surely needed just a quick zipper tug or a fallen strap before they, too, would slide to the ground, leaving just the underwear.

I would require additions to my wardrobe. They would have to look as though they'd been there right from the start – otherwise I'd look as though I'd tried way too hard.

What a problem! I had three days to find the perfect dress to take off. I didn't want to think about how I was going to manage to take it off in front of Anders. I wouldn't think beyond the dress for the time being. That was enough.

I'd seen a vintage store quite close to the apartment. I hadn't actually been inside because I'd felt it was too intimate a space to test my French language skills. The BHV had the anonymity of any large department store, but a second-hand shop – that required more work.

I asked Madame to loan me Napoléon.

'I am going shopping,' I told her, fulfilling her expectations.

'The sales have not started,' she cautioned. 'It is ridiculous, Lisette, to shop before the sales.'

'I'm shopping for vintage,' I said. 'Second-hand stuff won't go on sale. Anyway, I can't wait. I need something specific for Saturday.'

Madame Christophe's eyebrows arched.

'It's just a thing with the art students,' I said. 'I want something new.'

'This is not logical,' was all she said but I noticed she fussed around and changed Napoléon's collar from his plain blue to a smart tartan, as though that was more suitable for vintage shopping.

There were two vintage shops in the Marais. They were both full of designer vintage, which meant they were expensive. The first was staffed by two young women with impossibly perfect skin and hair. I was in and out of that shop in three minutes.

The second was staffed by two men who asked if I was Canadian and cooed at me when I told them I was Australian, then left me alone while they continued an argument in fierce, swift French. Beautiful dresses hung on the hangers – Gucci, Versace and more – but at the back of the shop was a section of clothes that weren't designer but still second-hand.

This was the section I wanted. The clothes didn't even look like they'd been worn. I pulled a couple of halter-neck dresses from the rack and flourished them at the men behind the counter, who directed me to a tiny fitting room that was wall-papered in red velvet.

Eventually I chose a rockabilly style dress that was made from a blue fabric printed with cowboys riding broncos. It wasn't the baby-doll dress that I'd imagined – but at least I could slither out of a halter-neck. Also the neckline made me look slightly bustier than I really was. I wasn't sure if that counted as false advertising but it wouldn't really matter as I'd be taking the dress off anyway. I shuddered at the thought. Too late to back out now.

Years ago I'd asked my mother how she felt when my father left her. She was only twenty-two, pregnant and about to be a single mother. Not your ideal future. She said she'd been devastated but simply had to lift up her chin and swagger through it as though it was all fine. I'd cherished a vision of my mother, very pregnant, sashaying through her own mother's rage and disappointment in those fringed boots.

I would have to swagger on Saturday. I had the dress. Now I just needed the shoes.

Even though it was too hot for cowboy boots they were all I could think of. I explained my need to the two guys behind the counter who consulted each other and drew me a map, warning me that the boots, even though it was summer, wouldn't be cheap.

Their map led to a small shop cluttered with shoes and

boots of every size, colour and description. It was like stepping into boot heaven. The woman behind the counter sported a pair of tooled boots. They were red and matched her fringed skirt perfectly, as though she'd just left the rodeo.

Between us we found a rather plain tan pair that fitted me exactly. She insisted I try them on with the dress, and they were perfectly nonchalant.

'Of course, you will need the right handbag,' she said, 'something that is different. I have nothing ideal. You should try the flea market at the Porte de Vanves. There you will find everything – except boots of this quality.'

'Porte de Vanves,' I repeated. 'Thank you. I'll check it out.'

The boots were so wonderful I wore them home. They added a certain kind of flair, I felt, to my tartan skirt. I'd spent a lot of money, but I was still within my travel budget.

When I'd planned my trip, I'd worked out exactly what I needed to live on for three months in Paris, then I'd added a buffer amount for emergencies. This was an emergency.

Just before I'd left, the lawyer's letter had arrived. It announced that William Harris Lewis was dead. The name meant nothing to me, even though the letter was clearly addressed to Lisette Addams. William Harris Lewis had left his only child Lisette Alicia Addams ten thousand pounds. I read the same paragraph three times. Then I shoved the letter at Mum.

'It took him long enough to be responsible,' she said. 'It's not as if there was any support when I was raising you.' She sat down suddenly on a kitchen chair. 'Poor Will,' she said softly and there were tears in her eyes. 'It's not easy for an artist to save that kind of money. I wonder if his wife will have to sell anything so you get this inheritance? I do hope not.'

I read the letter again. So that was my father's name: William Harris Lewis. I'd never known his full name. Mum referred to him only as Will when she talked about him – which was rare. My father was a no-go zone and always had been. Once, when I was twelve and Ami and I were in super sleuth mode, we'd searched through her filing cabinet looking for clues. We'd found my birth certificate but the space next to Father was simply blank. Later I found out that if the father isn't around to sign the documentation, that's what happens. He's a blank.

'Doesn't it prove that he loved me?' I'd asked. 'Look. Ten thousand pounds, for me. He left that to me. He never forgot me.'

'Of course he didn't forget you,' Mum had said. 'He wasn't responsible, but he certainly wasn't forgetful.'

'Well, how would I know? He never got in touch.'

Mum turned away from the conversation to fidget with the flowers she was arranging. They were early tulips, as pale as breath. She was putting them in my great-grandmother's green vase, which matched the leaves exactly.

'Mum?'

'He may have tried to get in touch. Once, when you were a toddler. I said there wasn't any point. He couldn't be a proper father when he was living in Wales. Of all places! Why was Wales so much better than Melbourne? I didn't want you to

79

be hurt the way I was. Then after he'd married that woman he sent a letter saying how sorry he was about the past. I suppose she made him do it. Closure. When you were sixteen, he wrote to say that he was sure you were accomplished and beautiful. Well, you were, of course. No thanks to him.'

'He wanted to see me?' Would I have wanted to see him?

'He was only briefly back in Australia – and not even in Victoria.'

'So? Couldn't I have gone to see him?'

'I didn't think so at the time. I was scared.'

'You were what?'

'We were such a tight unit, you and I, Lisi. I didn't want him intruding. He could have unsettled everything. Oh my God, he was so young.'

I could have swept The Vase from the counter, but I didn't. It was an Art Nouveau vase. Like The Jacket, it was a religious relic. 'Why didn't you tell me?'

'I've told you. He was nothing to us then. He had run away. If it hadn't been for Greatma, I don't know what we would have done. My mother – well! It was the end of our relationship. She'd had us married, of course – she'd assumed. Well, so had I. I'd designed a beautiful wedding dress for a pregnant bride. Serves you right, my mother said, you should never have taken up with an artist. We'd been together nearly two years. I'd just thought it was a matter of time.'

That was the beginning of the argument that raged for five days until I left Australia. Even thinking of it now, sauntering through the Marais in my new cowboy boots, made me feel like punching something. It wasn't that I'd thought it would have been a grand reunion. He'd left Mum when she was pregnant. He hadn't been 'ready' to commit. What did that even mean? Yeah, it would have been awkward, but hadn't I deserved to at least see my father *once* – particularly if he'd wanted to meet me? He was part of my DNA.

When I'd stormed at Mum about that, she'd managed to find some photos. Who knows where she had them hidden – Ami and I certainly had never found them, for all our furtive searching. I'd brought them to Paris even though they weren't really mine. I wasn't ready to frame them or anything, but they were safely in my top drawer and I'd studied them, checking out the similarities between me and this strange but familiar man whose full name I now knew.

'Come on, Napoléon,' I said, 'let's reward ourselves with a walk in the Place des Vosges.'

Napoléon perked up immediately. The Place des Vosges offered new smells. It was busy when we got there and all the sunny seats were taken. On one square of grass, a photographer was taking shots of a model, who was wearing what would probably be called a dress on anyone significantly shorter. At one stage she pulled the top of the dress right down, revealing a bit of lace, which may have been a bra. The photographer threw her a fur coat and she shrugged that over the lace. At that point two security guards became interested in what was going on and wandered over. They may have been reprimanding the team for using the grass, or they may simply have been interested in the woman's breasts. I suspected the latter.

She was certainly not uneasy about displaying her assets in public. At one word from the photographer, she pulled the dress and the lace down entirely, opened the coat and lay back on the grass in full sight of the security guards, a group of teenagers eating gelati and two businessmen, who both stared at her while they talked on their phones. Between shots, a stylist arranged her hair just so on the lawn.

I watched surreptitiously. I hoped to get some tips, but it seemed to be just a matter of glorious confidence – and fur. Not that I was going to wear a dead animal. However, I could probably borrow a live animal. Napoléon might be a good distraction. I could thrust him in Anders' arms and command that he find somewhere for him to lie down and then – voilà! By the time Anders had settled Napoléon, I'd be naked.

Naked. I gulped. What had I let myself in for? I thought briefly about simply leaving Paris. I could catch a train some-where. I could visit Monet's garden. I'd simply text Anders and tell him I was out of town.

Or, I could tell Anders the truth and say that I'd decided I couldn't model for him. I wasn't the right type. It would be a disaster. He needed someone with more experience.

Or, I could pull on my new cowboy boots, and stalk into the studio, chin lifted because I was Lise now, not Lisi, and all artists needed models. It was just another job, after all.

The model on the grass pulled her clothes back up to their rightful places and then threw a shirt dress over the whole ensemble. The shoot was over. She and the photographer air kissed. When she walked off, she glided across the grass without her stilettos sinking. The stylist packed the fur into a suitcase, gesturing to the photographer. I'd have preferred to be the stylist, I thought, even if you had to haul around a lot of gear. At least you weren't getting your gear off.

Chapter

8

The rue de Rivoli is full of women whose handbags match their shoes and who drape a scarf, just so, even on the hottest day. Parisian style. Only my skull skirt saves me – and it is a borderline, umpire-whistle save. I am unravelling.

'I need to borrow Napoléon again,' I told Madame Christophe.

Madame Christophe gave me a narrowed-eyed look that made me think she knew far more than she should. She pursed her small, scarlet mouth.

'It could be amusing,' she acknowledged and for a wild moment I thought that Napoléon was her familiar, like a witch's cat, and had been reporting the events of our walks back to her. 'It could amuse him,' she corrected herself and Napoléon shrank back to his normal handbag size.

So, on Saturday, we set off to Anders' studio together. I was wearing my dress and the cowboy boots, and Napoléon his tartan collar.

'Very interesting,' Madame Christophe said of my dress. 'You will not forget that he eats an early dinner?'

'No, Madame,' I said, 'I won't be home late. It's a daytime thing.'

I got to the studio early, but there was nowhere to wait – outside the building was a covered walkway where at least a dozen people were still sleeping, on the ground, so I wasn't going to hang around. It stank of pee and I'd already stepped over trickles that I knew weren't water. No wonder Paris was a city of stilettos! I punched in the code, found Anders' studio and knocked before I panicked and ran away.

Anders opened the door. He was unshaven and shirtless. I really was too early.

'I'm so sorry,' I said. He had another tattoo on the left-hand side of his chest. Shirtless he was even hotter than I'd imagined but I didn't want to look as though I was checking him out. 'That's a cool tattoo. What does it say?'

'You can't read German so it might not be cool at all. It might say I love my mother.'

'I meant the lettering.'

'Come in.' He motioned me inside, holding the door open.

'Great place.' I tried to sound casual.

Anders shrugged. 'It does the work,' he said. 'The architecture is banal but it's free. Coffee?'

'Thanks.' Was he ever going to put a shirt on? Apparently not. He stuck an espresso maker on the electric hotplate. There was nowhere to sit. The two chairs in the room were covered in magazines, books and clothes.

'*Und die Lieb' auch heftet fleißig die Augen*,' he said.

'What?'

Anders pointed to the words that flowed over his skin. 'It's from a poem,' he said, 'by the great Friedrich Hölderlin. "And love too fixes keenly its eye". Do you know the poet?'

'I studied English lit and French, not German.'

'He is a favourite of mine.' Anders moved the stuff from the chairs to the floor. 'He will not wee?' He pointed at Napoléon, who was inspecting the clothes.

'No,' I said, 'he's my landlady's dog.'

'I thought you had bought yourself the essential Parisian accessory!' Anders rescued a T-shirt from the floor, sniffed it dubiously, and then shrugged it on. 'There are three washing machines here,' he said, 'and over two hundred artists. One or two machines are always kaput. In Germany we would fix quickly but here . . .' He shrugged, lifting his hands up in a French gesture of mock resignation. He heated some milk in a small saucepan and when the coffee was done, he poured it into two bowls. They didn't match, but they were both old with gilt flowers on them. 'Café au lait bowls, also for hot chocolate. Charming?'

'Charming,' I agreed.

'I buy from the flea market at the Porte des Vanves,' he said, sipping the coffee contemplatively.

'Yes, I've heard of that,' I said. 'Napoléon and I will have to go sometime.' I wasn't sure why I'd involved the dog in the flea market trip. Nerves. I wondered if Anders could hear the strain in my voice.

'Napoléon?'

I pointed at Napoléon, who had curled up on one of Anders' T-shirts.

'That's a big name for such a small dog.'

'I know, right? And Napoléon wasn't even French. But he was short.'

Holy crap. I was out of small talk and Anders was not contributing. I studied my coffee as though the meaning of life was in the small bowl. Should I drink it fast or slowly? I decided on the former. At least if I was posing, I wouldn't have to talk. The silence stretched out. Why didn't he at least play some music?

'Well,' I said, putting down the coffee I could hardly taste, 'shall we start? Where do you want me to stand? Or do you want me to sit?' I jumped up before Anders could say anything. His easel was empty, but surely he'd put something up on it once I was posing? I dragged my chair opposite the easel. Anders still didn't say anything. I was going to have to take the initiative for everything. I wasn't good at that but it was too late now. I started to undo the straps behind my neck. The top fell down and revealed my bra.

'Wait!' Anders held up his hand and then there was a knock at the door. I clutched at my dress as Goldie walked in. A small wail escaped from my mouth. She was wearing my dress too!

'I don't understand,' she said. 'Am I interrupting?' she asked and then said to me, 'You're nearly wearing my dress?'

'You're wearing *my* dress,' I said. 'The dress I *was* wearing.'

'Is this a joke?' Goldie asked.

My face was flame red.

'I think Lise has misunderstood,' Anders said.

'Where did you get my dress?' I asked Goldie. It was easier to deal with that than with whatever else had happened.

'Let's all sit down,' Anders said. 'I will get you coffee, Goldie.'

'I think it looks lovely on you,' Goldie said, drawing a chair up to the small coffee table. 'We could be sisters. Do sit down, Lise.'

Maybe she hadn't seen my bra? I quickly retied the halter straps. No, of course she had. I wanted to flee but Goldie was sitting between me and the door.

'I understand.' Anders smiled as he delivered a bowl of coffee to Goldie. 'Lise thought I wanted to draw her.'

'Well, that's what artists do, isn't it?' I demanded.

'That is true,' Anders admitted, 'but what I want is to film you and Goldie for an installation. And now, you have both made it perfect. Like twins. It could not be better.'

'I'm so embarrassed,' I said. 'I'm so . . .'

Goldie got up and put her arm around my bare shoulders. I could feel tears prickling behind my eyes. 'Don't be,' she said. 'Where I come from, we dress in the same clothes as our best friends often. It is to say to the world that we are sisters.'

'I bought it at a vintage shop,' I said. 'There shouldn't be another like it.'

'The vintage shop in the Marais, with the gay boys?'

'Yes, that one!'

'They make them up, out the back. I like your cowboy boots.'

'Thank you,' I whispered. 'I thought I had to pose nude.'

'You are very brave,' Goldie said seriously. 'I would not do that, except maybe for a boyfriend.'

That made me feel better. Then Anders told some obscure German jokes that neither Goldie nor I understood and then he became serious and there was no room for embarrassment any longer. It was exhausting. Anders had a vision. To make that work, Goldie and I had to do everything perfectly in time. Then we had to lie down on the floor with our eyes closed.

'Our dresses!' Goldie exclaimed.

'Goldie, this is my vision.'

When Anders had filmed enough of his vision, my stomach was rumbling. 'See,' Goldie said, pointing to it, 'Lise is hungry. You can hear how hungry she is. We've had it, Anders.'

'I will buy you both lunch.'

'As a modelling fee? Anders, you are cheap.'

'I am thrifty,' Anders said. 'Come. They are making lunches in the courtyard. We shall have a picnic.'

'I can't come,' Goldie said. 'I have to work. You can buy me lunch another time, Anders. Don't worry, I *will* hold you to it. Enjoy your picnic.'

'She is a worker, that one,' Anders commented as we carried our takeaway lunches across the road. 'The glass is like a lover for her.' He lifted his arm and put it around my shoulders. The gesture was so unexpected I nearly stopped walking. 'She is very serious,' he continued as though we strolled like that all the time, 'but so are we all.'

I couldn't put my arm around his waist; I was holding the plastic bag that contained the couscous. I could transfer the plastic bag to my other hand, but I was too self-conscious to make that move. It was already awkward enough – every step we took bumped our hips together, the plastic bag swung and hit Napoléon, who growled a little.

I gave myself up to the moment. Anders smelled good. It was a forest smell – pines and something else woody. He wore striped espadrilles, which were beachy, and his jawline was faintly stubbled. He would be the perfect European boyfriend.

'It went well today,' he said suddenly. 'I am happy. These exhibitions make one work for a deadline. How are your photographs, Lise?'

'I'm enjoying them,' I said. 'Of course, I'm not an artist, but I'm loving the little accidents.'

'What are you, Lise?' Anders asked. 'What do you think you might be?'

'I don't know,' I said. 'I suppose I'm here to find out?'

'I think you are like a clear canvas,' Anders said. 'You stand in front of yourself, not knowing where to begin.'

'That's silly, Anders.' I followed him to a seat overlooking the river. 'I'm already *someone*. I'm my mother's daughter, a friend—'

'What about your father?' Anders said. 'You never mention him.'

I shrugged. I wasn't going to tell Anders my family history. I didn't trust him enough. 'Of course, but the matriarchal line is stronger.'

Anders rolled his eyes. 'All these strong women. Men have been belittled. We have handed over our power.'

'That's such crap!'

'Easy for you to say.' Anders fed Napoléon a small piece of sausage and then lapsed into silence while we watched the tourist barges go by. He didn't try to kiss me again.

'I like stuff,' I said, surprising myself, 'you know – like your coffee bowls. Things other people have owned.'

'Well, there's a mark on your canvas,' Ander said. He didn't sound entirely convinced. 'Not a particularly large or useful mark but one should not judge an unfinished artwork.'

'When we're finished, we're dead,' I said sharply. 'Honestly Anders, you are so patronising.'

'I am wise,' he said. 'Come on, Lise, let's do something. You have nothing planned?'

'I have to get Napoléon home early for his dinner, but that's all.'

'Let's go to the Père Lachaise,' Anders said. 'This will appeal to you as you like old things.'

'The cemetery? I didn't mean *that* old!'

'It's very picturesque, very beautiful. Fabienne will enjoy hearing about our visit next week. Everyone should see the Père Lachaise. Even Napoléon will enjoy it.'

'Okay,' I said. Anders' enthusiasm was catching. 'I guess we could do that.'

'We'll buy some beer,' Anders said, 'so we can toast the departed. There are so many great people buried there.'

'Are you sure you can drink in a cemetery in daylight?'

'This is Europe, Lise. We drink everywhere.'

I still wasn't used to being allowed to take a dog on the metro, but Napoléon was obviously comfortable with the whole thing and curled up on his own seat as though he'd paid for his ticket.

'He is very French,' Anders said, with a slight note of disapproval.

The Père Lachaise was huge. I'd never seen such a big cemetery. Not that I spent a lot of time in cemeteries. There'd been once when Mum decided she'd better make sure they'd put up a plaque for Greatma and we trundled off with a bouquet of flowers. It was sad but in an unreal kind of way. The plaque had nothing to do with Greatma. It was just a bit of metal with her name on it. Then there'd been the Saturday afternoons that Ami and I had photographed cemetery angels for visual arts. They were my experiences. Of course, I had not been to my father's funeral – I hadn't even known it had taken place.

This was more of a tourist attraction than a proper cemetery. There were tourists everywhere and all of them were searching for Jim Morrison's grave.

'It's the big attraction,' Anders said dismissively. 'We will not worry about him. Oscar Wilde is the other most visited. His grave we will find. But it is Héloïse and Abelard I enjoy most. These we will toast.'

I hadn't heard of Héloïse and Abelard, so Anders told me the story of the doomed lovers and how they'd castrated Abelard when he was caught with Héloïse, his student. Anders shuddered theatrically as he told me and pretended to clutch his groin. 'See how we are emasculated!'

'It still happens, of course,' I said, 'in Australia.'

'They castrate men?'

'No, I don't mean that! But if you're a teacher and you're caught with a student, you can go to jail.'

'And that is the end of the romantic stories,' Anders said. 'Where are we without forbidden love?'

'I think it's seen more as paedophilia,' I said sharply.

'But do you think so with Héloïse and Abelard? We have their passionate letters as witness to their love.'

'It was different back then,' I said. 'You married younger.'

'That is true,' Anders said, uncapping the warm beer, 'but I think with these two' – he motioned to the old grave – 'it was more about class difference. That still happens.'

'Not in Australia,' I said stoutly, taking the smallest sip of the warm beer.

'So, if you or your family were very rich, they'd be happy for you to marry a penniless artist?' Anders grinned at me, swigging his beer.

'I don't see why not,' I said. 'It wouldn't really be their business, anyway.'

'Things are the same in Germany,' Anders said seriously, 'but there can still be . . . problems. Statements, remarks that sting.'

'You're speaking from experience?' This was turning out

to be the most revealing conversation I'd had with Anders. It was clear he was the penniless artist. Perhaps that was why he was in Paris and grumpy about women. He was nursing a broken heart. Could I be the one who mended it for him?

'Don't be so serious, Lise! I am no Abelard, believe me!' His loud laugh attracted the attention of a couple, who both frowned as though laughter was forbidden in the cemetery. It wouldn't have surprised me – we'd already seen cemetery officials zooming around in carts reprimanding people for sitting on the lawns. No rest in this cemetery!

'I didn't mean that.' I was offended. It had been what Ami called 'a moment' and Anders had backed away.

'Come.' Anders held out his hand. 'Let's go and see the great Oscar – another doomed lover.'

'Surely the fact that everyone is here,' I said, gesturing over the graves, 'indicates that we're all doomed.'

'Oh, Lise! You have the angst. But it is true, of course. No matter what we do we end up here. All the more reason to enjoy this day, this company.' And leaning forward Anders kissed me for the second time. Just when I'd begun to relax and think about kissing him back, he pulled away. 'There,' he said, 'that is to cheer us both up. What better than a kiss among the dead?'

Napoléon was home for his early dinner, as was I. I had hoped the afternoon would turn into a proper date. I'd thought we might have dinner together at one of the cafes I never went to. We'd sit side by side and order the smoked salmon. Or I would; Anders would eat something more meaty like the charcuterie platter. We could share. But that didn't happen and nor was the kiss repeated. At the Châtelet Métro he waved me goodbye, saying he had an exhibition opening to catch and walked off, leaving Napoléon and me to walk slowly home in the opposite direction. Instead of smoked salmon, I ate two-minute noodles, watched the street from my apartment window and marvelled at how sadly glorious it was to be in Paris alone and – maybe – falling in love.

Chapter

Mum said everyone should own at least one smiling dress – the dress you put on when all is right in your world and you want everyone to know you're smiling inside. Mum's has lots of flowers embroidered at the hem. I left my smiling dress at home. It's scrunched up at the back of my wardrobe where I balled it up and threw it when Mum 'found' the photos of my father. It's the floral shift Mum made me last summer, before I knew my father's full name or that he'd wanted to see me.

I wasn't prepared for the open studio to be so busy. Anders was hyped and I could see why – people kept arriving. It looked as though the plastic cups would run out and the remaining food began to look sad on the industrial china plates. Goldie and I had both been instructed to wear our 'vintage' dresses, which we did and everyone *oohed* and *aahed* over us as though we were celebrities.

The video of us was projected against one bare wall of the studio, and on another wall were stills from the video, blown up and superimposed with collages. Some of them I liked more than others. The one where we were nearly covered by a photo of Paris pigeons was creepy.

Fabienne turned up in a sheer lace mini dress. You couldn't help but see how slim and toned her tanned legs were.

'So it was planned, this wearing of the dresses?' she asked Goldie.

'Tonight, yes, but on the day, no. It was a happy accident.'

'But what a disaster for you both. Arriving alike!'

Goldie shrugged. 'We didn't mind,' she said mildly, 'did we, Lise?'

Fabienne was genuinely shocked. 'If that happened to me, I would . . .' Her English failed her. 'But of course, there is no real fashion in your countries.'

I didn't know whether to laugh or make an angry retort but Goldie just shook her head slightly so I let it go.

Mackenzie arrived with a tall Canadian boy who she introduced as Ethan. She was wearing her new bra. I could see the straps when her T-shirt slid off one shoulder. He chatted to me for a while about environmental issues in Australia. I was pleased for Mackenzie's sake that he was such a decent guy and sorry when they both left. That left me at a loose end. Goldie was flirting with someone I didn't know. I made small talk with an Italian girl from the French class, but it was hard going with limited French. I was beginning to feel bored and lonely when Anders came up with a beer.

'It's going well,' he said, 'don't you think? Thank God it is nearly over. Then we can party.'

'So what is this?'

'This is not the party. This is the ordeal. When it is over, the people I like most will stay, we open more beer, I find the secret food and we philosophise and get drunk.'

'You have more food?' I was indignant – and hungry.

'Of course! I shopped today at the Bastille Market, some for the studio, some for our party. You are staying, Lise?'

I thought that if you had just come in the door of the studio, you might think we were a couple. Particularly if you then noticed that I was one of the girls on the wall.

'Yes, of course. I wouldn't want to miss a party!'

'I wouldn't want you to miss the party,' Anders said seriously, and dropped a light kiss on the top of my head, before moving away to greet another arrival. I looked around and saw Goldie. She was frowning at me. The boy she had been talking to had disappeared. Was she jealous? Then the boy came back with beer and claimed her attention again. It was hot in the studio so I went out to the courtyard and wandered around, looking up at the still-blue sky. I wasn't lonely anymore, just waiting. I tried to look casual, or as though I was thinking about art. Finally, Anders came out.

'I think you're right, Lise,' he said. 'This would be the best place for us all to be. Nearly everyone has gone. Will you help me set up?'

Anders had stashed the small studio fridge full of food. We washed the heavy china plates and I arranged cheese and fruit, cut up baguettes and put olives into a couple of little bowls. I felt almost like a proper girlfriend, except that I didn't know where anything was kept.

There were soon about ten people in the courtyard, clustered around the table. I wasn't surprised that Mackenzie and Ethan had left but I was surprised that Fabienne had stayed. She sat cross-legged on one of the bench seats, her dress riding up to her thighs and talked to an older guy Anders had introduced as one of the printmakers. I wondered whether I'd ever be as confident as Fabienne and doubted it. Goldie came to sit with me and was about to say something serious – I could tell by her face – when Anders strolled over with a platter of cherries. She gave him a long look that I couldn't decipher. Had there been something between them?

Anders sat down beside me and put his arm around me as though it was the most natural thing in the world. I thought I heard Goldie sigh, but I wasn't sure because the guy Fabienne had been talking to picked up a guitar and began to play.

'This is living,' Anders said somewhere close to my ear and I relaxed against him, letting the music fill the night. It was sad, wild music and when the guy began to sing I knew he was lamenting a love lost to him forever. The sky darkened imperceptibly as twilight inched towards night. After that song, the music shifted and even I recognised a flamenco.

A girl kicked off her shoes and got up. Despite the jeans she was wearing, when she danced you could imagine her skirt ruffling up and hear the castanets as she clicked her fingers. Fabienne stood up too.

'But she's French, not Spanish,' I whispered to Anders.

'She can do anything,' Anders said in my ear, watching her.

She was ridiculously sexy. She and the girl circled each other, mirroring each other's movements haughtily.

'You're right,' I admitted. 'She can do anything!'

'We should have a go,' Anders said.

'No!' I said it louder than I had intended. I didn't want to be shown up by Fabienne.

'Come on, it's just a dance.' He stood up.

'No.'

'Where is your gypsy soul?' He dismissed me and joined Fabienne and the Spanish girl. He didn't know the flamenco – that was clear – but he was muscled, arrogant and proud, and the music changed ever so slightly to include him. The women gathered him up in their movements until the dance was about rivalry. I wouldn't have been up there dancing for anything but without Anders I felt conspicuous, as though I was a child who'd been allowed to stay up past my bedtime.

'Lise,' Goldie hissed at me urgently, 'Lise, we're going. We're off to have a coffee. Do you want to come?'

'No,' I said, 'I'll stay for a little longer. Do you have to go?'

'Yes. I have to clear my head. I've had too much to drink. Come with us, Lise.'

'No, I haven't said goodbye.'

'You can wave.' Goldie was standing over me, swaying slightly. 'You don't have to say anything. It's a party. No one says anything.'

'You go. I'll be fine.'

'Don't . . . you know—'

But I didn't hear the rest of what Goldie said because everyone was clapping and the dancers and the boy had tugged her away. Then Anders was back by my side, sweating slightly.

'Magnificent!' he called to the guitarist and raised his beer bottle. 'You are a virtuoso!'

'You should dance more,' Fabienne said. She wasn't even sweaty, just slightly flushed and glittery. 'Germans should always dance, it loosens them.'

I wondered how much she had had to drink but Anders just laughed.

'I drink now,' he said, 'that is also loosening, Fabienne.'

He'd put his arm back around me and I was safe. When he talked, I heard his words rumble through his chest. I didn't have to say anything. I could just sit there and be a part of it all. The guitarist, Salvador, kept playing between drinks. Sometimes Fabienne and the Spanish girl danced, sometimes they just sat, tapping their feet. The talk was about politics and art. No one, including Anders, really talked to me, but I didn't care. It was enough to be there, close to him.

Eventually someone from a nearby studio called out that people had to sleep and Salvador packed away his guitar. Fabienne came over to say goodnight and Anders released me and stood up. They embraced briefly and she kissed him rapidly on both cheek, but I counted three kisses, rather than two. I stood beside him but only received two airy kisses.

'We are continuing on,' she said to Anders, gesturing to Salvador, the other dancer and another couple, 'you can join us.'

He shook his head. 'I have to work tomorrow.' I wasn't invited, which would have stung but I was sleepy and warm.

'Take care,' Fabienne said to me and it wasn't clear whether it was a warning or a farewell.

The courtyard was empty. I yawned. 'I have to go too,' I said reluctantly, 'it must be late.'

'It's still early,' Anders said, 'the sky isn't dark yet.'

'The sky is never dark in Paris. I thought you had to work?'

'I have time to sit for a while with you.' Anders pulled me down, so I was on his lap. 'I've been wanting to do this all night,' he said and he kissed me firmly on the mouth. It was not like his other kisses, fleeting and light. This was a proper kiss, teasing but insistent. His arms were tight around me and I hoped he couldn't hear me breathing more quickly.

His hands moved over my bare back. I wished we weren't in such an open space. I didn't want to do anything half-undressed in a public space ever again.

Then Anders' phone beeped and he stopped kissing me and fumbled for it instead.

'Ah,' he said and I couldn't identify the tone of his voice. 'You must go home now, Lise. I have to attend to this.' He practically pushed me off his lap as he stabbed a message out on his phone. I straightened my dress. What was I supposed to do? Kiss him goodbye? Just leave?

'Well, bye, then,' I said, giving an awkward wave that Anders didn't even notice.

'Goodnight, Lise,' he said, still focused on his phone. He made no effort to get up from the seat.

I didn't understand. I paused outside the studios to think about it, but the people who regularly slept under the colonnades were laying out sleeping bags and cardboard and I didn't want anyone to think I was staring at them, or for them to ask me for money that I didn't have. I kept my gaze straight and my walk steady until I was well away.

It must have been Goldie who texted, I thought. She hadn't approved of me sitting with Anders. She'd frowned at me. It made sense – she'd texted Anders from the club or wherever she'd gone and . . . I couldn't guess what she'd said. She shouldn't have interfered! Anders and I were adults. We could make up our own minds about our behaviour.

Perhaps it wasn't Goldie, but Fabienne. Yes, had Fabienne sent Anders a message chastising him for making out with a fellow student? No, that was ridiculous. Fabienne wouldn't be so . . . parental.

It wasn't so much the message that annoyed me as the way Anders had dismissed me. He could have at least stood up and given me a hug.

What bad luck that Anders got that message just when I was prepared to – well, to do whatever he wanted? The world did not want me to have a boyfriend. Look what had happened with Ben. Timing – it was never on my side. I was even wearing my second-best bra, which didn't, of course, match my undies, but at least they were my lacy ones, not my daggy everyday undies. I'd almost been prepared.

It was a lonely walk back to the apartment through streets full of people laughing together and kissing under the lights. The Hôtel de Ville fountains were lit up and people sat around them, enjoying the warmth of the night.

By the time I was in my apartment I was angry with Anders. It didn't help that when I checked my email, my mother had sent me a reminder that she hadn't yet received a postcard from me and had I remembered to visit where Chanel used to live and take a photograph? Of course I hadn't. I ignored the email and went to bed, where I spent hours composing cutting text messages that I didn't send to Anders.

My phone buzzed the next morning and I sprang on it like a lion catching prey. It had to be Anders explaining about the night before – and it was Anders. He offered no explanation or apology, however. He just said it was a perfect day for shopping and did I remember offering to help him with a difficult purchase?

I thought about simply ignoring the text. I thought about it for all of thirty seconds and then I said sure. I hoped the single word was dignified and gave nothing away. If Anders wasn't going to explain, I wasn't going to ask. At least, not in a text. We agreed to meet at a cafe. He said he wanted a good breakfast but I decided he was nervous about encountering Madame Christophe again. I was too, and I evaded her questions, talking instead about how striking Fabienne was and telling her what she had worn to the opening.

'She has style,' Madame Christophe acknowledged, 'but she has not yet – and it pains me to say this about my friend – comprehended that her age demands a little . . . restraint. In this she reveals her Italian father. No matter. For the moment she is safe.'

I thought of the lace dress and wondered exactly who was safe? No matter. I had evaded questioning.

Chapter 10

PARISIAN LINGERIE

When Mum took me shopping for my first bra, she also bought me a lingerie bag that she handed to me as though it were a religious relic. Despite that I'm usually pretty casual about underwear. Unless there's a chance it might be seen.
Ami, on the other hand, only ever buys bras with matching knickers. Boy scout preparedness, she says when she's in a good mood. Delusional optimism, when she's not. I hope she got the stay-ups I sent.

Anders was waiting for me at the cafe. Although when I say waiting, I'm exaggerating slightly. He was eating sausages, drinking coffee and consulting his phone. He was wearing a pale striped T-shirt and he hadn't shaved. Despite that, I felt slightly frayed around the edges. I'd rescued my shorts and teamed them, rather hopefully, with the stay-up plaid stockings. The plaids clashed, but in an edgy way. I was beginning to think wistfully of the wardrobe Mum had wanted to make me and of the sales in Paris. Could I afford new clothes? Or something *really* vintage?

'Guten Morgen,' Anders said. 'Coffee? This is a difficult assignment, Lise. We must find something special. Something very French. I hope your shopping talents are up to it.' I thought he was examining my outfit with suspicion and I tugged at the bottom of my shorts surreptitiously. I didn't want to show too much lace.

'So who's the present for?' I asked.

'A person of total discernment.' Anders smiled as he took my hand. 'That's why I need to employ a shopper. Gabi is total chic.'

'And Gabi is?'

'My sister. It is her birthday and she wants something French.'

'A scarf?'

'We have scarves in Germany.' Anders dismissed the idea with a wave of his sausage-laden fork.

'Perfume?'

'Too obvious.'

I was getting cranky. He'd ditched me the night before and now I was supposed to instantly come up with brilliant ideas for his sister's birthday present? 'What happened,' I began, 'one minute—'

Anders' phone dinged and he held up his hand. 'Ah,' he said, 'the woman herself has spoken. She requires lingerie. French lingerie.'

'Your sister wants you to buy her lingerie?'

'Why not?'

'I don't know. It's just a little odd?'

'Not in my country. Let us search.'

I thought we'd go to a large department store, but instead Anders strode off in the direction of the Louvre. From there we turned right into streets filled with small, expensive shops. It was designer territory. The windows of each shop were works of art and I wanted to linger in front of the patisseries where piles of rosy macarons nestled next to gleaming tarts filled with whirls of dark chocolate.

Anders paused at a window filled with haughty manne-quins pretending to be wearing more than their scanties. 'Here,' he said and I followed him in.

The lingerie was laid out in glass cases as though the barely-there bras and panties were museum artefacts. I grabbed Anders' elbow. 'It's going to be expensive,' I hissed.

He was unperturbed. 'Gabi *is* expensive.'

An attendant glided up to us, murmuring in French. When Anders spoke, she instantly switched to English. 'For mademoiselle?' She indicated me with a glacial smile. I pulled at my shorts again.

'Not for me,' I said in French, 'for his sister. It's her birthday.'

'And the sister, she resembles your boyfriend?'

I looked at Anders. I had no idea. 'Anders, what does Gabi look like? Is she like you?'

'No, not at all. She is shorter, with dark hair and pale skin.'

'So completely unlike?' I was surprised.

'She takes after my mother,' Anders said, 'I take after my father. This is genetics, Lise.'

It must have been clear from my ignorance that I knew nothing so the attendant switched back to English and led Anders to the counter where she rapidly laid out wisps of lace in dusty pinks, scarlet and silver-grey. 'It depends on the look,' she said as she all but stroked the bras, 'perhaps not too sexy from a brother?' and she deftly removed the scarlet push-up from the silky pile.

'Romantic,' Anders said, 'definitely romantic. With a hint of sexy, but above all, something elegant. Not red or black – too obvious.'

He clearly didn't need my help. Why had I been invited along? As the attendant flourished bras at Anders, I pretended it was my birthday. We'd been together for six months, I decided, long enough for a European man to choose underwear for his girlfriend. I knew the set I wanted as soon as the attendant held it up. Unlike the others, this wasn't all lace. It was a silk balconette bra in blue polka dots, but what made it perfect were the ruffles. Sure, you'd only be able to wear it with certain clothes – but it would be the best bra to show off. The knickers had rows of the same ruffles forming a boy leg.

'I like those.' I nudged Anders.

'They are not sleek,' he objected. 'And they are not Gabi's colours.'

Sleek turned out to be the barest-pink semi-sheer lingerie set decorated with floral lace. I noted that Gabi was smaller than me but took a C cup. I was impressed that Anders knew that – or was it creepy? I couldn't decide – I was an only child. Would I want my brother to know what size bra I took? Perhaps I would if he was prepared to spend as much on me as Anders spent on Gabi. The attendant wrapped the delicacies in the palest green tissue – almost the exact shade of the leaves that curled around the flowers.

'Your sister is very lucky,' the attendant said, and then to me, 'It might be your turn next.'

'Lise wears only tartan,' Anders said, taking the slim box, 'we would have to buy her underwear from Scotland.'

'That's not true,' I began to protest, but my words were lost in the flurry of the attendant opening the door for us and telling Anders was a wonderful brother he was.

'So, to thank you for your help, I should buy you something,' Anders said, taking my hand.

'I didn't do anything,' I said sulkily.

'You provided moral support,' he corrected. 'Also, I wouldn't have entered the shop without you. Come, we will get you something special.'

For one bold minute I allowed myself to hope – but the special thing turned out to be a pastry from a nearby cake shop. I was still smarting from the tartan underwear comment so I chose an elegant lemon tart even though I actually wanted the opera cake, which looked amazing. Predictably, that's what Anders ordered. We sat outside, facing the street. Every woman who passed us was elegant. No one wore stay-up stockings with shorts.

'You are gloomy,' Anders said. 'Why, Lise? Has no man ever bought you pretty lingerie?'

I shook my head. 'I don't think an Australian guy would be game,' I said, 'or if he did, it would be something dodgy – you know, something *he* thought was sexy, not something a girl would like to wear.'

'You need to find yourself a European man,' Anders said, patting the box on the seat next to him, 'we think of the woman.'

'Last night you didn't,' I blurted out, 'you just kicked me out. More or less.'

'Ah, this is what makes you sad?'

'No. Well, sort of. It was a little abrupt.'

'I am sorry, Lise. There was something I had to attend to. It was a shame. I did enjoy kissing you.' And just like that he leant over and kissed me on the mouth, despite the crumbs of lemon tart. I didn't have time to push him away, even if I had wanted to. 'You taste like lemons,' he said, 'lemons and sugar. I wish I had more time today, Lise. I would be able to show you just how much I enjoy kissing you, but today is full of urgent errands for me. Perhaps later?' He signalled the waiter for the bill. 'I must hurry away now. You stay here, finish your coffee. There is no rush for you.' He kissed me again – this time on the top of my head – and before I could protest, he had marched off, holding the box of lingerie.

What did later mean, I wondered, ordering a second coffee. Did it mean that evening? Or later in the week? Still, he *had* kissed me. I replayed our conversation in my head for the rest of the afternoon as I sauntered through the Tuileries, watching the children play with the little boats, and the couples lounge in the sun. If I hear three people speaking German, I thought, Anders will text me. He didn't, even though I heard four people speak German. If I see two Bichon Frisé dogs, Anders will text me. I cheated on that one – I saw one and a rather plump poodle. Anders did not text. If I remember all the conjugations of aimer, Anders will text me. Even the subjunctive of aimer didn't work.

Later obviously did not mean that day or even that night and I ate two-minute noodles again sitting on my bed, watching a movie on my laptop. It was part of Ami's going-away present and it made me miss her. I left a Facebook message for her, asking what kind of man buys expensive underwear for his sister. When I woke up, she'd replied, *An incestuous one.* I knew that Ami had just meant to be funny, but it wasn't. I didn't reply.

Chapter 11

MENSWEAR - WHO CARES?

You may think you don't – but, trust me, you do. Ami says
she doesn't mind a good T-shirt collection, but they have to
be what arthouse movies are to blockbusters. Mum says every
man should own at least two suits – one for funerals and one
for celebrations. The funeral suit needs to be classic, the
celebratory one can be fashionable, within reason. I like
a guy who isn't afraid to wear a shirt with a collar.
A guy in a shirt has the potential to be a man.

When my phone buzzed the next day I expected it to be
Anders but it was Goldie, asking me to her studio for lunch
that day. She'd bought too much from the market, she texted,
and needed to share. Please say I could make it.

It was better than nothing, I thought, and a chance to see
Goldie's artwork, so I said yes. I took my fish-eye camera. She
was on the fourth floor of the main block of studios. It wasn't

as good a position as Anders' courtyard studio. I wondered if Goldie envied him.

She was waiting for me. The standard studio table was covered with a bright sarong that made the thick white china look rustic. 'I'll make coffee first,' she said. 'You must sit.'

I prowled around instead, admiring the glass objects that were scattered on every surface. Goldie made miniature female figures, which she arranged in coloured landscapes. At one end of the studio there was a large sculpture that reminded me of a Japanese Zen garden, except that the glass reflected the light in a hundred different directions so it was distracting, rather than restful. I liked the little women, however. There was something self-contained about them, as though they were simply content to contemplate their own beauty.

'I haven't any wine.' Goldie emerged from the kitchen. 'It doesn't mix with glasswork. All right for the painters to drink during the day, but if I make a mistake it will mean pain.'

While we ate, I felt as though Goldie were watching me. We talked – I learnt Goldie *was* from the Philippines, and had two siblings, both of whom worked in IT. Her ex-boyfriend had called off their relationship before she'd left for Paris on the grounds that she might meet someone and that he had to be free, too. After this revelation she came to a standstill. It was obviously my turn to speak but there was nothing I could think of saying other than the question I'd been asking myself since the night of the open studios, which I now blurted out.

'Did you text Anders the other night, after the opening?'

'No. Why would I?'

'I don't know. I thought – a message just came at an inconvenient time. That's all.'

Goldie nodded. 'I'll make more coffee?' She turned away.

'I wish I knew who it was,' I complained. 'It was really weird.'

Goldie busied herself at the sink and brought back the refilled plunger.

'I think you should know,' she said, 'that Anders is a bit . . . unreliable.'

'I know.' I laughed. Goldie's tone of voice had made me suspect she was going to tell me something far more serious.

'Not like that. You must listen, Lise. There's a girl. They have some kind of . . . arrangement.'

'An arrangement?'

Goldie got up from the table, even though she'd just sat down, and rearranged a glass landscape on one of the shelves. Absently she brought the little woman back to the table and fiddled with her as she spoke. 'It's complicated, but Anders – he flirts with someone. Like you. He did this before, right?'

'Before what?'

'Before you. Then, just when it seemed as though it was going to go somewhere, Anders called it off. The girl, Sophie, was devastated. The next thing, Anders arrived with this German girl. He introduced her as his girlfriend. Sophie didn't finish her residency. She just left. Anders said it wasn't his problem, he didn't promise anything. It was flirtation only.'

I held on to the table and stared at Goldie. Her eyes were soft and worried.

'He has a girlfriend?'

'She arrives when she feels threatened, perhaps? Who knows? I wanted to tell you before . . . before you were hurt.'

'Do you think it was the girlfriend who texted Anders? Do you think she knew about me?'

'It's possible. Mackenzie thinks it's a game they play.'

'It's an awful game,' I said, 'and I was so close to . . . you know.'

Goldie nodded. 'I didn't think things would go that far. I tried to say something, but I didn't want to make a fuss.'

'That's why you glared at me?'

'I didn't mean to look cross. I'm sorry.'

'Not as sorry as I am.' I got up and went to the big windows. There was no breeze to cool my face. 'I can't believe it. I know he can be arrogant but sometimes he's so nice.'

'He is,' Goldie said quickly, 'but as a friend, not a boyfriend. Or maybe he is nice to Gabi?'

'That's her name? Gabi? He told me that was his sister,' I wailed, remembering the expensive silk. 'We went shopping together for her birthday present.' I had known something was wrong with a brother buying his sister lingerie.

'That's not nice at all.'

'He told me stuff about her. How she was beautiful and elegant. I was so pleased she was only his sister, not his girl-friend. I knew I wouldn't have had a chance if he'd been interested in someone like that.' I didn't want to cry in front of Goldie but then she was beside me, her arms around me, and I was crying into her shoulder before I could stop myself.

'It's not the end of the world,' she said, after a few minutes. 'He's only this one guy, Lise. You don't even know him that well.'

'Maybe,' I sniffed, 'but I wanted to.'

Goldie shrugged. 'He is good-looking,' she acknowledged, 'but what interests do you share with him?'

'He helped me buy my camera.' I felt like a snotty kid.

'How difficult was that?' Goldie asked. 'How much time did it take from his day? Did he buy it for you – of course not. With Anders you jump to his tune. Is that what you want, Lise? To be like your little dog?'

'Napoléon's not like that,' I protested. 'He can be quite snarly and he's very independent.'

'So maybe you should be *more* like him? Snarl a little.'

'If Anders is with someone else, it doesn't matter what I do,' I said mournfully.

'Still, you can use this,' Goldie said.

'What do you mean?'

'To learn,' she said firmly.

'That's the kind of thing Madame Christophe would say.'

'Oh Lise, I know it's horrible. It is *so* horrible, but it only stays that way while you let it hurt you.'

I didn't know how to stop it hurting but there was no use telling that to Goldie. She insisted that we'd spent enough time on Anders and made me take photos of her even though with my tears I could hardly see through the lens. She said it would make me feel better and strangely enough it did. I knew Ami was going to love seeing the photos and I told Goldie about her and how I'd sent her some plaid stockings. Talking about Ami didn't make me feel homesick, despite the whole Anders thing. I missed her, of course, but Goldie was right. I was in Paris and I'd be home soon enough. Maybe by then Anders would be just another travel story?

Chapter

12

Ami wanted to have a cool affirming quote tattooed onto her wrist but she was worried her wrists were too small for anything worthwhile. She said 'breathe' was stupid as it was an involuntary act but I think sometimes it would be a reassuring reminder.

I left Goldie's studio a couple of hours later with a film full of photos and one of her little glass women. The humid air hit me and so did my loneliness. I didn't want to go back to the apartment where I'd be tempted to Skype Mum and get a lecture on male irresponsibility. I found myself in the Place des Vosges with its serene, ordered hedges. I sat on a bench and watched the pigeons.

There was a group of people my own age sitting on the lawn and eating. From their accents I could tell they were Irish and one of the girls had that auburn hair that always goes with pale, beautiful skin. She looked ethereal. Was Gabi as beautiful? As more friends joined them, the group on the grass jumped up and kissed or hugged each other before making the picnic circle bigger.

I had never felt quite so alone. Serves you right, I told myself, viciously scrubbing away tears before they could fall. Serves you right. You're so stupid. Just a stupid little girl whose own father didn't love her. Except now I knew that was no longer true. My father had loved me and he'd never forgotten about me. I could no longer chant the old mantra I had used when everything went wrong with Ben.

After Ben, before VCE finished, I'd seen a counsellor. Ami was doing psychology and diagnosing everyone. She'd pronounced me depressed and urged me to see someone. It was true that I wasn't sleeping well. I was stressed and anxious, but you could have said the same for nearly everyone in our year level.

It was actually a good move. The counsellor didn't lecture me for wasting her time. She listened to me and then suggested some strategies. She asked me to check in with her regularly to see if those strategies were working. She also explained how Ben wasn't the cause of it all. It was natural to carry around a fear of abandonment if one of your parents was absent, she explained. But, I could work on that by changing the things I told myself. That would be a start.

I am not stupid, I told myself now in the kindest tones I could manage. I am not stupid. I am good at some things. I know quite a lot about art and fashion history. I'm smart. I found my apartment in Paris even though it was the first time I'd ever been overseas. My father loved me. My mother loves me. I have good friends. I'm okay. Really, I'm okay. Anders is the jerk.

I sat there for about an hour, repeating my new mantras to myself, trying to believe them. Every so often I'd glance at the Irish group and wish that one of them would notice me and invite me to join them. They didn't. In between mantras, I'd check my phone. Just in case Anders had texted me. He hadn't.

Paris seemed grey and empty. Which was absolutely ridiculous. But I didn't tell myself I was being ridiculous. I told myself that I was in shock and that I was grieving and it was fine to feel this way for a while. If nothing worked out I promised myself I could go home early even though I knew I couldn't – not without wasting a lot of money. I'd been through all that with Mum before I left.

'But you won't want to leave,' she'd said. 'Paris for three months – the time will fly!'

'What if I get homesick?' This had been before the lawyer's letter, before our fight and before my world had shifted.

'You'll manage.' Mum had patted my face. 'You'll get through it, Lise. You've got a stubborn streak just like . . .' She'd paused and turned away. At the time, I'd thought she'd meant her mother. Now I suspected she'd meant my father, my stubborn father.

Anders and his stupid idea of me as a clean canvas could jump in the Seine, I thought savagely. I was so much more than that. Who knew where my passions would lead? People might laugh at my knowledge of fashion history, but somewhere it would be useful.

I could have told that stuck-up shop assistant selling lingerie something she didn't know. I could have told her that the first report of a brassiere was in American *Vogue* in the early 1900s and that an American first patented the bra. Take that, Paris, fashion capital of the world. Out-engineered by the USA! I should have casually leant on the counter, with just the tip of my elbow – like Audrey. 'Of course, once you'd have been buying a bust bodice,' I'd have said. Except Anders wouldn't have cared what a bra had first been called. Stuff like that didn't interest him. Stuff like that didn't interest any guy.

I put the little glass woman Goldie had given me on the park seat. I didn't really want to keep her. I felt guilty about it but she would always remind me of the moment when I knew I'd been played. She was too lovely to just throw away. I could simply leave her there to be found by someone she would delight.

I thought I could walk down to the Seine and see whether the Paris-Plages beaches had been constructed yet. I could take some more photos and then I could go back to my apartment and make some postcards. Or even Skype Mum, if it wasn't too late. I had been avoiding her but now I wanted to hear her voice. I wouldn't tell her about Anders. I just wouldn't mention him at all.

I walked past the Irish group. It was their last night in Paris before returning to study. I loved the accents – it sounded as though they were reciting poetry even when they were just passing plates of food around.

My phone buzzed. A message. From Anders. My mouth was dry and my stomach churned. I didn't want to know what it said but I couldn't just delete it without looking.

'Excuse me,' a voice behind me said urgently. 'You have left this. Your object of art.'

I turned and there was a skinny boy not much older than me with thick, ragged hair and almond-shaped eyes. He wore a proper shirt, but it had come untucked from old-fashioned suit trousers. When he handed me the glass woman, I could see that his cuffs were frayed and the arms slightly too short. His French was fluent, but careful, and I heard an English accent behind it.

'Thank you,' I replied in French. I didn't want to admit to having left it behind deliberately. I took it out of his palm and put it gently in my bag.

'You're not French,' he said in English now.

'No, Australian.'

'Oh, Australian! Hugo. English. Originally from Camden.'

'Lise.' I shook his hand. His bitten down fingernails made his hands look as though they belonged to someone younger, although this was belied by the bony strength of his handshake.

'Such a pleasure,' he said. 'I've been speaking French all day and my brain is going to explode.'

I was torn between wanting to talk to him and reading Anders' text. Maybe he was messaging me to explain? Maybe Goldie had made a mistake? Maybe this time things were different? I glanced at my phone pointedly.

'Oh,' he said, 'I'm sorry. You're calling someone?'

'A message,' I said. 'I'm kind of . . . Do you mind?'

'Of course not.'

'There are some Irish students back there.' I gestured to the group on the grass, but even as I did so I noticed that most of them had drifted off. 'They all speak English.'

'It's okay.' He smiled and I noticed the smile caused two small creases to appear next to his mouth. 'Not really an issue. It was just that I thought – hoped – you might have a gelato with me. But you're busy and why wouldn't you be? It's Paris. No one comes here by themselves! Well, except me. And really I'm on business. Have a lovely evening, Lise.'

He half-waved and walked briskly away, leaving me slightly confused. He was in Paris on business? He wasn't dressed like a businessman but nor was he like any of the hipster artists I'd met. There was nothing studied about his clothes or appearance. It was more as though he'd borrowed someone else's once-quality garments.

My phone buzzed again. I steadied my hand and then opened the message. *Meet me at the falafel?* That was it. No apology, no explanation. Had Goldie told him what she'd revealed to me? What if she was wrong about him? What if he'd broken up with Gabi? I'd turn up and he'd be romantic. He'd have flowers – dark roses. Or maybe some exquisite chocolate truffles dusted with gold leaf. I'd seen some that looked like fairytale bird's eggs. I had to give him the benefit of the doubt, didn't I?

I just had time to whiz back to the apartment, apply some make-up and change my clothes.

I was five minutes late at the rue des Rosiers but my eyeliner was perfect and my messy bun the result of half an hour of hard work. Anders was slouched against a wall examining the queue already forming for falafel. He greeted me with a kiss – not an air kiss, but a real kiss on the mouth. I couldn't pull away. He smelled of that nearly familiar forest fragrance and he put his arm around me straight away, as though we were already a unit.

'Shall we queue?' he asked. 'Or shall we go the rivals?'

'Is there a difference?' I didn't want to talk about falafels. I wanted Anders to tell me the truth about Gabi but I couldn't just blurt out everything Goldie had told me.

'I don't think so, but then for me food is fuel. Perhaps not the Berthillon gelato or my mother's stollen, but falafel? The difference is too subtle.'

That was my opportunity. I could ask how he felt about women. Were our differences too subtle? I was trying to form the words in my head when I had to decide whether or not I wanted spicy falafel and garlic sauce. It seemed too trivial to compare myself to chilli flakes so I just accepted the falafel and Anders and moved on.

'I can't eat this walking,' I said. 'I'll spill it.'

'We'll find somewhere. But you must walk quickly, Lise. I don't want my fuel getting cold! Come, there's a square near here.'

It was not the Place des Vosges, but a small, barren square dominated by a large mural of a ghostly woman. We sat beneath her and were immediately mobbed by pigeons who stood defiantly at our feet, waiting for tidbits. Eating was serious business for Anders and he didn't talk. I followed his lead and concentrated on my falafel. He'd put his arm around me. He'd kissed me gently. He wasn't a jerk. He wasn't a player. Goldie had it wrong. Maybe she'd lied? Maybe she was keen on Anders? She had said he was good-looking. But Goldie was my friend – she'd never do that. And Anders was my friend too, wasn't he? I didn't know what to think.

After Anders had folded our empty wrappers carefully together and disposed of them, he settled back on the park bench, and nestled me against his chest. 'This is perfect,' he said. 'Such a beautiful evening with a beautiful girl. What more is life for?'

'Family? Your sister? Art?' I lifted my head up and, as though in answer, he bent his head down and kissed me. It was a long, slow, deliberate kiss. A voice in my brain shrieked, *this may not be right – what about Gabi?* But, no matter how strident that voice was, my mouth went right on kissing Anders back.

'It is good,' he said, eventually pulling away, 'that we both had the garlic sauce.'

It wasn't a very romantic thing to say but I didn't feel I could point that out to him. I laughed nervously instead.

'Here,' he said, 'smile!'

He aimed his phone at us, his mouth against my cheek. 'I'll send it to you?'

The whole thing was surreal. 'I didn't think you were the selfie sort?'

'I don't like Fakebook,' he answered, fiddling with his phone, 'but that doesn't mean I don't wish to remember good times. And also, I know that all you girls love photographs. Proof that you have won our hearts.'

'That's not true.' I twisted away from him. 'I hate selfies. Well, that's not true, either. It's okay when everyone's posing for fun.'

'Shall we take another and you can do that hair shake thing?'

'I'm wearing a messy bun,' I said. 'I don't want to shake it out. What would be the point of putting it up in the first place?' Everything felt wrong.

'What's the point of anything?' Anders asked in a tone that was at least half condescending. 'Ah, but I know. Come back with me to my studio.'

Back to his studio! That could only mean one thing. Was that what I wanted? Should I mention Gabi?

I found myself saying, 'Okay,' as though I was under a spell.

'Beautiful Lise,' Anders murmured, stroking the side of my face, 'so beautiful!'

He lifted me to my feet as he kissed my neck and shoulders. They were fluttery kisses that matched the butterflies bursting to life in my stomach. I could feel the muscles in his back and chest as we stood up and I was forced to hold on to him for balance. We kissed again and it was the perfect moment, pressed up against Anders, the mural above us and, surprisingly, for Paris, no one else in the square.

Then his phone rang. He broke away. 'Sorry, Lise. I need to take this call.'

I couldn't believe it. I would have let my phone ring out, but no, Anders was not only answering his, but walking away from me and talking in German, leaving me with the pigeons until he came back.

'That is dealt with,' he said. 'It was just my sister.'

'Your sister?' The butterflies in the pit of my stomach solidified into a thick mass I felt I'd vomit up any second. I tried to keep my voice light when I said her name. 'Gabi?'

'That's right.' Anders smiled, but a small muscle beside his mouth jumped. 'Gabi. She is coming to Paris.'

I took a deep breath. It all made sense. The selfie had been part of the game. He'd sent it to Gabi.

'That's fabulous,' I said, my voice unnaturally bright. 'I'll meet her?'

'Gabi is a whirlwind,' Anders said. 'She will have plans for every minute. Shall we go?' He took my hand but I stood my ground.

'But you've told her about me?'

'I have,' he said confidently. 'I've told her how beautiful you are, Lise.'

'Did you send her our photo just then?' Was I sounding as innocent as I hoped?

Anders gave me a slightly puzzled look. 'Yes, I did,' he admitted.

'So she rang when she received the photo? She must want to meet me.'

'Of course, but she also wants to see my exhibition. It finishes next weekend. Gabi is very . . . supportive of my work.'

'Well, what *sister* wouldn't be?'

'Lise, why are we standing here discussing Gabi when we could be walking back to my studio contemplating far more pleasurable pursuits?'

'Because she's not your sister,' I said and my voice shook.

Anders released me straight away. 'What?'

'Gabi is your girlfriend, Anders.'

'It's not like that,' Anders said, but he'd already moved a step away from me. 'It's complicated.'

'That's a Facebook cliché,' I said.

'Who told you? Who interfered?'

'That's really not relevant. Why did you lie to me? I thought you were my friend.'

'It's complicated,' Anders repeated, 'and I don't conduct my relationships like some teenager. I don't think in those boxes – girlfriend, boyfriend.'

'How convenient,' I said, 'and how progressive. Well, I like those boxes.'

'You are so young, Lise.'

Tears stung my eyes. 'I don't think it's a question of being young,' I said. 'I think it's more about trust. I trusted you and you betrayed me.'

'But if I had told you from the start that Gabi and I were open to other . . . complications . . . you wouldn't have been part of it,' Anders said.

'That's right,' I said, 'I wouldn't and you knew that.' The tears made my voice thick and even shakier. 'You're just a user, Anders. Just a jerk.' I couldn't say anything else. It was stupid to cry for a relationship that had never even happened but I wasn't just sad, I was also really, really angry. I turned away. I thought I might throw up.

Chapter 13

It can take ten hours to make a few centimetres of lace the traditional way. Mum knew someone who made her daughter a lace bridal veil. It took over two thousand hours. Mum and I worked out that was about two hundred and fifty full working days. She began the veil when her daughter was born. Imagine being so certain your daughter would get married – and wear a veil. What if she'd been a punk? Or didn't want a traditional wedding? Or just didn't want to get married at all? I guess people don't ask those questions when they begin something so enormous. Something so big with love.

I wanted to rant. I needed to tell someone. Mum was my first thought. But did I really want her to know that I'd been taken in by a smooth German player? Also the time difference was no longer on my side, which cut out Ami as well. Instead, I went for a long walk along the river.

I pretended I was a heroine from a classic book or one of Mum's favourite old movies, walking along the Seine. Except if I'd been a nineteenth-century girl, nearly ruined, I may well have considered throwing myself in. I thought of this as I leant on the parapet, looking at the beginnings of the Paris-Plages. It was incredible to think that each summer a fake beach was built in the centre of Paris. I couldn't even guess at how much sand was being dumped. Dumped. I hadn't even had a chance, this time, to be dumped.

'He's not worth it,' a faintly familiar English voice behind me said, 'and it's not like in the books. You wouldn't drown – all Australians can swim – but you'd end up in hospital with some dreadful bacterial bugs in your system and die a lingering, expensive death.'

'Thanks for that,' I said. 'I was actually watching them make the beach. Did you find someone to talk English with?'

'I have now. It must be my lucky day.' He stuck out his bony, nail-bitten hand for me to shake again. 'Hello again, Lise.'

'Hi, Hugo.'

'So, meeting you here means one of two things – your date didn't work out or you were lying to get rid of me the first time.'

I sighed. He was watching me carefully, his face a studied blank. 'My date didn't work out.' I offered the truth and he beamed at me.

'Sub me in?'

'Sub?'

'You know, substitute me. I'm more than happy to be runner-up. It's not glamorous, but someone has to do it. Feel like an ice-cream?'

'Not Berthillon.'

'Don't tell me – you used to go there with him. Isn't it the best ice-cream in Paris? Not that it worries me. I'm English. Our tastebuds are genetically stunted by generations of chip butties, lager and Woodbines. I'll settle for second-best ice-cream. Or third-rate. Or no ice-cream but a beer.'

'I was just going to walk,' I said, although the idea of beer with this strangely attractive guy was appealing. Was he only attractive because I was on the rebound? Could you even be on the rebound from something that hadn't happened?

'Let's walk, then,' he said. 'Do you know, if we walk far enough we can see the dinosaur.'

'The dinosaur?'

'Someone's building a dinosaur. It's art.'

'Wow, I didn't know that.'

'Good thing you subbed me in. I'm a wealth of local knowledge.'

Despite myself, I was cheering up. 'So you live in Paris?'

'I visit. I'm from England. Formerly of Camden, latterly of ooop North. Hugo Sandiland of Sandiland and Nephew. I'm the nephew. Antiques, bric-a-brac, rare books, you name it, if it's worth something and it's old, the Unc and I will attempt to make a quid out of it.'

'Antiques. That's great. So you're not a student?'

'Of life and the antique trade, of course. But not of any smaller institution, no. And you?'

'Gap year – well, gap three months. I'm here learning French and studying art – historical stuff, sort of.' And artists, I thought.

'Art? So we're in the same game?'

'I'm not really in any game yet!' We'd fallen into step now and were heading towards the Tuileries. Hugo's nonstop talking reminded me of Mackenzie and that alone made me feel easy with him. 'Actually, I came largely because my mother persuaded me to. It was her dream.'

'Which you inherited?'

'I guess. We learn French together. She's a seamstress.'

'Not just a dressmaker, but a seamstress?'

'Correct. She worked for a while in haute couture, but not in France, of course. In Melbourne. That's when she started learning French. She might have come to France but she got pregnant to my dad. Then she had me and a business and it was just too hard to travel as a single mother.' Why was I telling him all this? I stopped.

'Ah,' Hugo said, 'so you thought you should step into her dancing shoes because you'd effectively mucked up the original tango?'

'It takes two,' I said sharply.

Hugo laughed. 'Touché!'

'So why are you in Paris?'

'Unc sends me over to do deals. His French is too proper. They rip him off.'

'So you come over here to buy stuff?'

'A little here, a little there.'

'That's fantastic!' He seemed far too young to be entrusted with business, but even as I thought that, I wondered if that wasn't part of the point.

'It's a living. More or less. Actually rather less in the current economic climate, but we do the best we can.'

'That would explain your shirt,' I said without thinking. 'Oh, sorry!'

'My shirt?'

'The frayed cuffs,' I said apologetically.

He stuck one of his wrists out. 'Hmm, I see what you mean. Didn't notice myself. Unc and I are becoming a tad shambolic, I fear. It's batching together. Not good for our sartorial ship-shapedness at all. Still, my clients probably haven't noticed. Not the most sartorially minded themselves. You, on the other hand – well, a seamstress's daughter.'

'I wasn't being critical,' I said.

'Not at all.' Hugo took my hand in his, as though it were the most natural thing in the world. I should have tugged my hand away but instead I let him tuck it into his elbow. Maybe it was an English thing? 'I think observant is the word. A necessary quality if you're studying art history.' Maybe to distract me from the fact that we were now walking close together, he kept up a high-speed account of his past few days in Paris. It was a bewildering list of names and places completely unfamiliar to me.

'So where are you staying?' I asked, when he paused for breath.

'Ah, good question, that. First up, I stayed with an old amour of Unc's but her daughter arrived out of the blue – broken marriage. So now I'm couch surfing for a couple of nights. I was lucky enough to find somewhere in the seventh.'

'Couch surfing? But aren't you working?'

'I'm buying,' Hugo said, 'not selling. Yet. You have to have the money to spend money to make money. What district are you in? Are you in a hostel?'

I told him about Madame Christophe, French lessons and Fabienne. I told him about Mackenzie and Goldie, but not about Anders.

'There it is,' he said suddenly. We both stared at the metallic dinosaur. 'It's not as big as I thought it would be. Disappointing.'

'I think that calls for a beer. Drown our sorrows?' I suggested. I discovered I didn't want to turn back home. I wanted to find out more about Hugo.

'Now you're talking!' He found a bar effortlessly. It was a punk bar run by a middle-aged woman with a full-sleeve tattoo. Hugo ordered our drinks and chatted to her in fluent French. He must have told a joke because she laughed a throaty smoker's laugh and, later, brought out a small plate with salami, cheese and baguette. She said in English, 'Your boyfriend is a charmer,' and winked at me. Hugo ducked his head and blushed.

'Do you know her?' I asked.

'No,' he said. 'We share some of the same music tastes though. It's a Camden thing.'

'I thought you lived in Ooop North?'

'Good accent,' Hugo said. 'I do now, but you can't take Camden out of the boy.'

'So, where is Ooop North?'

'Yorkshire, lassie. Way ooop North.'

'Oh.' It was my turn to blush. 'I thought ooop North was a place.'

Hugo laughed. It was an unabashed sound. It made me sort of proud to have caused it. 'It's a place and more – an attitude, a way of life, a way of talking and so slow it drives anyone from Camden crazy. But I kind of like it there, now. Unc needed me and I've always loved old things.'

'Isn't that strange? I mean, I love old things too. But for a guy?'

Hugo shrugged. Unlike Anders, his shoulders were thin and where the seam was giving out at the top, I caught sight of his blue-white skin. I looked down at the plate and took a piece of salami. The glimpse of skin had made me feel as though I'd eavesdropped on an intimate conversation. 'Half the antique dealers I know are men,' he said. 'I like things that were precious once to someone else.' He leant forward to make his point. 'When we weren't such consumers, gobbling everything up and then tossing it out, even ordinary things were chosen with care. You didn't just buy, say, salt and pepper shakers. You thought about them. You imagined them sitting, just so, on your favourite tablecloth.

There was meaning there. That's what I like – feeling the meaning.'

'We still do that,' I said, 'Mum and I. We talk about stuff before we buy anything. It can be frustrating because it takes us so long but in the end we get something we really want. I think it's because we didn't have much money when I was born. But maybe it's because we lived with my great-grandmother.'

'With your great-grandmother? Isn't that strange for an Australian?'

'I guess,' I said defensively, 'but my grandmother didn't want Mum to have me because she wasn't married. It worked out for Mum and Greatma, though, because Greatma was getting forgetful. Not dementia – just forgetful. Also she didn't drive and she hated Meals on Wheels. She called me her little blessing because Mum moved in with her and looked after us both.'

'Is she still alive?'

'No, she died when I was ten. I still miss her sometimes. She had a whole lot of old stuff, antiques and bric-a-brac. Mum kept nearly everything.'

'How wonderful.' Hugo seemed genuinely interested. 'What a fabulous childhood that must have been in so many ways. I mean, shame about your grandmother and all, but a great-grandmother – that's something. You'd have been so spoilt!'

I knew what he meant. Greatma had never been too busy to read to me, or make me doll's clothes or play Scrabble.

'Yeah, maybe, but not in a princess way. When she died Mum lost her voice for about four weeks. The doctor said there was nothing he could do. It was grief. She croaked around the place wearing Greatma's aprons. We told each other stories about Greatma and cried every night.' Embarrassingly, my eyes were filling now. I took a big swallow of beer and willed the tears away.

Hugo reached over and covered my hand with his. 'It's hard to lose people,' he said. 'Unc says this life is a vale of tears and it's remarkable that we keep slogging on through the misery. Mind you, he's an Eeyore.'

I laughed. 'Does that make you Tigger?'

Hugo laughed too, the welcome sound filling the small bar. 'That's what he says,' he admitted. 'I think of myself more as the wise Owl. He fought in the Falklands.'

'The Falklands?'

'Yeah, we forget it wasn't really a world war. It was just a British thing – before you and I were born, of course. But it was still a war. Unc came back a lot more pessimistic, Mum says, and a lot quieter. PTSD.'

'PTSD?'

'Post-traumatic stress disorder – most soldiers have it.'

'Oh, yeah, of course.'

'He doesn't go out much. I'm his runner.'

I nodded. 'My mum doesn't go out much either,' I said. 'I mean, she's not agoraphobic, she's just self-sufficient. I used to worry about her. I wanted her to meet someone. Ami and I tried to set her up on OkCupid, but she wasn't impressed.'

'So she hasn't got a boyfriend?'

'No. I don't think she's ever had one – well, not since my father. She has lots of friends, though.'

'If she's anything like you,' Hugo said, 'there would have to be a man somewhere. Sorry, Lise, that's not really a compliment – it's just a fact.'

'I look like my dad,' I said.

'Do you have photos?' Hugo asked.

'Back at the apartment. Only a few of him.'

Hugo fished out his phone. If you'd asked me what kind of phone Hugo would have, I'd have guessed something old with a cracked screen, but this was a new smart phone in a leather case, which he flipped open to reveal a proper French metro card, not just the paper tickets I bought by the tens. He must have seen my surprise.

'Chosen with care,' he reminded me. 'I'm techno savvy, as any Camden boy should be. Course this phone just might have fallen off the back of a lorry but that's the perks of the trade, luvvie.'

He showed me photos of his uncle, an older version of Hugo with the same dimples when he was smiling. I saw the shop they ran with the sign, *Sandiland and Nephew*, hanging up in ornate ironwork. I saw photos of his uncle's cat. Then I saw photos of his mum and his sister. 'Hairdressers, both of them,' Hugo said, pushing his thick fringe away from his eyes. 'Mum said I was a crime to hairdressing. Double crown, thick hair. A nightmare. I was banned from the shop in case her customers thought she was responsible.'

'You're joking.' The woman in the photo had hairdresser hair, perfectly tinted and styled in a deliberately messy updo. Her lipstick and nail polish matched. It was hard to imagine Hugo as her son.

'Of course I'm joking!' Hugo said with undisguised affection. 'Mum's okay. She looks a bit Stepford wifey but she's not. What you can't see in that photo are the two tatts she's got – Hugo inside her left forearm and Olivia inside the right. So she doesn't forget who we are when she's old and demented, we say.'

'She's got tattoos?'

'It's a Camden thing,' Hugo said. 'You'd love Camden, Lise. You should come across the channel. See somewhere other than Paris while you're on this side of the world.'

'I'd love to go to London,' I said. 'I'd love to travel everywhere but this trip is all about Paris. Mum said you don't know somewhere properly unless you live there for a while. And I'm taking French lessons.' As soon as I said that, I thought, oh no: I'd have to go back to French class and Anders would be there. Damn. 'So what about your dad?' I asked, not wanting to think about that embarrassment.

'He's okay. We don't see a lot of each other these days.'

'But you do see him?' I pressed.

'Yeah, on special occasions. Don't you see your dad?'

'He's dead.'

'Oh, I'm sorry.'

'It doesn't matter. I never knew him. He took off before I was born. Went to Wales, England.'

'Wouldn't you like to see where he lived?'

I thought of the painting hanging in my bedroom. Those mysterious hills wearing hats of low cloud. 'Not this trip,' I lied. 'It was all arranged before I knew where he even lived. This trip isn't about him at all.'

'Really? But you're only a hop, skip and a jump away. Just saying.'

I changed the subject and Hugo let it ride but I knew I'd dwell on what he'd said when I was back at my apartment.

The sky was just darkening by the time I returned. I'd had one beer too many, I decided, as I tried to focus on the numbers of the security code. It was a good thing that Madame Christophe wasn't still awake. I negotiated the flights of stairs and flopped on my bed. Hugo had tried to walk me home but I'd put him off. I needed to clear my head.

'Are you sure you'll be all right?' Hugo asked.

'It's Paris,' I said, 'it's not even late and the Marais is a gay district. I'll be fine, Hugo. Hey, let me ask you one question. Do you know what a bust bodice is?'

'A bust bodice? If this was a trivia game, I'd have to guess that it was a kind of bra?'

'You're exactly right!'

'There you are – I'm not just a pretty face. Let me give you my number.'

'I need to be alone,' I said, 'but you do get a prize for the right answer.' And I'd kissed him. Just a little kiss but on his mouth. Which was surprisingly soft.

'Whoa!' he said. 'That was unexpected. And lovely. But maybe you've had too much to drink?'

'Just one beer too many,' I said, 'but I meant the kiss. You're very sweet, Hugo. Very. Just remember that, won't you?'

Lying on my bed, I cringed thinking about that moment. The walk – and pretending to be more sober than I felt – *had* cleared my head. I just hoped Hugo had accepted what I'd said as a real compliment, and not just the kind of drunken, condescending statement a girl makes to a guy she's subbed in for someone else.

Chapter

'A time to reap, a time to sew' – Greatma embroidered those words on a needlework sampler. It's a misquote from the Bible. I imagine her stitching, pushing her hair from her face the way my mother does. At ten she was making something that would outlast her, something that would be cherished. All the women in my family have sewed. It's genetic. What else is genetic?

Mum Skyped me early the next morning, afternoon her time. It felt as though months had passed since we'd spoken. We didn't talk about my father or the money he'd left me or the fact that she had kept photos of him that she'd never shown me. Instead she told me how the weather was becoming colder and that she had made a cape for one of her clients that looked exactly like Red Riding Hood's coat. I let her talk. I was slightly hungover. I told her about Hugo, but not about Anders.

'An antique business?' Mum was excited. 'Oh, how wonderful, Lisi. And over in France buying for his uncle!'

'He was very nice,' I admitted, 'but not, you know, boyfriend material.' There was silence, although I could see Mum's fuzzy frown. I knew what was coming next. 'Not that I'm looking for a boyfriend. That would be stupid.'

'Difficult,' Mum agreed. 'You'll be home before you know it and then it will be university and a whole new cast of people. No, you need to concentrate on your French and soak up all that culture, Lisi.'

'Have you seen Ami?'

'Yes,' Mum said, 'we had dinner together the other night.'

'She's never on Facebook,' I said. 'I keep leaving her messages.'

'She's been working for her uncle – it's uni holidays.'

'What are they doing?'

'Some kind of catering thing,' Mum said vaguely, 'you know – office morning-tea parties. Apparently he got some green tea cheaply and they're experimenting with baking with it.'

'Baking?'

'For the catering.'

That sounded just like Ami's uncle – and, knowing him, it would turn out to be really popular. It also explained why I hadn't heard from Ami, other than the briefest of messages like waves from a passing car. Then Mum's phone rang and we hung up. We'd managed the whole conversation without saying anything narky to each other.

By the time I got down to breakfast, Madame Christophe had nearly finished eating and my coffee was lukewarm.

'You need to go to the Porte de Vanves,' she announced. 'Today.'

'Why?'

'You will enjoy it and you will find your mother a present from Paris.'

I had a perverse need to rebel. 'I could go next week,' I said, pouring more coffee. 'I'd be better prepared.'

She shrugged. 'You can certainly go next week,' she said, 'but you also need to go today. You can take Napoléon. He will help you haggle. Also, he adores flea markets.'

Napoléon's world opinions were flexible and opportunistic; however, I loved stepping out, dog in tow. I gave Napoléon a conspiratorial wink while Madame Christophe fussed over his flea-market-suitable collar, which turned out to be a rather smart navy blue number decorated with silver paw prints.

'Take cash only,' she said, 'you will not be able to use a card. Be careful in the metro – it is not a good line. There will be thieves.'

Porte de Vanves reminded me of parts of Melbourne – it was more modern than the Paris I had become used to. There were no sweet alleys and old buildings but tall modern apartments and office blocks, and there was a tram. I stood there gaping at it. A tram! I took a photo to send to Ami.

The market stretched up one street to a coffee cart, then it turned the corner, meandered along that street and across the road was another length of stalls. It was just after ten when Napoléon and I arrived and the market was bustling. There were all sorts of vintage things for sale. The first stall had ugly vases, empty picture frames, and a plastic tray full of costume jewellery. The next had linen: embroidered tablecloths, napkins and rolls of faded ribbon. Another stall sold nothing but perfume bottles and the Chanel and Bulgari gifts that you sometimes got if you spent enough money, blingy bracelets and necklaces, a wallet and a travelling jewellery pouch. They weren't free on the stall, of course. Other stalls sold doll's heads. They seemed sad, piled up without their bodies. Then I overheard the price of one and sadness was replaced by incredulity.

I could see so many things that Mum would love. Madame Christophe had been right – this was the place to buy her a French present. Perhaps an Art Deco tea set? She would adore that but of course it was entirely impractical. I needed something precious but small. There was a stall of handbags and one of them was vintage straw decorated with bright yellow daisies that I knew would have matched the yellow in my cowboy dress. I picked it up twice, to the stallholder's displeasure. She hissed the price at me and I replaced the handbag reluctantly. I hadn't bargained on the market being so full of wonderful things and my cash was limited. Mum's present would have to come first.

I was nearly back down the row when I saw it – a marcasite brooch. A poodle. It was half kitsch, half gorgeous and fully vintage. It was wholly perfect. I asked the stallholder how much it was.

She eyed me up and down. 'It's marcasite,' she said, 'and it's very old.'

I knew it wasn't that old, but I just nodded. 'It is the ideal thing for my mother,' I said.

'It is one hundred and twenty euros,' the woman said, smiling and reaching for the brooch. 'Shall I wrap it for you?'

'That's too expensive,' a familiar voice behind me said. 'Chérie, it's a little gaudy, don't you think?' Hugo plucked the brooch from my hand and turned it over. 'I mean, it's cute, if you like this kind of thing.' He shrugged and returned it to the stallholder. 'But too expensive, regrettably.' He pulled me away.

'I wanted that,' I hissed as he marched me from the stall.

'I know you did and so did she. It was all over your face. You need to bargain, Lise. It's only fifties marcasite. Although it is sterling, I'd give you that, and the poodle is very French. It's a perfect gift for your mum.'

'But you stopped me from getting it!'

'Ah, no, but I have a plan. A cunning plan.' He was leading me back up the hill to the coffee cart.

'I knew it was fifties, by the way,' I told him, 'and I guessed it was silver. I'm not stupid.'

'I don't think you're stupid at all.' Hugo stopped and the crowd of shoppers swirled around us. 'I think you're sharp, Lise. You're clever, stylish, brave, quite beautiful and I bet you wouldn't say no to a hot chip?'

His abrupt change of subject was disconcerting. 'Well, thanks. I mean for the compliments. And, yes, I guess to the chips. But I want that brooch, Hugo. What if someone else gets it?'

'Then you shrug philosophically and say, ah well, there is always another market, another brooch.'

'You said yourself it was perfect and you don't even know Mum.'

'Okay, okay. Just wait. Let's order chips and while they cook I'll get your brooch. Deal?'

He ordered the chips and I sat down at a rickety table with Napoléon at my feet, growling slightly at a feisty miniature schnauzer who was guarding the end of a bread roll.

'I'll be back,' Hugo said. 'Make sure the Hound of the Baskervilles doesn't eat all the chips!'

The proprietor came over with our food. 'Hugo's a good man.'

I was intrigued. 'You know him?'

The guy nodded. 'Always joking, even though life cannot be easy. His uncle is troubled.'

'Yes, I've heard.'

'But of course, the company of a young woman as lovely as yourself will make him cheerful.'

'We haven't known each other for very long,' I said hastily.

'Ah well, there is always the beginning,' he said cryptically and shuffled back to serve someone else.

'Voilà,' Hugo said, coming up behind me, 'your brooch! You owe me the rather less expensive sum of seventy euros.'

'Oh, Hugo – that's wonderful. How did you do that?'

'Charm and wit. I could have got it for less had you not so obviously wanted it.'

I unwrapped the brooch. 'How did you know it was silver?' I asked, turning it over as Hugo had done.

'See that?' Hugo pointed to a tiny imprint. 'That's the silver hallmark. You can absolutely guarantee anything with that mark is silver. I say, it is lucky we've met again, isn't it? This is our third meeting. That has to mean something.'

'It means that Paris is quite small,' I said.

'No, anything that comes in threes is symbolic. That's a rule of the universe. So, what else catches your fancy?'

'There's a handbag,' I said slowly, 'but it would be hard to pack. It's straw.'

'You're thinking of packing already?'

I rolled my eyes. 'Only in terms of shopping.' Actually, when I added up how many weeks I had left, I was dismayed. I would be leaving Paris in seven weeks. Seven weeks! Time was slipping past. I'd already been in Paris for more than a month.

'Yellow daisies?'

'Yes, that's it. How did you know?'

'We antique dealers know these things.' Hugo laid a finger beside his nose and nodded complacently. 'Come on, let's get you bargaining, Lise. The trick is to pretend to yourself as well as the stallholder that you don't care if you get the object of your desire or not. Just tell yourself there's something even more perfect around the corner. If that fails, pretend to be someone else – haughty and supercilious.'

We went back to the stall and Hugo launched into a stream of effortless French. Within seconds the stallholder had unbent and they were laughing at each other's jokes. I was pleased with how much I understood. Hugo had made me his girlfriend. He was against the buying of the bag, because it would be difficult to pack.

'But Hugo,' I said, placing both my hands on his shoulders and looking up at him in a girlfriendly way, 'I will carry it. It's a handbag!' The stallholder and I rolled our eyes at men in general, and this one in particular. His shoulders were bony under my hands. What would it be like to slide my hands down his back? I'd be able to feel every little knot of his spine. Instead I put my fingers on his mouth. 'Don't say another word,' I said. I rather hoped he'd kiss my fingers but instead he took my hand in his and held it.

Then it was over to me.

The stallholder named a ridiculous sum. I picked the bag up. I pretended to myself that I didn't really want it. I'd much rather a Birkin, I thought. I looked at it critically and picked at a loose bit of straw with a contemptuous fingernail. I examined the underside of one of the yellow daisies (so perfect!) and showed Hugo a discoloured spot on the fabric. We both shook our heads. I tested the handle and poked at one end that was slightly unravelling. Nothing I couldn't fix. I could already see exactly how it could be done with some stout linen thread.

'Regrettably, Madame,' I said, 'this bag is not in perfect condition. Look.' I flicked my fingernail at the loose straw and tugged on the handle, drawing her attention to the flaws.

She shrugged and lowered the price by five euros. I was a haughty Birkin-loving woman. I was enjoying myself. I eyed the bag speculatively. 'Packing it will be a problem,' I said, 'and not just for me, but for anyone. Only a tourist, after all, would be interested in such a piece.'

'Oh, but not at all, Mademoiselle,' the vendor said, 'these are very desirable this season. Have you seen the latest *Vogue*?'

'I have, Madame,' I said – and I wasn't fibbing. I'd pored over it only a couple of nights ago, seeing if I could understand all the articles, but mainly examining the clothes. 'There was not a single piece like this, I'm afraid. This season it's all about neutral leathers and everything is oversized. We are carrying our life in our handbags. This is why you will only sell this to a tourist.'

'It is vintage,' the vendor said defensively, 'vintage is always *au courant*.' But she lowered the price by another five euros.

I managed to bargain her down by fifteen euros without Hugo saying a word.

'Your girlfriend is formidable,' the stallholder said grudgingly as she handed over the bag.

Hugo laughed. 'She surprises me all the time,' he said and then drew me into a hug. Without thinking I stood on my tiptoes and kissed his mouth. It was a soft kiss that I let last longer than I should have because the surrounding stall-holders and several passers-by clapped.

'You do surprise me,' Hugo whispered.

'Oh, that's right – you're English. That was a little too public for you?' I wanted to kiss him again and keep my eyes open this time. I wanted to see if he enjoyed it.

'Not at all. We've met three times. We'd probably have a kid by now, back where I was born.' Hugo grinned. 'I'll carry the bag for you. You've got Napoléon. You did really well, you know. I wouldn't have believed that was your first time haggling. You're a natural.'

'It was fun,' I said. 'I really, really enjoyed it. But then handbags are something I know about. Jewellery, not so much.' Hugo still held my hand. Kissing him had been an unexpected bonus. But I didn't say that out loud.

'It can all be learnt,' Hugo said, 'if you've got a feel for it and an eye – which obviously you do. I bet I could sell that brooch for twice what you paid for it. It's very quirkily chic.'

For a breathless moment I imagined the market life for myself, or maybe running a small shop. 'Oh Madame,' I'd say, 'such an elegant piece but with a genuine French je ne sais quoi.'

'Can we have lunch together?' Hugo interrupted my daydreaming.

'We've just eaten,' I said.

'Chips were the entree. Come on, there's a place near the metro. Cheap and cheerful. I want to know everything about you, Lise.'

He dropped my hand and then offered me his elbow. I tucked my hand in its crook and we sauntered off. Hugo didn't seem to be at all concerned that in his other hand, he swung a vintage straw bag covered in yellow leather daisies and sporting an enamel daisy clasp.

Chapter

15

The Romany girls I've seen in Paris have been dressed just as I'd imagined – flounced skirts, jangling bracelets and off-the-shoulder tops. Their eyes slide past me. I cannot imagine living as they do, so brashly identifiable and so obvious.

If you had asked me, I would have said that Hugo did most of the talking. He told me the local gossip in the town he and his uncle lived in. He told me about his uncle's dogs and how they were his uncle's excuse for not going anywhere, except for walks on the common. He talked about ordinary things, like the television programs he and his uncle watched and how his uncle had taught him to cook. In return I told him about my mother's afternoon teas with the rose-patterned Royal Doulton teacups, the sugar tongs and the teapot always turned three times.

'We have tea bags,' he said. 'Fancy being out-civilised by an Aussie colonial!'

'Mum doesn't like that the tea has to be bagged,' I said. 'It's environmentally unsound.'

'She's smart, your mum.'

'Sometimes,' I admitted, 'but she lives – well, Ami calls our place the House of Estrogen. That says it all, doesn't it?'

'That could be scary,' Hugo said.

'It's a bit like a movie set,' I said. 'Designated places untidy, otherwise cushions plumped, throw rugs on the furniture they exactly match, flowers always in the correct vase and candles at night.'

'Comforting, then? Unc and me – it's dishes in tottering piles on the sink, herds of empty beer bottles standing around and a month's worth of old newspapers in lieu of a tablecloth.'

'Disgusting' – I wrinkled my nose – 'but kind of fun.'

'That's behind the shop doors, of course. In the shop it's different. Sherry for the best customers. Old crystal glasses that Unc surreptitiously polishes on his shirttails. The English don't mind. Used to eccentricity. We embrace it.'

'Australians don't,' I said. 'We like everyone to conform and to be good at sport.'

'But you don't look like a joiner. Are you good at sport?'

'I play tennis. At school that wasn't good enough. It was all about netball or swimming. There were the popular kids, the sports jocks and the nerds. Then there was me and my best friend. We were a little hard to categorise.'

'Who likes school anyway?' Hugo said. 'Dreadful idea. Unc thinks we should all have had tutors at home. The old way.'

'In the library?' I imagined a dark room, floor-to-ceiling books and children standing around a large desk that was covered, perhaps, in a map.

'Oh my God, the library!' Hugo pulled out his phone. 'I have an appointment. Phew – there's time.'

'Do you have to rush off?'

'The book market. I'm sorry, Lise.' He rifled through his wallet. 'I thought I had a card. Damn. Do you have a pen?'

'Probably.' I rummaged around in my backpack and found a biro.

'This is my number.' Hugo grabbed my forearm and wrote large numbers along my arm. 'I seriously have to run!' He dropped a kiss on my forehead and ran off with a strange, loping stride.

I made my way down to the metro wistfully. I'd expected the afternoon to continue with us wandering around together. I'd certainly wanted that to happen! I pushed through the turnstile, Napoléon in my arms, and when the train arrived I jumped on still thinking of Hugo. Napoléon bristled and I saw that I'd nearly stepped into a taut piece of rope at one end of which a thin, watchful dog hunkered down under a seat.

Across the aisle sat a woman dressed in layered rags, so dirty I wasn't sure of the original colour. Her feet were bare and her matted dreads were wrapped in a filthy scrap of material. Another dog sat under her seat. She and the dogs stared at me. I didn't want to back away but I didn't want to step over the rope, either. I wanted to say excuse me, but I couldn't find my voice. Finally she yanked the rope and the dog slithered reluctantly from under his seat to join her other dog. Napoléon's hackles rose and he growled but I hushed him and walked past. I whispered, 'Merci.'

It was the dogs that shocked me. Most of the dogs I'd seen on the street had been well cared for, even pampered. They were drawcards for money, as well as company for their owners. The guy begging next to the supermarket had two Pomeranians he brushed until their fur was supermodel shiny and when he stopped, the dogs nosed and licked him, before curling up on their sleeping mats. These dogs were wild and uneasy. Napoléon was on high alert and I hugged him close. The woman turned deliberately so she could keep staring at me. The other passengers all studiously avoided eye contact with either of us. I counted the stops before mine. There were too many.

Three stops later, she got up. Thank goodness! However, instead of going to the nearest doors, she walked right up to me, pulling the cringing dogs after her. I could smell the thick, unwashed stench of her. She spat a stream of measured invective at me in a language I didn't understand. With each word, she brought her face nearer to mine. None of the other passengers moved. I was on my own, apart from Napoleon, who growled. I couldn't hush him. I couldn't say a word. My throat was sandpaper.

I was mad, though. At every word, my anger rose. She had no right! I had done nothing. And those poor dogs. They slunk behind her, as far away as their ragged rope leads allowed. I would not cower from her. I returned her stare, found my voice and said, in French, that I didn't understand her. Finally, the train pulled up and the doors opened. She said one last, long sentence and then jabbed her finger at my forehead, despite Napoléon's snapping at her, and held it there. Her hand smelled of sweat and dog. I kept staring. Her eyes were full of anger and she could have been any age. It was impossible to tell under the layers of dirt. She may even have been pretty, if she was washed and loved. Just before the doors closed, she pulled herself away and yanked the dogs off the train, but she continued to speak at me through the window until we pulled out of the station. Napoléon bared his teeth.

No one in the train carriage met my eyes. It was as if they hadn't seen anything.

I was still trembling when I got to Madame Christophe's.

'Calm yourself,' she advised. 'Poor little Napoléon – he has had a shock?'

'He's had a shock! What about me? That horrible woman!' I told her the whole story.

'Yes,' Madame Christophe nodded, 'yes, I think you have been cursed. No matter. It will be fine. You should wash your forehead. She touches you so that your thoughts are hers, but that cannot be.'

'I don't want to be cursed. I don't even know what she cursed me with. She wasn't dressed like the other girls.'

'It will not be pleasant,' Madame Christophe said calmly, 'it will be the usual Romany curses – unhappy love, ill fortune for you and yours. They have been cursing people for centuries. Nothing changes. They do not all wear pretty skirts, Lise. There are others, perhaps not so lucky as to own a pretty skirt and some bangles.'

'Do you believe in curses?' I asked, subsiding onto her client chair. My forehead was hot where the woman's finger had been. I didn't want to believe it, but I was also, at the same time, spooked and thrilled. I'd been cursed! What a great story to tell! Hugo would love it, so would Ami.

Madame Christophe gave an elegant shrug. 'It is what they are good at,' she acknowledged, hesitating between her words. 'I would be foolish not to believe a little.'

'Can you lift it?'

'Not entirely, but I also have some power. You will wash your face with this.' She rummaged around in the desk drawer and drew out a gauze bag containing some soap. 'And then come back to me. I will prepare something. It will not disappear the curse. You will have always been touched, but that may be a good thing, who knows?'

The soap smelled of plain old comforting lavender. I checked in the mirror but there were no visible signs of the curse.

'It was the dogs I minded most,' I said when I'd finished, 'they weren't happy. They didn't want to be with her. That's why I stared back. I'd have been scared if it hadn't been for those poor dogs but they made me angry.'

Madame Christophe nodded. 'She didn't pick the right person,' she said. 'She didn't know you were Australian. We will cleanse you now.' She lit a stub of herbs and waved it around me and chanted something I couldn't understand. I wanted to laugh. I was in Paris, I'd been cursed by a Romany in the metro and now I was being smudged by a French clairvoyant wearing stilettos and a leopard-print scarf.

'It is done,' Madame Christophe said after a while. 'Of course, you have still been cursed. But we have done what we can to turn it.'

'Thank you.' I was wobbly all of a sudden. 'Thank you.'

'Go and rest. It is the smudging and the curse in battle. You will be tired.'

She was right, although I didn't think it was due to an internal battle between good and evil. I was still in shock. The smoke didn't help. Its slightly acrid smell was lodged in my throat and my eyes watered. I stumbled upstairs, drank a glass of water, pulled the curtains shut and slipped into bed. I registered how cool the sheets felt before falling fast asleep.

I woke when smells of cooking wafted up the stairs. There were a couple of other tenants who had stayed for the summer but they were mysterious beings. I hardly saw them – just caught the sound of a heel on the narrow stairs, or smelled their food. Someone on the floor below lived on Moroccan takeaway. I was hungry. Was it too soon to text Hugo? The yellow daisy bag was perched on my bed. It was so perfect for my Paris dress! I should at least text him and thank him again. Maybe he'd want dinner?

But when I stretched out my arm, the numbers had smudged, some even obliterated except for a faint trace of blue ink. How had that happened? I'd only been asleep, not swimming!

It was the curse.

I'd been stupid not to take it seriously. Despite Madame Christophe's cleansing smudge sticks, it had worked. I stumbled downstairs to the shop.

'Look!' I held out my arm for her to inspect.

'Ah, Lisette. Did you sleep?'

'My arm.' I waved it in front of her. 'Where Hugo wrote his number.'

Madame put her designer specs delicately on her nose and then held my arm still. Her fingernails were bright pink. They matched today's leopard-print scarf perfectly. 'Wrote his number?'

'He had an appointment. He'd run out of cards. He wrote his number on my arm. The curse washed it off.' I realised that tears had filled my eyes and I stopped babbling, ashamed.

'Alas, yes. There is only a fragment of the number left. But why is this so important?'

'Because . . . I don't know. He lives with his uncle. He listens. He understood the whole . . .' I paused, trying to work out whether Madame Christophe would understand 'House of Estrogen'. I settled on 'House of Women' instead.

Madame Christophe nodded, still holding my arm. 'So, you think he is important to you?'

'We've only just met.'

'But you are crying,' she pointed out, letting go of my arm and offering me a tissue from the packet for distressed clients that she kept in her drawer.

'I'm cursed,' I said, sitting down in her client's chair, blowing my nose. 'I'm cursed and he never had a chance to become important. She needn't have cursed me, you know. I was already cursed. My father never had a chance of being important either. Mum hid him. No wonder I'm crap at men.'

'Your mother hid him?'

'She hid his photos from me.'

'But you have them now?'

'Yes, but I could have seen them earlier. She could have told me more. I might have been able to meet my father. Now he's dead.' Tears welled in my eyes and I scrubbed at them with the moist tissue.

'Did you ask?'

'No,' I said, 'but she made it impossible. She wanted a life without chips or cracks. She didn't let me ask.'

'She was humiliated,' Madame Christophe said slowly. She sat down behind the desk and Napoléon jumped onto her knee. 'I think you understand humiliation, Lisette?'

Heat rose in my face. First Ben and then Anders and Gabi! Oh, yes, I understood humiliation. I nodded, shamefaced.

'It is difficult to simply brush off humiliation. Your mother, she would have thought everything was settled. She and your father would live together, happily ever after. He thought the same, perhaps. Then, when he thought that ever after would not, perhaps, suit him, he left her. She was seven months pregnant, Lisette.'

'I know,' I whispered, 'but he was my father. And now all I have is some of his money – well, I will have when the estate is settled. He got married, Madame.'

Madame Christophe nodded. 'I know this. But you are his only child. You were never forgotten.'

'But is that enough? What if Mum *had* talked to me about him, what if I'd tracked him down?'

Madame Christophe shrugged and scratched Napoléon behind the ears. 'We always expect the what if to be better than the what was,' she said. 'But it is not always true. Let us play a different version of this game. What if you had found him, and he had turned his attention from his painting – he was an artist, yes? – and said, very nice, lovely, now please, I have no time?'

'I would have – I don't know.'

'I think you, too, would have been humiliated. And then perhaps bitter and you would have thought, he does not love me and nor has he ever loved me. When perhaps the truth was that he did love you, in his own way. He did not forget you. When he made his will, he made provision for you. He would have thought, I will leave Lisette something, enough for her to find her way in the world as a young woman.'

'Maybe,' I said.

'Maybe,' Madame Christophe agreed. 'Now, Lisette, wash your face and put on your Paris dress that goes so well with your new handbag and let us proceed to dinner.'

'You and I are going to dinner?'

'With Napoléon, of course,' Madame Christophe nodded. 'It will celebrate surviving the curse.'

'But Hugo's number didn't survive.'

'I would not worry about that. You can always find him. You have wi-fi.'

She had a point. I could easily track Hugo down – if he and his uncle were the kind of businesspeople who had a website and checked their emails. That didn't really fit with my idea of eccentric antique dealers, but then I remembered Hugo's smart phone. Maybe I could do that. Maybe I would do that. I cheered up and the idea of dinner out – a real French dinner out – sent me speeding up the stairs to get dressed. My reflection smiled at me as though that young woman was ready for whatever life offered her. I blew her a kiss, just because.

Chapter

16

Mackenzie said that a mini-crini sounded like a fat-saturated, high-salt, hidden-sugar treat that the Americans would invent. I told her it was Vivienne Westwood's much-abbreviated take on the crinoline. It is so good to have a friend in Paris to hang out with. She and Goldie are the best, although I feel closer to Mackenzie. She's Canadian, after all. That's almost Australian!

The bistro was one I'd walked past a dozen times before but never gone into. Unlike the other cafes, there were no tables outside, and sometimes it was open and other times not. Madame Christophe sailed in and was greeted by the waiter with a warm kiss on each cheek. I was introduced and then Madame was called out from the kitchen to meet us. Madame was a short, fat woman who rolled her 'r's' with a guttural passion. When she gently pinched my cheek, as though checking whether or not I was ripe, her hands smelled of lemon and flour and I was suddenly very hungry.

'I will order for us, yes?' Madame Christophe didn't wait for my reply, but conferred with both the waiter and Madame, whose accent made it impossible for me to understand anything. I smiled and nodded, hoping my enthusiasm made up for my lack of comprehension. Everything on the menu was discussed at length and then everything that wasn't on the menu was also deliberated over until, eventually, choices were made that caused everyone pleasure.

'This is food from the real France,' Madame Christophe said. 'We will eat like peasant royalty tonight, Lisette. This is the last place in Paris you can eat food that tastes of the countryside, the soil that grew it. You will let your mother know of this – it will interest her greatly.'

The waiter appeared with a bottle of wine and poured a little into Madame Christophe's glass. He beamed at her as she tasted the wine.

'Superb,' she said, 'which is what I expected. Lisette – to your health.'

'And to yours,' I stammered, raising my glass.

'Lisette was cursed by a Romany this afternoon,' Madame Christophe confided to the waiter, 'but I did a cleansing and now she is left, perhaps, with only the wisdom of the curser. Who knows?'

The waiter tutted and exclaimed and there was talk of the healing power of food and then toast arrived along with a chunk of some kind of terrine. Madame Christophe smiled and fed Napoléon a small corner. 'You will never taste terrine as good again,' she said, 'it is all about the choice of pigs.

Madame has a brother. He takes the pig foraging. They are pigs that are delighted with life. You can taste their delight.'

The terrine was salty with a slight tang of aniseed. Did delight taste of apples and hazelnuts? I hoped so, for the sake of the pigs.

By the time we finished our meal, we were the only ones left in the bistro and I was practically in a food coma. The waiter came to the table with a tray of coffees, an unmarked bottle and some glasses. Madame came out of the kitchen and I noticed through my daze that she'd taken her apron off, swiped on some lipstick and tidied her hair. Coffee was passed around, more alcohol came out and they both sat down with us. I'd have thought that the alcohol would make it harder for me to understand Madame, but it was as though it had loosened not just my speech but also my hearing. I stuttered out my thanks for the wonderful meal and told her that I understood she'd been brought up on a farm and had learnt cooking from generations of country women. Both she and the waiter crowed over my French as though they, themselves, had taught me. More of the sharp, warm liquor was poured and Pascal made a toast to Madame, whose name was Jeanne. Then the table was cleared and Madame Christophe produced some tarot cards and began to read their fortunes, while I sat back sleepily.

There was happiness due in Pascal's life, she told him, and he agreed. Proudly he admitted that his daughter was having a baby boy in early winter. Madame Jeanne, Madame Christophe prophesied, would receive good news from abroad. Madame made us all accept another glass of liquor. Her friend was coming from America, she confided. They had been corresponding by email and had decided it was time to meet in person. She disappeared to the kitchen and brought back – of all things – a tablet, found a Facebook page and passed it around so that we all had a chance to admire the photograph of a smiling, rotund man brandishing barbeque tongs.

'He has his own restaurant,' she said, 'but he is leaving it in the hands of his son and daughter-in-law. They specialise in Tex-Mex. France will open his eyes to the real food. I will take him to my brother's farm. He will learn.'

'So, how did you meet?' I asked through a fog of eau de vie.

'On the internet,' she said, 'that is how everyone meets these days. It is – what do they call it – a village of the world?'

'It is Lisette's turn,' Pascal announced. 'Madame Sylvie, you must read the cards for Lisette.'

'Ask a question,' Madame Christophe ordered, 'and shuffle the cards.'

The only question I could think of was whether or not I'd see Hugo again. I asked that and moved the cards around the tabletop. I thought it was a silly question – of course I wouldn't see him again, the curse had erased his number. I was destined to be single forever. I'd have to become a crazy dog lady. I asked anyway.

Madame Christophe began to lay the cards out and Pascal and Madame Jeanne leant in to see, as though my future was as important to them as their own.

'This is the foundation of your question,' Madame Christophe said. 'A young man, creative and business-minded.'

'Ooh.' Madame Jeanne gave me a knowing look. 'A young man! Is he handsome?'

I blushed. 'I suppose so,' I admitted, 'he has a nice smile, but I don't really know him.'

'This is in the past' – Madame Christophe flipped up another card – 'another man, but not so pleasant. This is someone who is cruel and wilful. He is a source of unhappiness.'

I pretended to be mystified but my colour heightened. It was clearly Anders.

By the end of the reading I still didn't know if I was ever going to see Hugo again but I had learnt that I needed to see beyond the superficial and that an unexpected gift was going to lead to happiness. Pascal and Madame Jeanne exchanged meaningful glances as though they could both see my future quite clearly.

'A good outcome,' Madame Christophe said, gathering up her cards, shuffling them and putting them back in the velvet bag. 'Yes, Lisette, a very good outcome. Fortune will smile upon you.'

I tried to be suitably pleased but yawned instead. 'I'm sorry,' I said, 'I think it's all the cognac.'

Madame Christophe nodded. 'Not to mention the curse. You are possibly still involved in internal conflict. It is tiring.'

'That woman did the devil's work,' Madame Jeanne agreed and crossed herself discreetly. 'The next time you pass a church, Lisette, you should light a candle.'

To my surprise, Madame Christophe paid for our dinner. She waved my protests away. 'I invited you,' she said, 'you are my guest. It was a pleasure, Lisette.'

Despite the food, the wine and the cognac, it took me a long time to go to sleep. I thought about what Hugo had said – how his uncle had buried himself in things from the past, to avoid the pain of his own past. Did my mother create order and perfection to make up for my father walking out on her? Sometimes her fussing drove me mad – I wanted to tear the petals off her roses or write something rude right across the mirror in the studio. At other times, walking in and seeing the pretty cups on a tray, the vase of fresh flowers and smelling the essential oils she vaporised made me calm and happy.

'So do you feel you're looking after your uncle?' I'd asked Hugo at lunch.

'I used to think he'd just disappear without me. He'd burrow so far into his books he'd never come out again. Lately, though, I've noticed he actually does have a life of his own. It was a bit of a shock, to be honest. I'd thought I was indispensable, but I'm not. He has friends. He goes to the pub. He plays snooker on Saturday nights and darts on Thursdays.'

'At least you're doing something real,' I'd said gloomily.

'For the next while,' Hugo had said. 'I might do something else in a few years. Anyway, you want to be an art historian, don't you?'

'I thought I did. But I don't know – it's all so remote, isn't it?'

'It's an education.'

'The problem is that all the art's hanging on gallery walls,' I'd said. 'You can't, you know, take it down, look at it properly. You can't touch it. That's why I like clothes. Or jewellery. I like things you can pick up, turn around or wear. I'd like – I don't know, to buy things for movie sets.' I had sounded so hopelessly young and stupid that I'd ducked my head in embarrassment. It was like saying you wanted to be a fashion designer – how many girls wanted that? Naturally, I'd wanted to do that, too. I didn't tell Hugo.

'Or go into the antique business?' Hugo said. 'That's what Unc and I do – pick things up, turn them around and then sell them. When we're lucky.'

It didn't sound like a bad job, I thought. I wasn't at all sure what I'd do with an art history degree, even if it was an education. Once I'd thought of it as a way to somehow get closer to my father – that one day, if we ever met, I'd be able to tell him I was working in his field. It was never going to happen now. We would never be able to have the conversations I'd imagined throughout my childhood.

In honour of my education, I decided the next morning I'd visit the Louvre. I announced this to Madame Christophe over breakfast. I thought she'd applaud my choice but instead she shook her head vehemently.

'No,' she said, 'no, you must visit next door – the museum of the arts decorative. There is an exhibition there of under-things. It will interest you.'

'Underthings?'

'Exactly,' she said. 'I would accompany you, but alas, I have clients booked. Perhaps you should ask that girl with the boy's name? She would enjoy it, I am sure.'

I stomped back upstairs to see what Madame Christophe could possibly mean and discovered that there was an exhibition of underwear, including crinolines and bustles, on at the Musée des Arts Décoratifs. Mackenzie *would* enjoy that, I thought, and Ethan had gone back to Canada, so she might want cheering up. I texted her straight away.

We met at the entrance of the museum.

'Thank goodness it's just fashion,' Mackenzie said. 'The more art I see, the less confident I become.'

Just fashion! I shook my head as we stepped into the dimly lit exhibition space. We ended up staying for over an hour. Who knew that underwear could also be a love letter? In the eighteenth century, a lover would have his declaration of love carved onto thin wooden or whalebone busks that were part of a woman's corset. In return, he might receive one of the ribbons that held it in place. So romantic! Or that sixteenth-century men had already discovered their equivalent of a sock in the jocks? Or that anyone would wear a wig down there? Seriously?

We tried on crinolines – not mini-crinis, but the full-sized ones – and took photos of each other. The best thing in the whole exhibition, however, was a doll-sized mannequin – a Pandora, the label read. They were sent around Europe so that fashionable women could choose their clothes from the doll's wardrobe. She was dressed only in her underwear, but the clothes she would have once worn were displayed beside her. Everything was tatty but I could see how exquisite she would have been and I longed to reach through the glass of the display case and touch her.

'A grown-up's doll,' Mackenzie said thoughtfully. 'Interesting.'

'Oh, Mackenzie, I want one!'

'I can see that!' Mackenzie said. 'Stop drooling on the glass, Lise. They'd be worth hundreds, probably thousands. If you could even find one.'

'I wonder if Hugo knows about them,' I said aloud.

'Hugo?'

'Just this guy I met. He's into antiques.'

'I thought . . . you and Anders?' Mackenzie said delicately.

I blushed. 'Goldie warned me off,' I said, 'and then Anders – oh, it doesn't matter, really. It was a near escape.'

'I would have told you,' Mackenzie said, 'but I wasn't sure. It was possible that Anders and Gabi had broken up. I'm sorry, Lise. I haven't been a good friend.' She reached out and touched my hand, her face sad and earnest.

'You've been a friend,' I said. 'Mackenzie – you're a great friend. Thank you.'

Her face cleared as suddenly as it had clouded and she wrinkled her nose. 'So this Hugo?'

'It's nothing,' I said, 'we've only just met and then the Romany curse erased his phone number from my arm.'

'Whoa' – Mackenzie held out her hand – 'stop right there, Lise. A Romany curse?'

I told her the whole story. It took two coffees each – Mackenzie's shout, she said, because it was such a weird story.

'Wow!' she said at the end. 'Lise, you come to Paris and stuff happens to you. Me, I come to Paris, do a few mediocre paintings and miss my boyfriend. You're an encounter magnet. Like, seriously, most people look at the Eiffel Tower, climb up to the Sacré-Cœur and see the *Mona Lisa*. You get a clairvoyant landlady, two men – okay, one's an arse, but the other one sounds fine – an authentic curse and your tarot read after a genuine French bistro meal.'

'I won't see Hugo again,' I said sadly. 'His phone number disappeared. I could contact him through the shop's website, but I don't think I should. What would I say? What if his uncle read it? Holiday romances don't last.'

'You never know,' Mackenzie said. 'Paris isn't that big. He might just show up again.'

I didn't have much faith in Paris being *that* small. Mackenzie's optimism was catching, however, and her version of me was much bigger and more interesting than my own. Perhaps because of that I found myself keeping an eye out for Hugo all the way home and even when I didn't see him, there was still a residual seed of happiness growing inside me.

Chapter

17

There are tricksy elements in designing dancewear.
You'll want a sexy, backless dress. But you'll perspire.
After your partner has jived, dipped and swung you across
the dance floor, he'll be all too familiar with your sweaty back.
This is just one of the reasons that I do not dance.
Mum and I once saw a movie where this married couple
dance together, around their bedroom, after a fight.
Mum started crying. 'That was the kind of husband
I wanted,' she said. 'Someone you could just fall into
step with, after the shouting.'
I get that now. I totally get that.

Only two days later I was window-shopping, dreaming of
mini-crinis and corsets and thinking of how romantic it
would be to receive a carved busk from a beau, when my
phone pinged. Mackenzie – *It's Paris-Plages. There's dancing!*
Tonight!

To say the idea didn't thrill me would have been an under-statement. On the other hand, what else would I do?

I did wonder what on earth Mackenzie would wear, but she showed up in jeans with small-heeled shoes that sparkled.

'Ballroom shoes,' she said. 'Ethan and I do ballroom dancing, back home. We met doing the salsa.'

'Wow! I didn't know that you were into dancing.'

Mackenzie grinned at me. 'It's so much fun,' she said. 'Let's go. Goldie's meeting us there.'

'Hang on a sec,' I said. 'Do we have to dance?'

'That's what it's all about.'

'I don't actually do that.' I cleared my throat. 'Not in public.'

'So what?' Mackenzie said. 'You're in Paris. You have to dance in Paris. You have to dance at Paris-Plages. They put speakers up. People come from their dance classes. It's a summer ritual. You only have to dance once, just to say you've done it. You can take photos the rest of the time, if you want.'

'You're kidding, right?'

Mackenzie just smiled.

There was already a crowd down by the river. Children were playing in the sand that had been dumped for the fake beach. The misters were on and kids ran in and out of them while a teenage couple stayed underneath, glued together by kisses and spray. Couples strolled past eating ice-creams, or sat on beach chairs watching the tourist boats and barges on the river.

A portion of the boardwalk had been constructed into a makeshift dance floor. Two large speakers were erected on some scaffolding and they blared out up-market lift music. People were already congregating at the edges of the stage, subtly checking each other out. They were mostly older women.

'Here you are!' Goldie found us. 'Jeans, Mackenzie?'

Mackenzie laughed. 'It's all I've got, apart from yoga pants. I'm wearing good shoes, at least. That's all that counts.'

The music changed to something with definite rhythm and a couple moved to the centre of the boardwalk. They were an unlikely couple. Even though he was definitely middle-aged, if not frankly old, he wore long dreadlocks that were looped around his shoulders. He was tall and far more casually dressed than his stout companion who wore a silky hot-pink blouse over a tight black skirt with kick pleats. His shoes, however, were sharp – narrow-fitting and highly polished.

'They're going to be good,' Mackenzie said. They were good. Even I could see that. They moved as though they'd spent all their lives entwined in that loose but confident embrace. 'Ooh, I want to dance with him.' Mackenzie sighed. 'Oh God, it's a tango! Come on, who wants to get up? I can lead.'

'Not a tango,' Goldie said. 'No way, Mackenzie. You have to know something to do that!'

There were more couples up on the stage now. Mackenzie gave a running commentary on the abilities of each dancer. It was obvious that she was longing to get up and dance but I pointed out that there was no one even close to our age dancing.

'It doesn't matter who you dance with,' Mackenzie said, 'once they know you can dance. The point is the dance.'

Finally Mackenzie managed to drag Goldie up for a salsa and I saw what she meant. The other dancers watched her, just as she'd watched them. They were definitely judging Mackenzie, but she was every bit as professional as the hot-pink woman. She led, making up for Goldie's hesitations and stumbles.

Mackenzie was a star. She had partners lining up for her after that. First was the dreadlocked man, who when Goldie shook her head slightly at Mackenzie's invitation to dance the next number, smoothly intercepted and swept Mackenzie away. His previous partner sat on the sidelines, fanning her face, clearly pleased to sit out the faster number.

'Was it fun?' I asked Goldie when she joined me.

'Sort of,' she said. 'But I'm happy to be here. Let's take photos instead.'

Mackenzie was not without a partner for the next thirty or so minutes and then, flushed and smiling broadly, she came down to rehydrate.

'I had completely forgotten how much fun that is!' she said. 'I just love it! Lise, you have to come up!'

More and more people arrived and there were always at least five or six couples spinning and dipping. One woman arrived with her partner dressed as though they had both come from a fifties-style wedding. She wore a hat with a tulle veil and a skirt layered with petticoats that flew out as her partner, in a three-piece suit, spun her around.

'It's amazing,' I admitted. 'Mum would love to see this.'

'She can see the photos,' Goldie said. 'Mackenzie, I really have to go. It's been great, but I have to get to an exhibition opening.'

'You'll stay, Lisette? We haven't even danced yet!'

I wanted to go too. Sweat had trickled down my back simply watching Mackenzie, but I agreed to stay, cursing myself for my cowardice.

I cursed myself harder when minutes later I caught sight of the one person I had wanted to avoid. Anders. With a girl. She had to be Gabi.

Mackenzie had already returned to dance and I couldn't simply disappear. I ducked my head and fiddled with my camera. If I couldn't see him, he couldn't see me.

I held the camera up both to conceal my face and also to zoom in on Gabi. She was a pale glow underneath a pile of dark curls. She leant into Anders as though they had been waltzing together all their lives. They probably had been. They were so engrossed in each other it felt as though I were spying. I lowered the camera but I couldn't stop watching them.

Why on earth had he made a move on me when Gabi was a part of his life? It didn't make sense. I was out of her league. I was too young, too blonde, too Australian. I couldn't understand it. It was humiliating to think that I'd imagined us together.

Gabi blurred. I put the camera down to blink away my tears. Anders didn't matter so much. What stung was my own stupidity. What had I been thinking?

They'd stopped dancing. I blinked again. Gabi was pointing in my direction. She was tugging Anders forward. I looked for an escape route but I was hemmed in by tourists. Then suddenly they were right in front of me.

'This is your little Australian? Introduce us,' she ordered Anders. Up close she was not flawless although her make-up was very good. Underneath the concealer, a fine sprinkling of pimples covered her forehead and I didn't believe for one second that those full, long eyelashes were her own. I lifted up my chin. My clear skin was one of my assets and my own eyelashes were respectable. I was ready to snarl like Napoléon.

'So, Anders, this is your *sister*?' I said. 'How very European of you both. How very . . .' I paused and took a breath to steady my voice, 'incestuous.'

Gabi flashed a look at Anders, frowning. 'I am his girlfriend. Always.'

'Not what he told me. Enjoy the new lingerie,' I said. 'I thought it was quite . . . pretty . . . if that's what you like. A little traditional for someone whose relationship is not so conservative.' I fluttered my fingers at them both and sidestepped into a gap in the crowd. My knees were shaking but I had done it. I had shown my teeth.

'I hate to intrude,' a voice with a distinct English accent said, 'but your clairvoyant told me to find you here.'

I whirled around. It was Hugo. I could have flung my arms around him. 'Hugo! I'm so sorry I couldn't call. A Romany woman cursed me and your number faded on my arm.'

'It always happens.' He nodded. 'I mean, if it's not a curse, it's a dragon abduction or an army of ogres. The things that keep me from the girls of my dreams!'

'It's true,' I said, 'there was a woman in the metro. Madame Christophe had to perform a cleansing smudge.'

'Is that an oxymoron?'

'With sage or something herbal.'

'So not charcoal and art therapy?'

'No. She's a clairvoyant, not an artist.'

'She's amazing. I think we bonded. Napoléon was the glue – he remembered me.'

'How did you meet her?'

'I could say it was an accident, and then I wouldn't sound like a stalker, but I'm happier telling the truth. When you didn't call I researched clairvoyants in the Marais. There are surprisingly few. Actually, there's one. Yours. So I went there and she told me you'd be here and . . .' Hugo stopped. 'And here you are,' he finished.

'I didn't tell her I was coming here,' I said. 'In fact, she was out when I left. There was a sign on the shop. How did she know?'

'She's a clairvoyant,' Hugo said, shrugging. Then he looked at the dancers. 'So that's him,' he said after a few seconds.

'What do you mean?' I asked cautiously.

'The guy who stood you up? The one who caused you to contemplate the lonely river?'

'I wasn't contemplating the river! Also, how do you know that's him? Or that he's even here?'

'Intuition. I'm a wheeler-dealer, remember. He's obviously a bit of an arse.'

'He *is* an arse and she's not as beautiful as she looks from a distance.'

'She looks high maintenance,' he said.

'Come on, Hugo, how could you even tell?'

'Just a feeling. Do you care about them?'

I considered the question. Did I care? 'I regret being deceived,' I acknowledged. 'They were actually in a relationship but he told me . . . he told me lies. That's what hurts – and that I believed him.' I looked at Anders. He was slightly self-conscious. His shirt sleeves were a little too neatly rolled. His hair had been gelled.

'I think we should dance,' Hugo said.

'Dance?'

'I'm not that great at it,' Hugo said, 'you know, Camden boy – we pogo. But we can give it our best and have a bit of fun, yeah?'

'I don't know. I haven't danced since the school formal.'

'I have been told I resemble a windmill on speed,' Hugo admitted but he already had my elbow and was leading me to the dance floor. 'On the other hand, that's better than looking as though you've a poker up your arse.'

'I've always liked windmills,' I said.

The music had changed to something Latin but that didn't deter Hugo. He watched for a minute or two and then grabbed me and we both attempted to follow the couple nearest to us. As it happened, they were the wedding couple who were so much better than us that what they made look easy tangled our feet in an instant. Hugo grabbed me and pulled me to him.

'We'll improvise,' he said in my ear, before swinging me out again.

Eventually we stopped fretting about what everyone else was doing and managed to dance together, roughly in beat with the music, inventing our own steps, which at one point definitely included something pogo-ish. When the music changed again to a slower number, Hugo opened his arms and I stepped forward as though it was the most natural thing in the world to be there.

His collar points were frayed and his shirt sleeves had half unrolled. He was wearing weirdly not-quite-vintage trousers. Where his shirt was open at the throat, I could see his white skin. He smiled at me, his eyes tender.

'It's not that difficult,' he said.

'It's not,' I answered and I knew neither of us meant the dance.

'You're not going to do another Cinderella on me, are you?' he asked.

'You're the one who ran off!'

'I had to. I nearly missed the whole reason I'm in Paris. Besides, I left you more than a glass slipper.'

'I was cursed!'

'Such a good story to tell our children. We nearly didn't get together because your mother was cursed by a Romany.'

'What? You're hopeful!'

'Always. Is that a friend of yours waving?'

'It's Mackenzie.'

'Mackenzie – good Scots name.'

'She's Canadian.'

'That explains it. Delighted, Mackenzie.' Hugo stuck out his hand for Mackenzie to shake.

'Hugo, Mackenzie. Mackenzie, Hugo.'

'I'd shake hands with you but I'm covered in sweat,' Mackenzie said. 'Shall we get a drink?'

'Sounds ideal,' Hugo said. 'I mean, I like dancing as much as the next chap, but there's a moment when your shirt feels as though it's just come out of the wash and that's when I prefer to stop. Beer? My shout.'

It was only when we were sitting down that I realised I'd forgotten about Anders and Gabi. At the same time, I noticed that Hugo had rested his arm on the back of my seat. He was waiting, I thought, for permission. I leant back and his hand came down on my shoulder. Mackenzie carefully smiled at her beer.

While Hugo asked Mackenzie about painting, environmentalism and her life in Canada, I wondered if Hugo and I were temporary, like Paris-Plages. Every so often Hugo's hand left my shoulder as he emphasised something he said. When it returned, warm and slightly sweaty, my pulse quickened as though my body was saying, *glad to see you again*.

'The thing is,' I heard Mackenzie say, 'you can't pre-empt the future, can you? I mean, you can't say, I shouldn't be doing figurative stuff because that's been done and it won't sell. You have to do what your heart tells you to do and trust that it will all come out okay.'

Mackenzie had nailed it on the head.

'I guess that goes for life as well,' I offered and Hugo squeezed my shoulder.

'It's all risky,' he said, 'risky and wonderful.'

How many days did Hugo have left in Paris? I couldn't remember when he'd said he was leaving.

'To wonderful risks.' Mackenzie held up her beer bottle and we clinked, echoing her words.

When she went to buy the next shout, Hugo turned to me. 'Will we risk it, Lise?'

'I don't know,' I said, but I felt a little giddy, as though I'd just drunk too much champagne rather than just one beer.

'I'm going to put your number into my phone. Then I don't have to track you through Paris. I'm going to drink this beer, walk you home and then I'm going back to Unc's friend because I promised to be in before midnight. Tomorrow I'm seeing my friends. They run a vintage store.'

'Can I come with you?'

'I would like that,' Hugo said seriously.

It didn't matter that in a couple of weeks the sand would be dumped back where it came from or that the bars would be taken down and the dancing stop for another year. I was here now, I thought. That's what mattered.

Chapter 18

Vintage – something from the past of high quality, especially something representing the best of its kind. That is seriously the definition of vintage and vintage shop owners should learn it by heart before they try to pass off old crap as vintage. Old crap is just that. Vintage is different.

'I'm meeting Hugo's friends today,' I told Madame Christophe. 'They are the Falbalas and they run a vintage clothing store somewhere.'

'They cannot be the Falbalas,' Madame Christophe said calmly, feeding Napoléon.

'I'm sure that's what he said.'

'*Falbalas* is a film,' Madame Christophe said firmly. 'It is not a couple. Although they may have chosen that name for their store, of course. It is a film about haute couture and very tragic. I hope they are not tragic people.'

I couldn't imagine Hugo being friends with tragic people

and I told Madame Christophe this. 'But I am pleased you told me about the movie,' I said, 'it would have been embarrassing to think that was their real name!'

'I do not think you could embarrass that young man,' Madame Christophe said. 'He is very – how will I say it? He is safe in his skin.'

I thought about Hugo dancing. Madame Christophe was right, although her English was obscure. 'Comfortable in his skin,' I said, 'that's what we say.'

'Comfortable, safe,' Madame Christophe shrugged. 'It is the same. You will take Napoléon? I have a client coming who he does not like. I would choose not to see this client but his problems are small and his pocket is rich.'

'Oh là là,' Hugo said when he met me outside, 'so French! We have the dog. Max and Edouard will be impressed.' He kissed me, first on one cheek and then the other and a third time, confusing me.

'Ouch.'

'Sorry.' Hugo ruefully rubbed his nose. 'I got carried away. It's Napoléon. Off we go to the biggest flea market in France, maybe the world.'

I had no idea where we were going but Hugo negotiated the metro, only interrupting his chatter to distribute money to various beggars and buskers.

'I can't give much,' he said to me, 'but I feel . . . well, what do I feel, really? Guilty, I suppose. So I have this policy. Anyone old, anyone with children and anyone with the right kind of dog.'

'So the wrong kind of dog disqualifies you?'

'I hadn't thought of it like that.' Hugo was worried. 'Disqualifies you? That's harsh. I guess I couldn't give money to someone with a dog who'd been beaten.'

I took his arm. I hadn't meant to question his system. 'It's great that you've given it so much thought,' I said. 'Most people simply ignore them.'

When we got out at Saint-Ouen, Hugo said, 'I need to get some flowers. I always take flowers. I also need to tell you something, so let's find a cafe and have a coffee.'

He bought a big bunch of dark pink and creamy white flowers, some in bud, some open. It was lavish. Opulent. I regarded it with suspicion. My chest was tight. What was Hugo going to tell me?

He didn't talk until the coffee arrived and then he took my hand and held it across the table.

'I want to tell you this before you meet them, so there's no confusion. Maxine and I – well, when I was younger, we had a thing. It was before Edouard. Maxine was the first woman . . . well, that I'd loved and everything.' He seemed to run out of breath.

I knew he was going to say that he still loved her. I tried not to glare at the flowers. His hand was sweating slightly and I pulled mine away from it. I didn't want to make this easier for him.

'First Anders,' I said, 'and now you.'

'What? No, no, not at all. Not even a little bit.' Hugo

grabbed my hand again, upsetting the sugar bowl and spilling coffee into our saucers. 'Damn!' He scooped the sugar back into the bowl. 'Don't look,' he said, but I kept staring at him as he swept the rest off the table with his napkin, then took my hand again.

'You're sticky,' I said.

'Sorry, you'll just have to put up with it while I tell you. You've got it wrong, Lise. Of course I love Max, but not like that. Not now. This all happened five years ago.'

'*Five* years! You're not that old.'

He grinned and ducked his head shyly. 'I was seventeen. Max is older by a couple of years. It was my first buying trip. I had strict instructions from Unc. He'd wanted to come but at the last minute he freaked out, so I arrived here with my schoolboy French, a list of things to look for and a budget. I was really flung in the deep end. Anyway, Max already had a stall at the Porte de Vanves. She felt sorry for me. I, of course, fell head over heels and mooned over her. For her it was a springtime fling with a boy. For me it was profound.'

The bands around my chest tightened. *Profound.* Along the street was some kind of African market – all I could see was a blur of bright yellow, green and red from the T-shirts hung up high like flags around the stalls.

'I wanted to tell you,' Hugo said, 'because I want you to know about me and why I buy Maxine flowers and why we're close – the three of us, Max and Edouard, her partner, and me. I'll always love Max – I'm so grateful to her. Not just for, you know – but also because later she put up with my emails and my drunk phone calls and she was nearly always kind when she needn't have been. I don't want you thinking I'm anything like that cheating guy.'

'What happened after Max?' I extracted my hand again. I was cold even though we were sitting in the morning sun.

'Nothing for ages.' Hugo laughed. 'I wrote emails in bad French and sent over things I'd picked up at the markets at home. Unc moved up North. I went on visiting flea markets. Then I met a Camden girl – very different from Max. She was my age. It didn't work. Not everyone understands vintage things, yeah? And they're kind of the point of my life. So now I've told you my sad story. Are we okay?'

'I guess.' Privately I thought that would depend on what this Maxine was like, but I also knew I didn't really have any claim to Hugo. I was a tourist – and not just in Paris.

'Just checking.' Hugo grinned at me. 'Come on. Let me wash your hand. I've got a water bottle.'

The Falbalas vintage clothing and bric-a-brac stall was in the middle of the huge antique market at Saint-Ouen. Hugo led me through a maze of different shops that sold everything from high-end Art Deco antiques to flea market goods until we reached a two-storey building. Max and Edouard were upstairs.

A woman, wearing a pantsuit straight from the late sixties that even had a matching waistcoat, looked up from her desk and leapt to her feet, shrieking over her shoulder, 'Edouard – it's Hugo!' She rushed at Hugo and triple-kissed him, leaving lipstick on his cheeks. Edouard emerged from behind a curtain. Like the woman, he was dressed in vintage wear but his clothing dated from an earlier period and he sported a waxed moustache. I tried not to stare.

'Hugo!' Edouard embraced him, ruffling his hair fondly as he did.

'Maxine, Edouard, allow me to present Lisette,' Hugo said solemnly, letting go of my hand as he gently pushed me forward.

'Enchanted.' Edouard took my hand and air kissed it close enough that his moustache tickled.

Maxine held her face against mine briefly. 'Delighted,' she murmured and we both checked each other out. She wasn't beautiful or even pretty, but she was chic. Her hair was cut very short and, despite the sixties outfit, the only make-up that stood out was the dark lipstick that contrasted with her pale skin. She was – I searched for a word and reluctantly found it. She was compelling. No wonder Hugo had fallen for her.

'I love this skirt,' she said, reaching forward to finger my skull skirt, 'it is very striking. An Australian designer? Hugo told us you are from Australia. So original.'

Was she talking about my skirt or Australia? I wasn't sure. What had Hugo said about me?

'Can we have lunch together?' Hugo asked, waving the flowers around.

'The flowers, Hugo!' Maxine reached for them. 'You will ruin them dancing like that! Look, Edouard – peonies. They are beautiful, Hugo. Thank you.'

'We will certainly have lunch.' Edouard produced a vase seemingly by magic. 'We'll close. Business is slow anyway.'

'But it's far too early. We could have coffee, unless you want wine? Edouard, find some chairs and water for the dog. Adorable. Trust you, Hugo – you find a girl with the perfect French accessory.'

Hugo put an arm around me. 'She's Australian – they learn to fit in.'

Edouard touched my elbow. 'Don't listen to Hugo – he is already taking you for granted.'

It was clear that I had passed some kind of test. Hugo's smile was as wide as the sky as he helped Edouard move chairs around the desk.

We were soon all drinking coffee from a fifties coffee set.

'This is interesting,' I said, checking it out. I'd wanted Mum to make the studio more fifties but she was all floral teacups. She said the fifties were ugly.

'Oh look, Edouard. She is examining our coffee set.'

'Sorry.' I put the cup down. 'It's just gorgeous.'

'Don't be embarrassed,' Edouard said. 'We all do it all the time, do we not, Hugo? It was on display but of course whenever anyone asked the price we'd put up it so far it couldn't possibly sell. Then I said to Max, obviously we don't wish to sell it. No wonder we make no money!'

Maxine shrugged. 'There is more in life,' she offered. 'And business with you and your uncle, Hugo?'

'Better after this trip,' Hugo said. 'I've been procuring something special for a distinguished client.'

'Ah, how we need distinguished clients!' Edouard laughed. 'Of course, I must be careful with this. Max does not like me to have too many distinguished clients.' He winked at Hugo. 'Lisette, you are interested in the trade?'

'I don't know anything,' I said, 'except about clothes.' I wondered what Edouard had meant by his comment. Was Hugo's client, who he'd been in such a rush to see, a woman? Was she interested more in him than his antiques? But then why would he tell me about Max – as a smokescreen?

Max clapped her hands. 'So perfect!' she said. 'Fashion, history of clothing. It creates an eye, does it not? That is clear from the skulls. You made this?'

'With my mother's help,' I said.

'You sew well!'

'Not like Mum. She's a seamstress.'

'And will that be your career?'

'I don't know,' I said honestly. 'I was going to go to uni and study art history. Now, I'm not sure. I'm worried that I just latched on to it for the sake of doing something.' I wasn't explaining myself very well but Maxine nodded.

'You need to feel it in your bones,' she said. 'Your skirt, you feel there? Clothes are art too. Ah, Hugo, this brings me to a moment of importance. We have clothes. We have been saving them.'

'I don't buy new clothes.' Hugo turned to me and then to Max and Edouard. 'Lise noticed my fraying cuffs.'

I stared at the pile Edouard produced. 'Some of these are beautiful,' I said. 'Hugo – this grey-green would suit you.'

'And this' – Maxine produced a shirt with pinwheels of colour all over it – 'would suit you, Lise. You must have it. Ooh, and also – where is that Audrey shift, Edouard? That would be perfect, too.'

Before lunch Hugo changed into his new old clothes. The shirt I had picked brought out the colour of his eyes. He lounged comfortably at the Moroccan cafe, his long legs stretched out in front of him. This was his world, obviously. Even his clothes, which looked slightly odd on the Paris streets, were just right at the flea market. I'd changed into the Audrey shift and Maxine had applied cat-eye eyeliner on me. I wondered if I looked at home like Hugo did.

'So,' Edouard said, helping himself to couscous, 'we have time to all go somewhere amusing? Perhaps to hear some music?'

'I have ten days left,' Hugo said, 'and then it's back to the UK.'

'And you, Lise?'

'I'm in Paris for another five and a half weeks and then back to Australia,' I said slowly. I hadn't spoken those words aloud before and the sentence stuck in my throat. Did I want to go home? I felt as though I was on the brink of some discovery. But what if I didn't find it in time? What if I went home before I'd worked it out? I wanted to reach out and hold Hugo's thin wrist or snuggle my head into his shoulder but how could I – we weren't really together and I was already on my way home.

Chapter

19

RULES

*There are fashion rules. When Mum was growing up,
her mother always told her she should never wear blue
and green together – blue and green, mustn't be seen.
My grandmother's shoes matched her handbag, her lipstick
matched her nail polish. A woman was always well-groomed.
It's all changed. What about Life Rules? You do what
you said you'd do. You marry the girl. You catch the flight.
You keep your promises. You don't mess up.*

I Skyped with Mum. 'I really, really like him,' I told her.

'So, he's become a boyfriend?' she asked. The connection
was bad and I couldn't see the details of her face. It was as
though someone had painted her with the colour laid on a
little too thickly. Was she angry or resigned?

'I suppose so,' I said, 'but we don't, we haven't . . .
you know.'

There was that weird Skype time-delay and Mum leant forward towards the monitor. 'You don't have to have sex with someone to be in love with them,' she said. As if I was twelve.

'I do know that,' I said. 'He goes back to England very soon.'

'You can stay in touch. I would advise putting the brakes on, though. You don't want to become too involved.'

'It's not even a romance yet,' I said.

'Exactly,' Mum said. 'Now, let's talk about other things. You'll never guess who came around the other day!'

'Who?'

'Ami's Uncle Vinh. With pork dumplings, beer and green tea. We had a meal together in front of the fire.'

'How's Ami?'

'She's doing fine,' Mum said, 'enjoying her course, apparently. Misses you.'

'She was there, right? Eating dumplings? Or was it just Vinh?'

'Oh, Ami wasn't there,' Mum said, 'she's started back at uni. It was just Vinh.'

'Why wasn't Ami there?'

'She was doing her own thing,' Mum said mysteriously.

After I'd finished talking to Mum, I wondered if Ami was seeing someone. Ami had said she'd never get a boyfriend without my approval. It wasn't fair to hold her to *that*, I knew, but I did wonder what excitement I'd missed out on. I Skyped her straight away.

'Are you going out with someone?' I said and then added quickly, 'I think I'm falling in love.'

'Uncle Vinh is seeing your mum,' Ami said, at the same time.

Then we both did that Skype *you first, no you,* three times each exactly.

'She's seeing him or going out with him?'

'She's going out with him. And staying in with him.'

'Wow! That's crazy. What about you?' I said finally.

'I'm staying in with my economics textbook. Not to mention my exam timetable. It's not crazy when you think about it.'

'It's just not fair. I leave the country for half a minute and she's taken up with some man.'

'It's not some man. It's Uncle Vinh. We all love Vinh.'

'That's why it's unfair. Mum's got a better chance of having a lasting relationship than I have.' Tears thickened my voice and I hoped the Skype connection didn't let on.

'He picked me up from your place ages ago. She made him a cup of tea – you know that blossom tea. You should have seen him, Lise. He took the teacups out to the kitchen for her. And then they made a cake together.'

'They what?' It was difficult enough to imagine a man in my mother's kitchen without having to also imagine him rolling up his sleeves to whisk eggs and measure flour. 'What kind of cake?' I asked. As if that mattered.

'Well,' Ami said, 'this is why I know it's serious. Sally was making a sponge and Uncle Vinh persuaded her to make a green tea sponge.'

'A green tea sponge?' Mum had always said there was nothing quite like a plain sponge. It was the little black dress of cakes. It was how you accessorised the sponge that was the key. Her sponges were whispered about by the customers. They put in shy requests for their favourites as they discussed fabric and drape. 'Oh, and if you could, darling,' they'd say, 'I heard the lemon curd sponge is a wonder. I've never tried it,' and they'd try not to drool on the watermarked bridal satin. But green tea? That was not Mum's style, no matter what size shipment Vinh had bought.

'With a coconut cream filling. It was delicious.'

I had a sharp pang of instant homesickness. I imagined my mother's kitchen and could almost hear the radio playing from the top of the cookbook shelf. I could smell ground coffee and the lemon verbena scent she wore through the summer. Of course, it wouldn't be summer. It was winter and she'd be wearing something spicier. 'Are they serious?'

'I think Vinh is. He consults me about what movies she likes. He's always talking about her. Sally doesn't talk much about him. But she doesn't hide the evidence, either.'

'The evidence?'

'Not gruesome evidence,' Ami said, 'not *our* kind of evidence. It's just little things. There were dumpling wrappers in her fridge and a new cookbook on her shelf – on making dumplings. Also a book on creatives and blogging. Vinh kind of things.'

'Wow.' I was stunned.

'I'm only surprised it hasn't happened before,' Ami said thoughtfully, 'but then I worked out that for those first years of high school Vinh wasn't even in Victoria. So I guess they've never really met properly. She's waved at his car. He's waved at her window. How romantic does that sound!'

'I guess.'

'You're not really jealous, Lise?'

'Of course not!' I lied.

'So who are you falling in love with?' Ami said. 'Is it still that artist?'

I sounded so shallow when Ami put it like that. 'No, but I'm sticking to boys in the arts field,' I said, aiming for flippancy.

'That's right, Vinh said there was an antique dealer?'

'How does Vinh know?'

'I told you,' Ami said patiently, 'they're dating. Your mum tells him things, he tells me things.'

'It sounds very cosy,' I snapped.

'Come on, stop being snarly and tell me about him.'

'He's . . . I don't know. He's just funny and sweet and kind of carefree. No, nonchalant. That's a better word. Even though he's really caring.'

'Nonchalant is okay,' Ami said after the Skype pause, 'so long as he isn't nonchalant with your heart.'

'He's not like that. He lives with his uncle. But he goes back to England in ten days.'

'You should go, too,' Ami said instantly, 'you could have a blissful time in England. God, Lise, you could even stay there.'

'Don't be ridiculous, I've got a return ticket. I come home in less than six weeks.'

'You can change it.'

'I can't change it. Remember all those terms and conditions?'

'So it costs money.' Ami waved that away with a careless, weirdly slow-motion hand. 'You've got money.'

'No, I haven't. I mean, I have enough to last me out in Paris. But not to change the stupid ticket.'

'You might have your inheritance,' Ami said. 'There was a letter from your lawyer on the kitchen bench.'

'Mum didn't mention that!'

'Well, she hasn't opened it. She won't open it, Lise. It's yours. But it's probably to tell you about the money.'

'Really?'

'Check your bank balance,' Ami advised. 'Have you even done that since you've been away?'

'Only my travel account.'

'Well, check your real one and see if anything has been paid in. They'd just do that, wouldn't they?'

I tried to remember the first letter I'd received. 'Yeah, I think so, but they said it would take time. They have to advertise the will and all sorts of other stuff.'

'It's been ages,' Ami said.

'Not legal ages.'

'Well, he sounds absolutely right for you. I'd go to England with him – even for a weekend.'

'I'm not going,' I said sharply. 'I don't even know if he was really serious.'

'Did he really ask you?' Ami asked

'It was just a throwaway line,' I said.

'I wish it was the kind of offhand thing boys said to me,' Ami said and then told me everything about nineteenth-century English literature, which she was enjoying studying much more than economics, as if I needed to know. Right at the end she said, 'You know, I could go and steal the letter, steam it open, read the contents and then seal it back up. Or, you could just be a grown-up and ask your mum to open it for you?'

'It won't be about the money,' I said, 'but, yeah, thanks for the heads-up.'

Chapter 20

There's always some item of clothing you associate with a person – and I don't mean Chanel's jacket or Alexander McQueen's black duck dress. I mean Madame Christophe's scarves, Fabienne's stilettos. I can pick a Hugo shirt from fifty paces. They are cotton, silk or linen and worn soft as skin.

I stopped going to French lessons. Hugo and I spent an afternoon window-shopping the antique stores near Madame Christophe's. The jewellery was more expensive than at the Porte de Vanves and displayed either on plump little cushions in the window, or in locked cabinets inside. Sometimes I knew more about the pieces than Hugo. Like when I guessed that a piece of bling was a Chanel giveaway.

'Yeah, I think you're right,' Hugo said. 'Who would want it, though?'

'I bet one of Mum's clients would,' I said. 'There's a woman who has three vintage Chanel handbags. She'd buy it.'

We talked about family. We talked about everything.

'My dad's a bit of a tosser,' he said one night, as we sat together eating ice-cream in a park. 'He's always got an idea that he thinks will make money and it never does, of course. He's charming, though.'

'So is he your uncle's brother?'

'No, Unc's my mum's brother. He practically raised my mum – their mum was sick all the time and their dad wasn't around.'

'Sick from what?'

A restaurant barge went up the river. People on board waved champagne glasses at us.

'I think she was depressed,' Hugo said. 'They don't talk about it much. She had migraines, they say. She drank too much. She stayed in bed all day. If you ask them anything directly they get evasive. As soon as Unc came back from the Falklands, my mum was onto him. Phone calls every day. Mental health checks every week.'

'I haven't got any uncles or aunts,' I said, 'or not that I know about. The women in my family are all only children.'

'Attention-seekers' – Hugo punched me lightly on the arm – 'drama queens, divas. What about your dad?'

'Not according to Mum. But how would I know? Like what if he did have a brother or a sister and she's just wiped them from her memory? I could have cousins I don't even know existed.'

'But she told you about your dad,' Hugo argued.

'Only when she had to.' I remembered the letter arriving. How light it was. How we'd stared at the envelope and Mum had said the solicitor's name aloud, both of us clueless. 'Only when he was already dead. Great, I've got a painting he did now. His wife sent it. But I will never know him. Her name is Sarah,' I told Hugo. 'My mum's name is Sally. Sally, Sarah – a little close, don't you think?'

'Have you met her?'

I shook my head. 'She lives in Wales,' I said, 'and anyway, *she's* not related to me.' There had been a note with the painting. 'Sarah' had said it was unfortunate that circumstances (like my father choosing to live on the other side of the world!) had not permitted us to know each other. She said that she hoped I had inherited my father's sense of adventure and playfulness. The sense of adventure, I'd thought, that took him away from me and my mother. The playfulness I'd never, ever seen. How could I miss a father I'd never known? But I did. I did. She'd also said I was always welcome wherever she was. As if.

'I think you should meet her.' Hugo turned to me. 'She'll open up part of your story to you. She can tell you what your father was like.'

'I think it would be too weird.' I hugged my arms around myself.

'Life's weird,' Hugo said. 'You could come to back to England with me. We could stay with Mum in Camden first and then you could meet Unc and then, when I've tied up some business, we could go to Wales. Easy.'

'I can't, Hugo. It's not that easy.' But even as I said it, I wondered – *could* it be that easy?

'Why not? You could stay for – what? Four weeks? – then come back to Paris and still catch your plane.'

'What about my French lessons?' I said.

'You've already missed some! Anyway, I can teach you French. We could speak nothing but French.'

I thought of what Mum had said about romantic involvements. I thought about leaving London after four weeks of Hugo's company, getting on an aeroplane and flying back to Paris and then the long-haul flight back to Australia. I couldn't do that. If I went with Hugh to England, I'd be saying something about us, wouldn't I?

Weren't those unspoken words already resonating in the way my fingertips traced the long veins inside his pale arms and held the sides of his face when we kissed? Wasn't each kiss saying something about us?

He dropped the subject and each kiss became more urgent, as though our mouths knew what our hearts were refusing to admit. It was as though we needed to know everything about each other, from the surface of our skin to the inside workings of our minds and history. I'd never asked anyone so many questions or answered so many myself. What was happening to me?

I showed him photographs of Mum's studio and he studied them attentively, admiring the Art Nouveau sweep of the front. He peered at the interior shots and said, 'Wow! Paper patterns, hung up properly. That's class, Lise.'

In return he told me his favourite Roald Dahl story about a valuable Chippendale chest of drawers being cut up by people who had just sold it to an unscrupulous antique dealer. They were worried it wouldn't fit in his car but he was actually cheating them.

'That's awful,' I said when he'd finished.

'You, Unc and I,' Hugo said seriously, 'we don't laugh at the story. Everyone else thinks it's hilarious.'

He told me about weekends spent visiting the Victoria and Albert Museum, when he could get away from the shop to visit his mum and sister back in Camden, and how he was researching the sixties. 'Everyone has to have a period, you know? A small but significant collection to call their own. The fifties is already out of my price range. I'm thinking the futuristic sixties. There are real gems out there. Imagine a world without mobile phones or Google. The future people were imagining then is nothing like now.'

When I heard the chimes of the shop ringing, I'd rush down the stairs, hoping it was him. He'd stand there, chatting to Madame Christophe, patting Napoléon and then we'd saunter out, arms wrapped around each other into the Paris afternoon or evening. We'd sit by the Seine, swinging our legs and talk until something he said, or I said, or the way he smiled, stopped us talking. We'd kiss and kiss. I'd feel his heart beating through the thin cloth of his shirt.

With Ben it had been all about sex. We'd kissed until my jaw had ached and my lips were dry. I'd wanted his hands all over me. We talked on and on about how we had to do it, because we loved each other. But it was impossible – Mum never went out and he had three younger brothers who were always around. When he got his licence, he'd borrowed his mum's car, to take me to the movies, he said. Being able to borrow the car was his reward for getting his licence first try. But really, *our* reward had nothing to do with the movies!

I hadn't told Hugo about Ben. I hadn't even invited Hugo to stay the night with me. I wasn't sure how. He'd apologised for not asking me to his place but I knew it was just a couch at his uncle's friend's studio. That was clearly when I should have asked him to spend the night at my apartment. I'd been tongue-tied and unexpectedly awkward, cursing myself later. Why was I so stupidly shy at that precise moment?

'I didn't know what to do,' I said to Goldie and Mackenzie.

They had claimed me for some girl time. There was a beatbox band playing at the Tuileries. It was some kind of German music festival, and I hesitated in case we bumped into Anders, even though he was no longer important. Friendship and crepes won out hands down.

'You just say to him, please stay the night,' Goldie said. 'What's the problem with that?'

'I know, but I was scared . . .' I stopped.

'You are making a problem where there is no problem,' Goldie said.

'I know that, Goldie. It just felt – feels – like a big thing.'

'It is, then,' Mackenzie said. 'Whether it is a big thing or it isn't, if you feel it is, then it is, because that's what your emotions are telling you.'

'That is so American,' Goldie complained. 'I don't even know what you're trying to say.'

'It's Canadian,' Mackenzie said. 'I wish everyone wouldn't confuse us with them. It's disheartening.'

We walked down to the pond and watched the kids, pushing little sailing boats around with their long sticks.

'We used to make paper boats,' Mackenzie said dreamily, 'every solstice. In summer, my mum would take us down to this picnic place. We'd make paper boats and write our wishes on them and then we'd sail them down the river. In winter, we'd write our wishes on paper and Mum would hang them carefully from a tree. Every morning, when I ate breakfast, I'd watch as my wishes twirled around in the wind.'

'That's so Canadian,' Goldie said.

'But not American,' Mackenzie said triumphantly.

'Anyway, we couldn't do that here. There'd be a law against it.'

'That's true,' Mackenzie said, 'it would be like sitting on the grass. So many parks where you can't lounge around! So French. But we could hire some of those toy boats? We could tell our Paris wishes to our boats and set them sailing.'

'It costs money,' Goldie said.

'And won't it seem odd?' I asked, even though I wanted to do it. The vintage boats looked magical and the children were like characters in a storybook. I wanted to be like them, not worried about anything except the fate of my little wooden boat.

'Who cares?' Mackenzie said. 'I'll shout. I'm a Canadian. That's what we do.'

'You can't shout all of us,' Goldie argued. 'That's not Canadian. That's just foolish.'

'I can, Goldie, and I will. Come on.'

Against all our protests, Mackenzie hired us each a boat and we took them down to where there were the least kids around.

'Now,' Mackenzie said, 'you have to whisper your wish to your boat and set it sailing into the world. Except of course, it's not really the world – but hey, it's the French way and we can adapt.'

I don't know what the others asked for. I stood there in the bright sunlight and I thought about my wish for what seemed like a long time. I didn't want to get confused. Madame Christophe had told me that most of her clients didn't even know what question it was that they wanted answered. I wasn't going to squander my boat wish on something I didn't really want. It made it difficult. Mackenzie and Goldie had already launched their boats by the time I shoved mine out into the water. In the end I sent it into the pond without wishing for a single thing. How lame was that?

Chapter 21

MORE RULES

All designers break rules. Coco Chanel took off her corsets and wore her signature pearl necklace backwards. Schiaparelli wore a shoe on her head. Vivienne made safety pins a fashion accessory. All artists break rules. Obedience doesn't create masterpieces. But nor does it create failures. It's like sewing with a pattern. You end up with something that looks like the illustration on the packet. More or less. It might not be the skirt you dreamt about, the one that swirled and swished and danced with you, but it will fit. Obeying rules means everyone is safe. More or less. But what about the rules you make yourself? Can you break them?

Hugo extended his stay by three days. 'It's fine,' he said. 'I've cleared it with Unc. I can't leave yet.'

I skipped another French class to celebrate and Hugo and I went to Versailles for the day.

'It's extraordinary,' I said so many times that Hugo stopped counting.

'Imagine having just one of those vases!'

'Or sleeping in those beds!'

'Sneaking through the corridors to visit your lover.'

'I'd get lost,' I said.

'You'd need Google Maps!'

We kissed near each fountain. I told Hugo it was an Australian superstition.

'You're just taking advantage,' he said.

'I don't hear you complaining.'

'I think it's a Camden thing that you need to do it twice,' he answered.

'I'm not objecting,' I said.

It couldn't last. He would have to go back to work. I had to get on with my life.

'We miss you,' Mackenzie said. 'You're the best student in the class. *Fabienne* misses you.'

'She doesn't even like me,' I said.

'She does, actually,' Goldie said. 'She likes anyone with a good accent. She asked after you on Tuesday. She said, "Where is the Australian?" and then she raised an eyebrow at Anders and said, "I hope you haven't scared her away."'

'Oh no!' I said. 'What happened next?'

'I told her that on the contrary,' Mackenzie said, 'au contraire, you'd met someone. I was pretty pleased with the au contraire. You need to come back, Lise, if only to say goodbye.'

'I'm not leaving for another four weeks,' I protested. 'I just need to be with Hugo while he's still here. You know that.'

They talked me into it.

I didn't want to see Anders. Somehow I felt that would taint the relationship I was building with Hugo. Would it be better to see him again when Hugo had left? The thought of Hugo leaving made me desolate. How was it even going to work? I'd go to the railway station and we'd cling together until the train tooted? I couldn't even think about it.

On the morning of the Great Return I was nauseous. I gave half of my breakfast croissant to Napoléon and then wondered if I felt sick only because I was actually hungry. Even my Falbalas shirt couldn't give me courage.

Madame Christophe regarded me sharply. 'You are return-ing to Fabienne's class?' she asked eventually. It no longer completely shocked me when Madame Christophe knew things that I hadn't told her.

'Yes,' I said, pouring another coffee for myself and adding a big splash of milk. 'It seems like time. Anyway, Hugo has a client to see.'

'It is time,' she nodded.

'Great,' I said.

Madame Christophe took a deep breath, almost a sigh, as though I had disappointed her in some way. 'You are not still worried about the German jogger?' she asked.

I shook my head. 'Not really.'

'So what is it?'

'Just life,' I said.

'Ah well, yes, life.' Madame Christophe gave her elegant little shrug. 'At least there is Paris,' she said as though that solved everything.

I met Mackenzie and Goldie. We were early to class and we took the three seats that directly faced the whiteboard. Goldie began an elaborate description of her latest glass constructions that required her to draw diagrams on her French notes. She was planning to make Paris scenes in which she'd place her naked women.

'It could be entertaining,' she said, 'or dreadful. You know – kitsch? I can't tell yet and so I keep drawing. I don't want to be kitsch, but I do love the idea of perching my little woman at the bottom of the Eiffel Tower. What do you think?'

'Kitsch,' a male voice said. It was Anders, of course. He'd walked in without us noticing. Goldie flushed.

'I think it depends on how it's done,' I said, turning to Goldie. I was surprised my voice wasn't shaking. It sounded certain and measured. 'I mean, if you're planning this whole Paris in summer theme, I think you'll get away with it.'

'So do I.' Mackenzie nodded. 'There's something celebratory about it, Goldie. I think an exhibition of them would be great – and they might sell.'

'Commercial,' Anders said, straight away. 'Selling out?'

I turned away from Goldie and looked at Anders. Yes, he was hot. There was no getting away from that. But his mouth was drawn into a mean sneer that made his lips thin and he'd narrowed his eyes so they were unkind. His shirt sleeves were too carefully folded up, as though he meant you to see his biceps. He saw me watching him and he smiled, but the smile didn't reach his eyes. My stomach jolted. I don't like you, I thought. I actually don't like you. My head spun a little and everything was floaty. I should have had more breakfast, I thought, and then, no – I'd been released. I'd seen through Anders.

At that moment Fabienne waltzed in, wearing tight jeans, her trademark stilettos and a sheer white shirt that revealed a lacy camisole. 'Ah, Lisette!' she said, and I was gratified to hear the warmth in her voice. 'We have heard your news!' she said theatrically. 'It is Paris, the city of romance.'

'Romance?' Anders asked me directly. His top lip curled.

I channelled Madame Christophe and shrugged one shoulder at him. 'I will have to consult my clairvoyant,' I said. 'I cannot see into the future myself.'

Fabienne clapped her hands, just once. I couldn't tell whether she was applauding or merely bringing the class to attention, but I suspected from her smile that it was the former. Anders pulled out his notebook and opened it noisily.

'So,' Fabienne said smoothly, 'what has everyone been doing? Goldie, you were talking about your art?'

Goldie sighed. 'It's hard to talk about art in another language,' she said, but she tried anyway. The class proceeded as though nothing had changed, but everything had changed and even when Anders began to describe his week, pointedly mentioning Gabi as often as he could, I didn't care. He'd been stripped of his glamour and what was left wasn't attractive.

When it was my turn I didn't mention Hugo. It was not anyone's business except my own. I did mention Falbalas, however, and the flea markets and was gratified by Fabienne's response.

'Ah,' she said, 'you are becoming a Parisienne, Lisette!'

I watched with some satisfaction as a couple of new students copied words from the whiteboard and asked halting questions about metro directions. I was careful to avoid all mention of being cursed. I didn't want to put anyone off.

'You were great,' Mackenzie said after the class. 'I'll buy you a beer for that effort.'

'I could do with a beer,' Goldie said. 'Did you hear how she made me describe the glasswork? Oof, I'm never going to learn French!'

'But you did it.' Mackenzie linked arms with us. 'You did it, Goldie.'

'I think I may have said I was going to have a woman in the Eiffel Tower,' Goldie said, 'or perhaps impale her on it?'

'It was a brief misunderstanding,' Mackenzie said. She caught my eye and started to laugh, which set me off. We were still laughing when we sat down in a Mexican cafe – chosen by Mackenzie, because who wouldn't want Mexican in Paris?

'To friendship!' I said, raising a toast with my beer. 'Thank you for being my Paris friends.'

'We'll stay friends,' Goldie said seriously.

'On Facebook,' Mackenzie said. 'Although, really, the world is a global village. You must both come to Canada.'

'I think it's too cold,' Goldie said. 'Aren't there bears?'

'You should both come to Australia,' I said, but my heart flopped when I said it. It wasn't an excited flip-flop but more of a belly whack. I didn't want to go home, but I had a return flight. I would go to university and study art history, whether I wanted to or not. I'd never be an artist but I would be educated. I tried to imagine myself saying to someone, a little sadly, 'Oh yes, I fell in love in Paris, but I had to come home. We still Skype.' I couldn't imagine who I'd say it to, I could only see Hugo's face in my mind's eye, the loose threads at his collar points.

'You're very quiet.' Mackenzie pounced on me. 'And you've hardly touched the corn chips. Are you feeling okay?'

'Yeah, yeah,' I said, 'I'm just. You know. It's all happening so fast. Time passing.'

We all ordered more beer even though that wasn't going to solve anything. Goldie launched into a long, complicated speech about a boy she had once gone out with and when they broke up he'd said that there was no such thing as a relationship that didn't work. It worked, he'd argued, for as long as it had worked. All relationships work. Then they might stop. It didn't make any sense, no matter how much beer I drank.

'Does that make sense to you?' I asked Mackenzie when Goldie went to the toilet.

'I think we need to order some more food,' Mackenzie said. 'I think food is seriously needed.'

'I just don't understand. Or am I overthinking it?'

Mackenzie studied the menu. 'Actually, I don't need food. I need to have drunk less beer.'

Goldie came back. 'I can't work this afternoon,' she said, 'not after this beer. What shall we do?'

'I know!' I said, waving a corn chip for emphasis. 'You guys can come with me and find Chanel. I promised my mother I would.'

'Chanel? You mean the shop?'

'Yes. The one where her old apartment is – I think the apartment's upstairs.'

'Do we have to go inside?' Mackenzie rubbed anxiously at a spot of salsa on her jeans.

'Oh come on, Mackenzie – you're Canadian. You can go anywhere.'

'Not covered in lunch,' Mackenzie argued.

'We don't have to go inside, necessarily. I just want a photo. That's all.'

My mother idolises Chanel. I don't, particularly, although I appreciate her role in haute couture. Nonetheless my heart skipped a beat as we stood outside 31 rue Cambon in front of the famous linked Cs.

'There's a shoe in the window,' Mackenzie said, 'and nothing else. I like the pastry shop windows better.'

'It's an expensive shoe,' Goldie said. 'There's no price tag on it.'

'Of course there isn't. That would be vulgar.'

'What's vulgar about knowing the price of something?' Mackenzie asked.

'Knowing is one thing, displaying is another.'

'Come on,' Goldie said, 'this making me nervous. I bought a pair of knock-off Chanel sunglasses in Manila. I could be arrested. Let's just take the photo.'

'Can you tell the difference?' Mackenzie asked curiously.

'I don't know,' Goldie said, 'I've never seen original Chanel sunglasses and I'm not going inside to find out.'

'I can't believe she must have stood here,' I said, 'and thought about her windows and wondered about the angle of a hat or the drape of a skirt. That's pretty extraordinary. I'm standing where Chanel stood. Mum should really be here.'

We took photos as discreetly as we could – not that it mattered too much. A whole bunch of tourists came up and madly photographed each other, a couple holding their white Chanel bags aloft.

'I think it's a little too perfect.' Mackenzie waved at the shopfront. 'I don't think I'm comfortable with perfect.'

I wondered, was that why Mum loved Chanel so much? The Vase often featured white camellias, one of Chanel's signature motifs. I preferred overblown peonies, Schiaparelli's wit and Westwood's audacity. I told Goldie and Mackenzie about the camellia.

'She had a signature flower?' Mackenzie was outraged. 'That's ridiculous. Why didn't she buy a bit of forest and save some trees instead?'

Goldie and I looked around at the buildings and cobblestones. 'I don't think trees were such an issue back then,'

Goldie said gently, and then to me, 'It's a fair point, though. Is haute couture still relevant?'

'It's as relevant as art is,' I said hotly, 'and as beautiful.'

'And as inaccessible to most people,' Mackenzie said. 'At least art gets into public galleries.'

'So do clothes,' I said, 'and anyway, what are you going to do with your art, then? Plaster Paris with it – or try to sell it?'

'I know, I know.' Mackenzie threw up her hands in defeat. 'But when I get home, I'm planning some environmental art pieces that will become part of the landscape. I won't be able to sell them, they'll be public art.'

'I just think there's room in the world for beauty,' I said, 'and for people who spend their lives making it.' I thought of Hugo's stories of his uncle lovingly polishing silver spoons. 'Or caring for it or collecting it,' I added.

'If you had a signature flower, Lise,' Goldie said, linking arms with both Mackenzie and me, 'it would be a strong flower that didn't give up easily.'

'I'd be a weed,' I laughed.

'You'd be a bougainvillea,' Goldie said, 'vibrant, beautiful and tough – a survivor.'

'We don't see them in Canada,' Mackenzie said, 'but that sounds like Lise.'

I thought, I'll remember this forever, the day I was told I was vibrant, beautiful and tough – three new words I could use to describe myself.

Chapter

22

Before Fashion Week, every big house operates 24/7 getting ready. They are on a countdown. Hugo and I were on countdown, too. But we weren't going to march it proudly down any catwalk. We were going to end up destroying what we'd been so carefully making.

'Come on,' Hugo said, 'ten best movies of all time. And one has to be a Star Wars.'

'You won't know the ones I like,' I said, a little self-consciously, 'a lot of them are kind of weird and old.'

'Try me.'

This was the type of game we played. Ten books you couldn't live without. Three favourite birthdays you'd had. Most vivid childhood memory.

'*Mary Poppins, My Fair Lady* – for the costumes – *Breakfast at Tiffany's*—'

'My mum has the DVD.'

'We have it, too. Shall I go on?'

'Please.'

'*Amélie*, another French one, *The Embroiderer* – it's really long and slow but she embroiders. It's . . . the colours? I don't know, there's something about it and she is pregnant and alone. Maybe it reminds me of Mum? But it has a happy ending.' That was the thing with Hugo. I told him more than I'd ever told anyone except Ami.

'That's five,' Hugo said, 'and you haven't picked the Star Wars movie yet. Mine, in no particular order, are Tarantino's *Pulp Fiction*, two by the Coen brothers: *O Brother Where Art Thou?* and *Fargo* – the former for the music, the latter for the black humour – and because I love the pregnant cop, but not in a kinky way. Okay, that was awkward but you know what I mean, right? *The Lord of the Rings* – that has to count as one, yeah? Also, and I know this isn't cool and sophisticated, but the first Harry Potter movie. It was like seeing one of my favourite books come to life.'

'What about *The Lion, the Witch and the Wardrobe*?'

'Doesn't make top ten.'

'*Atonement*,' I said, 'talking of films adapted from books. We studied it at school but I still love it.'

'Yeah, that could be on my list,' Hugo said. 'Mum, Unc and I went to see it. They cried.'

'I was furious at the ending. But that green dress! *Factory Girl*, about Edie Sedgwick.'

'Haven't heard of it,' Hugo admitted cheerfully.

'Andy Warhol's muse,' I said, 'she was one of the sixties icons. I think *The Lord of the Rings* would make my list, too.'

'See, we have films in common,' Hugo said cheerfully.

'Only two,' I said.

'And our Star Wars film? Go on, tell me it isn't *A New Hope*?'

'It is – but only just. The one with the Ewoks nearly beats it.'

'You're such a girl,' Hugo said and leant over to kiss me.

'Come on, Hugo! I bet you had a teddy bear. You'd have been just the kind of boy who refused to go to sleep without his teddy!'

'He had a sailor suit,' Hugo admitted. 'Actually, he's still wearing it. He lives in my old wardrobe at Mum's.'

When I stopped kissing him I could see the little blue pulse at his throat jumping.

'What will we do?' I asked.

Hugo shook his head and half turned away before he said, 'I haven't taken you to my favourite museum.'

'I've probably been to it already,' I told him.

'I bet you haven't been to this one.'

'Bet me what?'

'If you haven't, you come home with me.'

'Yeah. Sure. I bet your uncle would be thrilled. You know I can't do that, Hugo.'

'Okay, just to London. Just for the weekend. And, for the record, both Unc and Mum would be cool. People go from Paris to London all the time.'

'I know that, Hugo,' I said crankily. 'But what happens after the weekend? I come back to Paris, by myself. We can't keep crossing and re-crossing the Channel until I go back to Australia.'

'Couldn't we play it by ear? You don't have to come back to Paris by yourself.'

'My plane home leaves from here. So, are you saying you'll come back to wave goodbye to me from the Charles de Gaulle?'

'I'm saying why should you have such fixed plans at all?'

'It's called a ticket, Hugo. You can't change this kind of ticket just like that. It's not like a train ticket. It's a *plane* ticket.'

'You're sounding middle-aged,' Hugo said, 'as though your entire life is dependent on catching this and catching that. People forfeit tickets. People move halfway across the world. Your dad did.'

'I'm a responsible person,' I snapped. 'I made a commitment. Le Voltaire's busy season starts again in spring. They'll be needing me.'

'It's a hospitality job, Lise.'

I wanted to slap him. 'It's a *French* restaurant and I'm my mother's daughter,' I said and turned away.

'Oh wow. So it's not Maccas. What about us? Don't you think we're worth taking a chance on?'

'I think about us all the time,' I said. We stopped arguing then but the hurt simmered between us.

The museum was filled with weird things like shop signs that normally I would have loved but Hugo and I marched through it in silence. We didn't even hold hands.

After half an hour, Hugo checked his phone. 'I have to go,' he said. 'I have an appointment.'

'You didn't tell me that before.'

'No. Well, I don't have to tell you everything, do I? Anyway, you'll be able to find your way back, won't you?'

'Of course,' I said, 'I just thought we'd be able to spend more time together.'

'So did I,' Hugo said. He didn't even wave properly, just loped off without looking back.

I walked back into the museum. It was better to cry in a museum than on the streets of Paris. I went into the garden and sat on a seat and tried to breathe calmly. He had a cheek being angry with me, I thought eventually. I didn't care if I never saw him again.

But I did care. That was the whole problem. Why was I so intent on staying in Paris?

When I'd stopped snivelling I went home. I avoided Madame Christophe and even Napoléon. As soon as I was in my room I got on Skype. I sent Ami an urgent message telling her I needed to talk and then I waited.

'He says just for the weekend,' I told her. 'But what happens then?'

Ami rolled her eyes. 'What happens whenever?' she said.

'Ami! I'm serious. After the weekend I'd just come back and Paris would be awful without him.'

'So stay with him.'

'Don't be stupid. How can I? I've got a ticket home.'

'I know all about the stupid ticket, Lise. You've told me about the ticket a hundred times. So, you've got a ticket.

Have you asked your mum about the letter yet? Have you checked your bank account?'

'No. Not yet.'

'So, if it's about the money, that's what you need to do first.'

'It's not about the money.'

'Then what *is* it about?' Ami peered at me. My laptop had pixelated her face but I could still see her forehead crinkling in exasperation.

'I don't know,' I said. 'Failure? Like, you know, I go with him and it turns out there's a girl. A Camden girl. A Yorkshire girl. Or something else – his mum doesn't like me? Anyway, I can't just stay there forever.'

'As I see it,' Ami said patiently, 'you're jumping the gun a little, aren't you? The guy's just suggested a weekend in London and you're already talking about forever?'

'I know. It's stupid.'

'Just a bit,' Ami said. 'It could just be a weekend – or even a week sightseeing and then you could come back to Paris and then he might come back to Paris to see you the next weekend.'

'He's got a job. In Yorkshire. It won't be the next weekend. And then, anyway, I come back to Australia – and people don't do that all the time, do they? They don't cross back and forth to the other side of the world for the weekend.'

Ami examined her nails and then she waved them at me. 'Look,' she said, 'glittery, aren't they? But you know what? I can change nail polish it if it's too much after a week.'

'You're saying that you can change your feelings if they're too much? Shallow, Ami.'

'No, I'm not saying that. I'm saying you need to put things in perspective, Lise. Nothing needs to be permanent. Decisions don't. You have the power.'

Except Ami was wrong. I didn't have any power. Hugo had walked off without even waving goodbye. He'd left me for another appointment. Probably with his distinguished client. Who was probably a woman. That's what Edouard had implied: I remembered the wink. I hadn't had a chance to ask Hugo about that. It had slipped to the back of my mind, lost in the whirlwind of museum-going and park-kissing.

The more I thought of it, though, the more it made sense. He had a back-up plan. I had nothing, only French lessons, Madame Christophe (and Napoléon), a return ticket to Australia and work for the rest of the year – work so I could afford to go to uni to study something I wasn't sure I wanted to study. Hugo had a distinguished client who was probably pouring him champagne and clinking crystal glasses with him as I cried at my computer.

'You have the power,' Ami repeated stubbornly. 'What do you want, Lise? What do you really want?'

'I want Hugo,' I whispered. 'I want him but it's impossible, Ami. It's just not going to work out.'

Ami shrugged. 'You don't know that, Lise, you don't know anything. Anyway, I've got to go. I don't think I do want to sparkle for much longer. I'm going to ring the nail place and make a booking. Blue glitter is for mermaids. I want to be tougher than this. Lise, why don't you get your nails done? Or buy some more boots? Remind yourself that you *are* in control. That you can be tough – what happened to the girl who stomps around in her Docs? What happened to her?'

She's falling in love, I said to myself. She's falling in love and she's really confused. It's just a phase, like blue glitter or ox-blood Docs. Or is it something more?

Chapter 23

When Mum was a little girl, she had a collection of foreign dolls. One day she'd planned to give them to me, but when my grandmother died we discovered she'd got rid of them. 'Probably just op-shopped them,' Mum had said bitterly. She'd described the little Japanese doll with her collection of wigs. 'I'd change her wigs,' she'd told me. 'I'd make her kneel for the tea ceremony. She could have just saved her. Just her.'

I tramped through the Louvre all the next day – so huge. So exhausting. I'd woken up to a text from Hugo apologising and asking me to forgive him but I'd deliberately left my phone at home so I wouldn't text him straight back. I wanted him to be sorrier. I wanted him to suffer. When I got home I had the beginning of a headache and my feet were hurting. Hugo was waiting outside with a shopping bag of food.

'Please,' he said, 'let's call a pax?'

'Pax?'

'Peace. Let's break bread together. I'm sorry I was an arse.'

I let him follow me up the stairs. 'You just seemed to change,' I said. 'I thought we were being brave and bold and not worrying about the future?'

'It sounds okay in theory' – Hugo sounded gloomy – 'but in real life it's crap. Let's face it, Lisette. It's crap. I think . . . oh, never mind.'

'I don't know where we're going to eat this. On the bed?'

'Cosy,' Hugo said. 'That's one advantage of these maid's rooms. Very intimate.'

I raised my eyebrows. 'If we don't want intimate contact with crumbs, we'd better get plates.'

'So what do you want intimate contact with?' Hugo did a pretend leer as we settled cross-legged, facing each other on the bed.

'I think you know.'

Our knees were touching and I knew my skirt had ridden more than halfway up my thigh. A picnic in bed – that was practically an invitation, wasn't it? I wanted it to be, but I was also nervous.

'Is this how you've seduced all your other boyfriends?' Hugo fed me a piece of baguette.

'I thought you were seducing *me*,' I asked, putting an olive in his mouth. 'Also I haven't had many boyfriends, actually.'

'What about Anders?'

'He was never a boyfriend,' I said, 'he was just charming. For the wrong reasons.'

'But in Australia?'

Here was the talk I'd been avoiding. I'd alluded to boyfriends. Well, *a* boyfriend. I'd kept my inexperience secret. I'd let Hugo tell me about Maxine and the Camden girl while I'd evaded his questions. All he really knew was that I was single. He also knew that my home life hadn't been conducive to boyfriends, but I suppose he thought – as anyone would – that teenagers would get around that.

'Look,' I said to distract him. 'My blister! I told you I'd walked forever.'

Hugo cupped my foot gently in his hand. 'Poor foot,' he said. 'So, boyfriends?'

'Do you want some wine?' I asked.

'I'll open it,' Hugo said, 'you keep talking.'

'I don't know what to tell you.'

Hugo prised the cork out of the bottle and poured the wine. 'Have you been in love?'

The question caught me off balance. I'd expected something different. I thought of Ben, how my heart had beaten faster when he'd walked into the classroom. 'Yes,' I said finally, 'yes, I've been in love.'

'And?'

'Well, it didn't work out. Obviously.'

'But while it did?'

'It wasn't like what you had with Maxine or the Camden girl. It was just a school thing. Everyone knew we were together but we didn't go on proper dates. Sometimes I watched him play footy and then his mum or dad would drop me home after the game. Sometimes we went to the movies and my mum would drive him home. It was like that. He wasn't comfortable at my place with Mum always there. And his younger brothers wouldn't leave us alone at his house.'

Hugo looked confused. 'So what happened?'

'He got his licence,' I said, 'then we broke up.'

'Then you came to Paris? It must have been some break-up.'

'It was last year!'

'And then you had his love child, decided to adopt it out and have regretted it ever since?' Hugo waggled his eyebrows at me. 'Which is why you never talk about him?'

'I said it was a school thing.'

'He cheated on you with Shari who had a nose ring and you murdered them both and were subsequently expelled?'

I knew he thought he was making it easier. 'I don't know if I want to tell you.'

Hugo put his wine on the floor, rummaged through his backpack and took out a package that he unwrapped. He held up a small doll wearing torn undergarments. She had a painted face and her body was made from some kind of fabric. Her mouth was surprised and her dark hair slightly unruly. I leant over and smoothed it down. It was real hair.

'Oh, Hugo, where did you get her?'

'Lise, meet Babette. Babette, this is Lise. I've told you about her.'

'Pleased to meet you, Babette,' I said. Hugo's attention was firmly placed on the doll he'd balanced on his knee.

'About time he introduced us,' the doll said. 'I've been saying, you ashamed of me or what?'

I laughed. 'Hugo, I didn't know you were a ventriloquist!'

'Here!' Babette said. 'Don't pay him no attention. He's just along for the ride.'

Even though she wasn't a proper ventriloquist's doll and Hugo was holding her on his knee, there was something about her that was real in the subdued light of the apartment. 'I'm sorry, Babette.'

'That's orright, darling, you weren't to know. Come on, tell us the whole sorry story, then.'

'I don't know.' I glanced nervously at Hugo. 'You promise not to laugh?'

'I can't answer for him.' Babette's head jerked towards Hugo. 'But I won't, luvvie. Us girls have to stick together.'

'I won't promise,' Hugo said. 'But I'll try my best not to.'

'I'll bash him if he laughs,' Babette offered, 'and that's a promise.'

I took a deep breath. 'Okay. Well, because my dad didn't stick around to see me born, there was always an anti-boy vibe at home.'

'Boys,' Babette said, 'can't live with them, can't live without them.'

'Except my mum did – and I lived with her lectures about being careful and how you just couldn't trust men. In Year Nine Ami and I pretended we were lesbians just so we didn't have to produce a boy to moon over. It was funny at first and then it got a bit old. I grew my hair and Ami started wearing skirts, but it didn't change anyone's mind so we just lived with it. Then Ben came along in Year Ten. He was new to the school, kind of dorky.'

'There's hope for me. I'm the original dork.'

I remembered what Ben had been like in Year Ten: a weedy nerd with acne. He wouldn't have even made it onto my radar except that we'd been put on the same debating team and I felt sorry for him. He was so obviously at a disadvantage. Then I heard him argue – he was dynamite. Irritating dynamite because he thought he knew everything. That made me try harder to prove him wrong. We debated everything and realised we'd become friends.

'By Year Twelve,' I said, 'Ben had turned from an ugly duckling into a swan.'

'No hope for you.' Babette turned her head slightly towards Hugo. Her expression took on a slyness. 'You're still in the duckling phase, boyo.'

'Anyway, that's when he asked me out, at the beginning of that year. We made out a lot at school but it didn't go any further than that. Then Ben got his licence. We decided we should, you know . . . do it.' This was the part I didn't want to talk about, but I ploughed on. 'He borrowed his mum's car and we drove up the mountain – that's where you go, if you can't do it at home.'

'The old shag in the back seat. Doesn't happen where we come from, does it boyo?'

'No.' Hugo shook his head at Babette. 'Not so much. A knee-trembler after Friday night at the pub, maybe?' He sounded amused but he wasn't laughing. That was something. Anyway, I wasn't telling him – I was telling Babette.

'It should have been fine,' I said. 'Ben and I were excited but a bit scared. We talked about the future. Taking a trip together.'

'They do that,' Babette said. 'Let me tell you about the promises boys have made to me. Oops, sorry – it's not all about me.'

'It was Noosa,' I said, 'just a trip to Noosa.'

'It wasn't London.' Babette cackled. 'You've got the edge there, Hugo-boy.'

'Shut up, Babs.' Hugo was stern.

'Ooh, he called me Babs. He must be riled.'

'We'd been sitting outside but then it got a little cold, so we moved into the car.'

I remembered the aftershave he always wore. Everything was familiar and everything was new. The car had been cramped but we'd managed to get almost comfortable. We'd made out some more and then, half-undressed . . .

'You're in the car?' Babette's voice nudged me back to the present.

'Half-undressed and you know, nearly . . . and suddenly there's a light shining through the car window. I screamed.'

'I should bloody well think so.' Babette was indignant. 'Some pervert, love?'

'I couldn't see who it was,' I said. Even thinking about it still made the hairs on my neck stand on end and shivers snake down my skin. I had been utterly terrified at that moment.

'I thought it was a serial killer,' I told Babette. Her eyes seemed to flicker even though they were painted on.

'And it was a pervert?' she asked again sympathetically.

'A policeman.'

'Oh bloody hell.' Babette's voice sounded strained, as though she was choking back laughter. I couldn't look at Hugo.

'I understand that it's funny,' I said. 'Except it wasn't. I may have peed a little because I was so scared.'

'I always pee when I'm scared,' Babette confided. 'Nothing to worry about.'

'Ben and I scrambled into our clothes. Ben was swearing and I was crying. Then the policeman knocked at the door and Ben had to unlock it and show him his licence. The policeman gave us a lecture on having sex in a public place. We hadn't even got that far. If only Ben had laughed or we'd talked about it. I mean, I'd been terrified, but I would have seen the funny side later, I think. He dropped me home and said that he'd see me at school. But he didn't text me. He didn't answer my texts. Nothing.'

'See,' Babette said, 'men! What did I tell you? No finer feelings. No empathy.'

'I was responsible too. I was the one who had suggested Mount Dandenong. Who knew the police were patrolling the area? They didn't usually but there'd been a spate of drug-related crimes, petty things. We were unlucky. It still might have been okay. We might have been okay.' My voice cracked. 'But . . .'

'There's more?' Babette said. 'You go on, spill the beans. Got to get an experience like that off your chest.'

'He avoided me in class. I thought I'd give him space. I guessed he was cranky about the whole thing. Then he didn't turn up for debating. After our team won, Ami, Julia and I went back to Julia's. Her parents were away somewhere, so she'd organised for us to stay over because we all had spares the next morning. It was meant to be a serious study night – Julia wanted help with a photography assessment. I think Ami and I were pleased to have been asked. So we were all working away when her older brother decided to make some cocktails. He was studying hospitality.'

'So you got elephant's trunk and blabbed the whole thing?'

'Elephant's trunk?'

'Elephant's trunk, drunk. Rhyming slang. Bit of a cockney, our Babette.'

'Yes. I was tipsy and showing off,' I said miserably. 'Julia's brother is gay and funny and kept saying how charming we all were and didn't Julia have unusually intelligent friends. I told the story because I wanted to be funny too. Ben and I split up after that, of course. He finally sent me a text. Ending it. He didn't really ever talk to me again.'

'Oh love,' Babette said, 'but that's not the end of the world, is it? Got to get back on the horse, girl.'

'By the end of the year it had become a cautionary story. You know, my brother knew someone who went parking up at the mountain and was told off by a policeman. Also, no other boy took Ben's place. So, you know. I don't know that much.'

'You don't have to know that much,' Babette said and her voice was so kind it nearly undid me. 'In my experience, you follow your heart and things work out. More or less.'

I got off the bed and put the plates away on the kitchen sink. When I turned back, Hugo was stretched out on the bed, Babette lying beside him. His shirt had come untucked. I wanted to touch the skin that was revealed, trace my fingers over it.

'Come here,' Hugo said. He shifted to my end of the bed. 'Come and lie down with me.'

There wasn't really enough room but Hugo pulled my head onto his chest and I curled around him. I waited for a couple of minutes and then, tentatively, I put my hand on his stomach, just above the pulled-out shirt. I slid my fingers down to the gap where his skin was warm and soft. Then I tilted my head up to his and we kissed. We kissed each other breathless. He untucked my T-shirt and I felt, rather than heard, him sigh as he touched my skin. We paused for breath and then kissed again. And again. I'd undone his top three shirt buttons when he pushed me away.

'What? Hugo? Is something wrong?'

'The thing is,' he said after a long breath, 'I don't want to go that far if it just ends here.'

'What do you mean?'

'There are – I don't know – intervals in a relationship. You can walk away in the pause. You can say, oh well, that wasn't going to work out. I could walk away now. Sadly, of course. But I don't know how I'll cope if we become . . . more intimate.'

'I'm not sure what you're saying,' I said.

'I'm saying come home with me,' Hugo said, putting his hand over mine. 'Come to London and see what we're like. Give us a little more time.'

'My timing sucks,' I said. 'Don't ask me, Hugo. You know why I can't.'

'Are you living your own life? Or are you living your mum's life?'

'I don't know,' I said. I could feel Hugo's heart beating next to my cheek. 'I don't know what I want. I don't know if I should even go to uni. I don't know anything. I walked everywhere in the Louvre today. My head hurts and I have a blister.' My voice rose in a wail and tears ran onto Hugo's shirt. I was so tired.

Hugo stroked my hair and started to sing quietly. It was some kind of lullaby but the words were all wrong. Who called their kid Mucky? What lullaby threatened a kid with a whack? When the song ended I nudged him. 'More?'

I hadn't heard the end of the last song. That was my first thought when I woke up. One of my legs was half out of the narrow bed and Hugo was pressed against me. I could feel his breath on my neck. I had no idea what the time was but there was hardly any light visible through the crack between the curtains. My back was too hot with Hugo so close. I wanted to move away and I didn't want to move at all. His hand rested between my breasts. I'd never felt so close to anyone, I thought, not even Ben and certainly not Anders. I shifted experimentally and Hugo gave a little sigh, then his breath returned to normal. I stroked his hand and his body twitched.

I wanted to see his face. I squirmed around slowly. He sighed again and I stopped moving. Little by little I shifted gently until I was facing him. I was nearly off the bed by then so I put my arms around him to stop myself from falling out. In the half-light, I could see his face clearly. He looked younger asleep, his mouth just slightly open. His eyelids were almost blue and his eyelashes enviably thick. I wanted to kiss him. Would he wake up? I moved slightly and touched his mouth with mine. I kept my eyes open. His lids flickered and in half a second he was kissing me back, looking at me steadily.

We were half-undressed when Hugo stopped. 'I wasn't expecting this to happen,' he said. 'Have you got anything?'

'What do you mean? A condom? Well, no.' I didn't want to stop. 'Can we get one?'

Hugo kissed me again, and pulling away one hand, fumbled for his phone. 'It's so late,' he said. 'Nothing will be open.'

'Really?'

'Ssh. Let me think.' He put his hand on my mouth – as much to stop him kissing me again as anything else, I guessed. 'Nowhere I can think of. You're right, Lise, you are the queen of bad timing.'

'It's not my fault!'

'I know. It's equally mine. I'm sorry. I shouldn't have said that. Come on, let's get out here.' He pulled away and put his shirt on. 'Let's go and see a late night movie.'

'A movie?'

'Anything. Let's go for a walk. I don't care.'

'I can't walk,' I said. 'I've got a blister. I told you.'

'Well, I can't stay here,' Hugo said. 'We'll end up . . . and look what happened to your mum.'

'It's not contagious,' I said snappily.

'It might be genetic.' Hugo grinned at me. 'It's not worth the risk, Lise.'

'It just seems contradictory,' I complained. 'Come home with me, come to London. But let's not take a chance on this.'

'Lisette! Seriously?'

I looked up at him. 'Sorry,' I said. 'You're right. I'm just being sulky and stupid. I don't want to walk anywhere, though.' I held my foot up for him to see my huge blister.

'Can't you put a plaster on it?'

'I don't have any,' I said.

'I just need a circuit breaker.'

I tugged his arm. 'We don't have to do the full circuit,' I said. But the joke fell flat.

Hugo just looked at me before lying down next to me, his arms folded across his chest like some young, dead knight. 'You win.'

I scrunched myself up next to him. 'It wasn't very funny,' I admitted.

'It's all kind of messed up,' he said after a long silence.

I thought of what Ami had said after the whole Ben incident. 'No one's died,' I offered.

Hugo laughed. 'That's true,' he said. 'Come here.'

In the early hours of the morning he nudged me awake. 'I'm going now,' he said. 'I've got pins and needles in my arm, and a cramp in my leg, but really, I just don't think I can face Madame Christophe over breakfast.'

We crept down the stairs although I wasn't sure why we bothered when presumably, being a clairvoyant, she knew everything anyway.

'I don't care,' Hugo said, when I told him this theory. 'It's different her knowing from her magic crystal ball or whatever, to actually having her eyeball me in that French way over my early morning tea.'

'We don't have tea.'

'There – that's another reason. Oh Lise, don't look like that! Of course I'd sacrifice my breakfast tea for you.'

I waved him off down the street. I felt sad because I hadn't realised he was a tea-in-the-morning person and how would I ever get to know his habits if we said goodbye now?

It wasn't until I got back up to the apartment that I realised he'd left Babette there, propped up on my chest of drawers. She looked a little shabby and her eyes made her appear as though she were squinting. 'You really need some clothes,' I told her. 'It's disgraceful living in just your underwear – underwear you haven't actually changed for decades, by the look of it!'

The bed seemed much bigger without Hugo, and lonely. In the end, I put Babette in the space next to me. I wondered about the child who'd first owned her. I'd have to ask Hugo more about her, I thought. Where she'd come from and what he was going to do with her. For a brief second I let myself imagine Hugo buying dolls and me making clothes for them. Of course, I'd have to become a better sewer – but my hand stitching *was* neat. Mum had made sure of that. We'd live at the back of the shop, I thought sleepily. I'd become a tea-in-the-morning person and all my clothes would be vintage. I could go to university part-time and study costume history. I would bet almost anything there were universities offering that in England. Then I shook myself angrily. It was a daydream. That's all it could be.

Chapter

I had loved making doll's clothes when I was little. Mum cut them out for me and I'd sew them slowly by hand. Mum always said I was learning haute couture techniques at seven but I knew my stitches were sloppy. Is the rest of my life like that now? I know the theory, but my practice feels shoddy.

At breakfast I picked at my croissant and ended up creating so many flakes I just swept them onto the floor for Napoléon.

'You are feeling ill?' Madame Christophe asked.

'No . . . yes. A little,' I answered. 'It's hard to know. I don't feel myself,' I ended lamely with one of my mother's phrases. Madame Christophe leapt on my words and demanded I repeat them, in English. Then she cackled.

'That is very good to know,' she said, nodding. 'I shall tell some American customer that they do not feel themselves. It is so true, too. There are often times when one is not quite oneself, but the beginnings of someone else one might become. The difficulty is always stepping forward. Will it suit? What will be left behind? Many, many times what is left behind is nothing that was really wanted.'

I refused Goldie's offer of lunch and Mackenzie's invitation to coffee. I put Babette in my daisy bag. Her head poked out but I didn't care that I was too old to be taking a doll to the park. She was my talisman. I walked through the Jardin des Plantes. It was a hot, humid day. I'd looked up the weather in London earlier and seen photos of people sunbathing anywhere in the city there was a patch of sunlight, even outside the Tate Modern. Why had I looked up the English weather?

Big, clumsy bees that looked like oversized striped helicopters negotiated the flowerbeds. I wondered if they were bumblebees. There were cornflowers. They had been my Greatma's favourite flowers. I remembered planting them with her in the sunny corner of the garden. Mum and I kept planting them, alongside Queen Anne's lace. Mum said she supposed it was lovely, in a way, that Greatma was still so missed after that many years.

Missing people, grieving and mourning – my family was good at those things. How wasteful, I thought. How amazingly wasteful. Not my Greatma, of course – it was right that we missed her. She'd been a better mother to my mum than my grandmother had. Had my grandmother missed Mum? Who knew? Grandad used to visit secretly and bring chocolates, lollies and, once, a doll. My grandmother never unbent. Never apologised. When Grandad died, Mum went to the funeral and my grandmother didn't even say hello to either of us. We went to her funeral because, as my mother said flatly, 'I just want to make sure she's dead.'

Mum and Dad. She'd missed him even after what he'd done to her. Why else keep the photos? She'd missed him and she'd hardened her heart against him just as her own mother had clenched her heart against us.

Had I found Hugo just to lose him again? And why? Just because I was stubbornly sticking to a plan that was no longer relevant? Panic bubbled through me. He would be on a train in three days going back to London. I needed more time.

I couldn't stop thinking, so I walked away from the gardens only to arrive at another garden. I could just garden-hop around Paris, I thought, but I wasn't headed into the Tuileries with its lounging visitors lifting their faces to the sun. I went, instead, to L'Orangerie and sat in front of the Monet water-lilies for a long time, first in one room and then in the other. I didn't even look at the paintings properly, just let the colours wash over me like water itself. I was drenched in colour and that was enough to quieten my crazed mind. The questions stopped shouting at me and began to whisper, instead.

A text dragged me back to the real world. It was from a number I didn't know and, when I opened it, it was written in French. Maxine! I read through it three times before I was absolutely certain that she was inviting me to meet her so she could show me the best fabric stores in Paris that afternoon. No time to do anything but hop on the metro. I didn't even need a map these days! Of course, I was still carrying Babette but Max was probably used to people carrying around strange things.

And, indeed, she exclaimed when she saw the doll, 'Oh là là,' she said, 'she is fantastique. Hugo must have been very pleased to find her.'

'He didn't really say,' I said. 'I was wondering if I should make her some clothes.'

'But of course, she will be much more elegant that way. Do you know anything about her?'

'Nothing – except she's got real hair and her body's soft.'

Max nodded. 'This is correct,' she said, 'she is possibly from the late nineteenth century. A little worse for wear and those eyes are not her best feature. So not a Jumeau Bébé. Such a pity – that would have been worth something. Perhaps she is from a mystery maker – that is what they say when there is no maker's mark.'

'Wow! You know so much.'

Max shrugged. 'It is my business,' she said simply. 'You would learn, too, if you were in this world. You would learn quickly.'

'I'd love to,' I told her. 'I think I'd love that more than I would art. It feels more part of me. As though I could make it my own. There is something very personal about it.'

'This is true,' Max said, giving Babette back, 'this is very intimate, this handling of small, precious things. But, come – let us look at fabric. I want to buy something for new cushion covers – those I *can* make. You might find something for the doll?'

We headed to what Max told me was the fabric district of Paris – and she was exactly right. Each shop was filled with tables of fabric. There was one place that had five floors – one whole floor devoted to upholstery and home decorating fabrics. It was here that Max found some heavy cotton for her cushions. It was retro fifties print – abstract shapes, which reminded me of furniture, on a grey-green background interrupted by coloured brushstrokes of red and yellow. Then we looked for something suitable in the remnants pile for Babette.

'She should be wearing a . . . how do you say it?' Max outlined a crinoline shape with her hands. 'She is from that time.'

Eventually we found a remnant of some kind of heavy self-patterned brocade, some lace and some silk ribbon, which was delicately dyed.

'It is good,' Max pronounced, 'but how will you make the crinoline like a bell?'

'Wire,' I said, 'and look – these tiny buttons would be perfect, too.'

'She will need a hat. Women in those years would not go out without one.'

'I might make a bonnet. I've been looking up dolls on my laptop. Even the ones that weren't meant to model the latest fashions were beautifully dressed. I hope I can make something half as good!'

'I am sure you will,' Max said. 'Now, we must have a glass of wine, for that is what Parisian women do after shopping. If you have time, Lisette?'

We sat outside but Max directed her attention at me, rather than the passers-by. 'Santé,' she said and we chinked glasses delicately. 'So, Lisette,' she said after a sip of wine, 'Edouard and I have been wondering. It is not our concern, it is true, but we are fond of Hugo. We wonder what you are thinking – is it for you a holiday romance?'

'No,' I said straight away. I couldn't imagine having a holiday romance. That implied a resort and cocktails. It wasn't Hugo, lying in my bed, with my head on his shoulder. It wasn't him saying, *This is all messed up*. It wasn't *us*.

'But you are not joining him in England.' Max frowned into her wine.

'If I went to London with Hugo – then what? I'd come back to Paris by myself and then return to Melbourne? It would be worse than never going. At least here I have Mackenzie, Goldie and Madame Christophe.'

Max cocked her head and shrugged. 'A ticket?'

'I have to go home sooner or later,' I told her. 'There's the question of visas.'

'But is this what you want?'

'I don't know. Well, no. It's not what I want.' I'd said it. Out loud. The words hung between us. I could practically see them.

'Life.' Max patted my hand and smiled – although why I didn't know. 'It is sad, yes? But if you do not want things to be like this, you will find a way to make it different.'

That sounded to me like someone urging you to think positively as though that alone could change things, but

I liked Max and I wanted her to like me, so I smiled and nodded as though it were that simple.

When I got back to my apartment, I took out the fabric and haberdashery I'd bought and began a search on how to make clothes for Babette. One website instructed that an old doll would have to have authentic clothing and there was a warning to use only natural fibres.

I undressed Babette carefully and washed her underthings with my shampoo. I couldn't tell if they were authentic or not, but they were grubby. She didn't seem to have a mark on her, which meant that Max was probably right, and she was from a mystery maker. When I compared her to some of the examples I saw on Pinterest, I could clearly see her flaws – those off-centre eyes! – but I loved her even more.

I'd bought brown paper, scissors, a tape measure and a lovely fat pencil from the BHV. I carefully noted her measurements and then did some rough sketches. A crinoline was too hard, I decided, and one of the websites I consulted advised that these kinds of dolls were often dressed in a simple, low-waisted style of Edwardian dress. There were lots of examples. I knew the brocade would hold pleats well and so I worked out a rough pleated-tunic pattern. If I did that, I reasoned, I could fashion a jacket and no one would have to know the tunic had no sleeves.

I cut the pattern from the paper first to make sure it fitted. Then I cut it from the brocade. The best thing about making doll's clothes is that you don't need much space. I wouldn't have been able to cut out anything for myself in the tiny room, but I could simply use the top of my chest of drawers as a table for Babette's clothes. This was a familiar activity – Mum had taught me to sew doll's clothes before she allowed me to use any of her sewing machines. I had gone from painstakingly stitching along a pencilled line to making my own patterns, just as I was now. Why had I ever stopped? The last doll's clothes I'd made was an over-the-top Japanese streetwear outfit for a doll I had given to Ami for her birthday when we were both in Year Nine. She'd loved that, and pestered Mum until Mum had taught her to sew too.

I was trying to work out how to do the facing when Hugo knocked at the door.

'That's so fabulous,' he said when he saw the tunic.

'Do you think it looks too much like furnishing brocade?'

'They wore that kind of stuff, though. Heavy, so it wouldn't have to be washed as much. Lisette, don't you *feel* how right we are together?'

I snatched the tunic from him, nearly stabbing my finger with a pin. 'You can't ask me that all the time,' I said. 'You can't do this, Hugo.'

'I'm not asking you all the time. I'm asking one more time. That's all.'

'I can't go. And even if I did, I don't see how it would solve anything. We'd have a . . . holiday romance. That's what it would be, Hugo.'

'I'm not looking for a stupid holiday romance. What is that, anyway? And no, I don't understand. I'd do almost anything for this to work. I'd stay longer in Paris if I had an option to but I don't – I'm running out of money.'

'You're running out of money? Hugo – I have plans for my life. Why are my plans less real than your business?'

'You're undecided, aren't you? I didn't think you'd settled on what you wanted to do?'

'I've got nothing in England.'

'You'd have me. You've got your stepmother in Wales.'

'She's not my stepmother. I don't even know her!'

'Sorry.'

'I just thought that if you came with me, we could see what happened. See what we might be together. You never know what will happen if you don't take a chance.'

'We'd win TattsLotto?'

'It sounds stupid,' Hugo admitted, sitting on the bed. 'But I just thought having more time might present us with more options.'

'I don't see how.'

'I don't know either, but sometimes you just have to trust in the universe, or something.'

'Like think positively?'

'Why not? I might sell something big and make some real money. You might walk into a job. You might look around London or Yorkshire and think, this is where I want to be for the next while. We might look at each other and say this is who I want to be with. We might do that if we are together. Aren't you willing to risk that? I am.'

'No. No, I'm not.' My heart sank as I said it – but how

could I? How could I put my trust in something so intangible? How could I put my trust in this man, this *boy*, with his frayed collars and cuffs and his beautiful eyes? I wasn't my mother. But I also ignored the voice in my head whispering that Hugo wasn't my father either.

'I have to go,' Hugo said, standing up and reaching the door in one stride. 'I have to arrange some things. I'm supposed to be working. See you later, Lisette.'

'Hugo—'

'Don't walk me downstairs.' He held his hand out to stop me from moving towards him. 'I'm sorry,' he said. 'You can't take the risk. It's bad timing. I understand that.'

He was gone before I could reply, taking the narrow stairs two at a time. The front door crashed and I was standing by myself, cradling a half-made doll's tunic in my arms. I couldn't breathe – it was as though he'd taken all the oxygen in the room with him. I sat down on the bed. That was that, then. I'd let him go. I'd joined my family of mourners. There'd been something so final about Hugo's last words. He'd never talk to me again. I'd get a text – or maybe not even that. He was gone from my life.

There was half a bottle of rosé in the fridge and I drank a glass, leaning on the windowsill with Babette, now in her dried underthings, beside me, watching the Paris nightlife from my window. This was me, I thought. My mother made beautiful clothes for people who danced, flirted and fell in love. My mother measured hems and sewed on buttons. I'd come across the world to find out I wasn't any different.

Apparently I hadn't inherited any of my father's genes. If he'd only stuck around for even a little while, how would I have been changed? What would he have done if a woman had said, come with me? Make some more time for us? But isn't that exactly what my mother *had* said? Who was right? Why did all hurt so damn much? I drank the rest of the bottle and fell into bed. The room spun around and around and I felt nauseous if I moved, so I didn't. Eventually I slept, lying as I was, my arms straight by my sides like a soldier.

Chapter

25

In the Victorian era – about when Babette was made – when someone died, they made mourning brooches and wore them so they wouldn't forget their loved ones. They were often just miniature frames with a photo or human hair inside. My Greatma's mother had one containing the hair of her infant son, my Greatma's brother. It was one of the few things we sold after Greatma died. Mum said it gave her the heebie-jeebies. If I had some of Hugo's hair I'd put it in the silver locket Mum gave me on my sixteenth birthday. Not that he's dead, of course, but I'm in mourning. Clearly I should have been born in a different century.

I felt like a wounded solider when I woke up. My head ached and the morning light was too bright. No message had arrived from Hugo during the time I'd been asleep. I didn't even know why I checked my phone – he'd sounded so final when he'd left.

I didn't want to face breakfast with Madame Christophe. I didn't even want to face Napoléon. I trailed down the stairs forlornly, remembering Hugo leaping down them the night before as though pursued by a banshee. I could have wailed like a banshee.

Madame Christophe pushed the coffee plunger across to me. 'I cannot stay,' she announced. 'I have a Skype session with an international client. I said to her, no, Madame, I will not stay up until all hours of the night in order to tell you what you know already in your heart. If we are to Skype – such an ugly word – we will do it in my time, not yours. Napoléon will breakfast with you and you will pop him into his basket after.'

I breathed a sigh of relief. Napoléon sat silently beside me, eating my croissant while I drank coffee and water. Maybe I was coming down with something. I felt wretched enough. A summer cold – the worst. I sniffed experimentally. It wasn't a cold. I was kidding myself. This is what heartbreak and hangover felt like.

'No one died,' I told Napoléon firmly, but he looked unconvinced. 'Well, actually someone did if you think about it – my father died. I suppose I should find out what's in the mystery letter.' I left Napoléon in his basket and went back up the stairs. Would Mum be busy? If she was on Skype I'd tell her about Babette first and then ask about the letter.

'Good thing you called now,' she said. 'I'll be out later. You must be telepathic, Lisi – it's living with Sylvie.'

'I don't think clairvoyance is something you can catch,' I said.

'I was joking! I'm going out later, that's all. It's lovely to see you, sweetheart.'

'Going out?'

'Yes, with Vinh. You know, Ami's uncle Vinh.'

'Ami said you two were – you know.'

Mum leant into her laptop screen. 'Do you mind?' she asked earnestly. 'It won't change us, we'll still be the same, Lisi.'

'Well, we won't,' I said, 'but that's okay too, Mum. I think it's great for you. And for Vinh. I can see it working. I just don't understand why it didn't happen before.'

'It was one of those things. I suppose we were always preoccupied – me with you and Vinh with business. Anyway, enough of—'

'It just feels as though I had to leave the country for you to, you know, go out with someone.'

'Lisi, it's not all about you! I make my own decisions, you know.'

'Well, I know you try to make mine,' I said, but so quietly I hoped she hadn't heard.

'What have you been up to?'

When it came to it, I didn't trust myself to talk about Hugo, so I told her about the fabric district instead, without mentioning Babette at all.

'Interesting,' she said. 'Vinh tells me there are some wonderful fabric shops in Vietnam. Not the cheap as chips ones. Quality. You have to know where to go.'

'Which he does, of course,' I said rather drily.

'And beautiful handiwork – embroidery. Out of this world, he said.'

'Is there any mail for me?'

'Oh, Lisette, good thing you reminded me. There's a bank statement and one from the legal firm, those solicitors. I'll open that first?' I watched as she tore open the envelope. It was hard to tell on Skype, of course, but she was definitely different. Happier? Relaxed? There was silence while she read the letter.

'What does it say?' I asked finally.

'Well, it's amazing,' Mum said. 'Really, truly amazing.'

'What is it?' Had the money gone through already? Impossible.

'Sarah, your father's wife, has advanced some of the money to you.'

'What? How can she even do that?'

'She's the executor of the will, I suppose. I don't know – maybe it's her own money? Anyway, that's what she's done.'

'How much?'

'Five thousand dollars,' Mum said. 'That's very good of her, Lisi!'

'Where is it?' I asked. It was a rude question but I had to know.

'Hold on, let me read this again. Okay – the solicitor says that Sarah Grayson blah, executor of the estate et cetera, has requested, unusually, that you receive some of the money prior to the settlement and this has been deposited into the account you elected, so . . . it'll be in your bank account.'

'Can I access that from here?' There'd have to be some trick.

'I suppose so, Lisi, but you won't need to, will you? You aren't running short?'

'Not really, not exactly.'

'You'll have to write to her straight away and thank her. That is enormously generous. Did you tell her you were going to Paris?'

'Yeah, when I wrote to thank her for the painting.' I remembered my stilted note with shame.

'This really is extraordinary.'

'You'd do the same,' I said, loyally.

'I don't think I would,' Mum said. 'Grief can be so overwhelming. I don't think I'd even think about it. Of course, you could dip into it for a few souvenirs. Don't go crazy, though, Lisi. Actually, in some ways she hasn't done you a favour, has she? It will just be a temptation. You need to think about that being a nest egg for your university years.'

'I might use that money,' I said. 'I might use that money to go to London.'

'London? Why would you go there? Oh, no – Lisette – not the bric-a-brac boy!'

'He's not a bric-a-brac boy. He's an antique dealer.'

'That's quite irrelevant.' Mum's hand moved in slowmo as she brushed definitions aside – the same woman who insisted on being called a seamstress, not a dressmaker! 'Anyway, you can't go for long. What about your ticket home?'

'It's just a ticket,' I said.

'It's a ticket worth a lot of money,' Mum said. 'Listen, have you got Sarah's details? I'll give them to you now.'

I would have to contact her, I thought. I felt light-headed. Five thousand dollars!

'That's Vinh,' Mum said, listening to something I couldn't hear. 'Lisi – promise me you won't do anything stupid. Promise me you won't ruin your life over some boy. I love you. I don't want to see—'

'You're fading out,' I lied. 'I love you, Mum! And give my love and my blessing to Vinh. Bye!' I pressed end before I promised anything. Five thousand dollars. From a complete stranger. Well, almost complete.

The money could change everything. It could give us an option. I could change my ticket. I could go back with Hugo and stay for long enough for us to work out what we were together. What we could be. My father had bought us some time.

The only problem was that Hugo hadn't texted me. He'd said goodbye. He'd leapt down the stairs, two at a time, just to escape from me. He was probably chatting up his distinguished client as I was searching for my father's wife on Skype.

I needed to thank her in person – or as much person as I could, given that I was in Paris and she was in Wales. Even if nothing worked out, I wanted to tell her that I appreciated her thinking of me, even when she was overwhelmed with grief.

It didn't take me long to find her – she'd used her whole name and there was only one Sarah Grayson listed in her village. I sent her a long contact request. I was shaking. I received a message back more quickly than I expected. It said simply, *Delighted. Let me call you.* And then my computer buzzed and I was sitting in front of a woman I didn't know, a woman my father had loved enough to marry.

She looked older than Mum but – were those grey dreadlocks?

'Lisette,' she said in a deep, musical voice, 'how this unexpected encounter fills my heart with joy. You have no idea. You look so like him.' Her hand went to her mouth and for a minute I thought she was going to cry, but instead she blew me a kiss and smiled. 'Darling girl! So beautiful.' And she held her hands to her heart and shook her head so her dreads danced enthusiastically around her head. 'If only Will could see us talking now. And you in Paris! He would have been so proud!'

'How did he die?' I blurted out. I was shocked. I had not expected to ask that question so early in our conversation although it had been something I'd been wondering about.

'Oh, my dear Lisette. Shall I call you that? Such a romantic name!'

'I prefer Lise,' I said, 'but not Lisi.'

'Lise, then. It was quite sudden – thank goodness because Will would have hated anything slow – but terrible because it was so unexpected. It was a heart problem. Undetected when he was growing up. Nothing you need be concerned about,

Lise. I did ask so I could let you know if it was genetic. Can we talk about more cheerful subjects now?'

'I'm sorry.' I bit my lip. She was so much *warmer* than I had expected. 'I had to know.'

'Of course you did. But let's move on. Do you love Paris or are you suffering from Paris Syndrome?'

'From what?'

'Discovering your imagined Paris is nothing like the real city?'

'No, not at all. It's almost exactly as I thought it would be. Except better.'

'That rather sounds as though you have the other Paris Syndrome!'

'What's that?'

'Falling in love in the city of love.'

'Oh. Well, yes. Sort of. But he's not French.'

I hadn't meant to tell Sarah anything. I'd meant to thank her and, maybe, if she was okay about it, ask her something about my father but I found myself blurting out, 'I might come to England. I might change my flights.'

'Oh, I would,' she said straight away. 'Definitely. You're practically next door. Why the hell not? Come and stay here! Both of you.'

'How do you know . . .' I started uncertainly.

Sarah laughed, a warm, untroubled laugh. 'You just told me! You admitted you were in love but not with a French boy. So he's from England? Or does he just want to come here?'

I told her the whole Hugo story. I showed her Babette –
even though she couldn't see her very well – I told her about
Madame Christophe and Napoléon. I even told her about
Anders. By the time I'd told her everything, she'd swapped
her teacup for a glass of wine.

'But do you think he'll ever speak to me again?' I asked.
'He hasn't texted me since he left.'

'Oh, I should think he'll come around,' she said. 'But even
if he doesn't, do come over anyway. You'll love the UK and
it will love you. This is exactly what Will would have wanted
for you.'

'What was he like?'

'He was bold. Larger than life. Difficult. Prickly as cacti.
Wonderful. We were soulmates. The moment I met him,
I knew. Oh, Lise, I'm sorry. He did love your mother, but
he felt trapped. They were so young and she made all these
plans – she took for granted they'd be together forever.'

'What else would she think?'

There was a long pause and Sarah took a sip of her wine.
She looked thoughtful, rather than angry or sad. 'I know,' she
said finally. 'It was bad timing for them both. Your mother
must have struggled. It took a long time for Will to forgive
himself. But he had to do it. He wasn't ready to settle down.
Maybe if they'd met a few years later? Who knows.'

'I wish he'd let me into his life.'

'Well, he couldn't, actually. I know he didn't try very
hard – or, at least that's what it must feel like. He didn't try as
hard as he should have – I always told him that. But he didn't

want to hurt Sally any more than he already had. He did the best he could. Most of us do.'

I digested this.

'Mum worked really hard,' I said. 'She built up her business, all while looking after me.'

'I hope she was doing what she loved.'

I thought of the immaculate studio, The Vase always filled with flowers, the teacups on the table and the smell of rising sponge from the kitchen. I remembered the low chatter of the women as their hems were pinned, their seams adjusted. *It must be your sponge, Sally! I'm sure this was perfect when we measured it last week. I should never have had that second piece!* I thought of the nights when Mum and I and sometimes Ami would watch French movies, trying not to look at the subtitles. I thought of her now and the way she had of always touching anything soft, like petals, or my face, or velvet. Vinh would be in the kitchen, wearing a jacket, his tie slightly loosened. He was not prickly. He was not difficult. He was effortless, sincere and smart.

'Yes,' I admitted. 'She loves what she does. Always.'

'There you are. The best way to live. And speaking of love, I must show you more of your father's artworks. Hold on, Lise, I'll take you on a guided tour.'

I felt dizzy as I watched Sarah introduce me to my dad's artwork – there were big abstract landscapes with slashed colour and heavy lines, some that deliberately extended over the wide, plain frames as though nothing could contain their dark exuberance. A large red and purple nude was definitely

Sarah, but she didn't pass over it, just said matter-of-factly that she missed being his model.

'When you come over, I'll show you more,' she promised. 'We'll go to some galleries. Oh, I miss him so much. I know he's gone, but I hear him around. I talk to him in the evenings. When you're ready, come here – and bring your young man. Now, my chooks need feeding. The girls like a regular life. Lisette – I am so pleased my little family has expanded to include you. Go well, lovely human, travel light!' She blew me another kiss and was gone.

I sat back in my seat. I was dumbstruck. I tried to imagine those paintings on Mum's walls. I just couldn't see it. They'd have been too overpowering. Or Mum would have thought they were. But I could see a dark green piece, all ambiguous movement, like wind through scrub, or wind through water, even, being hung above The Vase without any problem.

But then I was the product of those two people. I swallowed. I could be bold. I could learn that from my father.

Chapter

26

Every fashion magazine in the world runs articles on packing light. There are whole blog posts devoted to reducing your wardrobe to a capsule of this-goes-with-that. My life spills out of an old ugly suitcase. It's never going to be perfect. It's never going to be manicured.

I waited all day but there was no word from Hugo. At least I didn't have to sit by a phone the way my mother would have sat, scared to leave the house for fear of missing a call. Did she do that? Did she sit there, day after day, her hand on her growing belly? She'd painted my room – an elegant blue-grey, rejecting the nursery colours advised by baby magazines. She'd quit her job in the ABC studios where she was only another dressmaker, not a designer. She'd put an advertisement in the local newspaper promising fast delivery, meticulous work and design flair. She cleared out the front room of Greatma's house and hung her brown papers on a rack. She didn't sit around.

I decided not to either but I did take my phone with me as I took some more photographs of Paris and did some shopping at the sales. Fabienne and Madame Christophe were right – they were worth waiting for. I didn't buy much. I was careful. I looked at everything first. I checked the stitching and the fabric. I thought about the buttons and the zippers. I was my mother's daughter, too. I didn't buy skirts – too easy to make. Instead I bought an intricately pleated fine linen shirt to go with my skulls, a jacket to go with the Audrey shift and a cheap-for-cashmere cardigan. It was winter in Melbourne. It would be autumn here soon. Toss a coin, I thought – heads or tails, where will you go?

Still Hugo didn't call. He didn't text. He wasn't at the apartment when I got back.

I rang Mackenzie and told her about Sarah.

'You're kidding!' she kept saying. 'So you're going to the UK?'

'I don't know,' I said. 'Hugo might already have left.'

'Call him. God, Lise – if you can Skype your dad's wife, you can call a guy you love.'

'I know,' I said. 'I know, right? Except that I can't. I'm scared I've blown it.'

'As soon as you hear his voice it will be okay,' Mackenzie said, 'seriously, Lise.'

It was silly calling him this late at night, I reasoned. He'd be out with Edouard and Max, drinking in some groovy bar, and they'd be telling him it was okay I wouldn't go with him – I was nobody. He was worth more than me.

I'd call him in the morning. I'd definitely ring in the morning. Or I'd text.

I didn't sleep. Babette and I watched the phone. It sat there, mute. At three a.m. I went to the window and watched Paris. A couple walked home. One of the homeless guys staggered past with a piece of cardboard. He was singing to himself.

At four I composed a speech for Madame Christophe. How much would she already know? At five I wondered whether Mackenzie had been right and that clairvoyants had a code of ethics. Maybe she wasn't allowed to look into my future until I asked her? Even then, would she tell me anything bad? At six I took up the hem of Babette's tunic. I really needed an iron, but I folded the fabric as firmly as I could and pressed it down with the flat of my hand. It was a pity she didn't have a hat. At seven I looked at Paris waking up. At eight I did all the yoga poses I could remember from when Ami and I had a crush on the instructor at the local aquatic centre. I tried to breathe the way he had taught us.

At nine I texted Hugo. *Please ring me. Please.* At nine-thirty I went down to breakfast. Even though it was late, Madame Christophe was there reading a magazine she put down as soon as she saw me. 'I have been thinking of your education,' she said, as though that was the most natural thing in the world to occupy her thoughts. 'I understand it seems like the plan of a featherbrain, but I applaud your decision.'

'My decision?'

'But yes, the decision to go to England. It is excellent timing as the usual occupant of your apartment returns to Paris early. There was an incident with some regrettable seafood. It made the vacation less joyful than anticipated.'

'I hadn't decided,' I said, plopping Babette on my lap as though she were Napoléon. Madame Christophe was kicking me out?

'Such a beautiful doll. You made her clothes yourself? You have talents you should bring into the light more often. Of course, you have decided.' She arched one eyebrow at me. 'Have you not?'

'Not exactly.' I was breathless. 'Hugo and I – I haven't heard from him.'

'But England, it would not just be for Hugo. It would be for you, also. An opportunity to see more, to continue this voyage of life.'

'Well, yes. It would.'

'I can refund the rent for the next few weeks. This is no trouble at all.' Madame Christophe smiled and placed her hand on my arm. The rings on her fingers glinted gold and glittered with small precious stones.

'Thank you, Madame. That is kind.'

'Paris will always be here. For the haute couture it is irreplaceable. I think you will learn more about yourself in England. When Destiny elbows you, it is wise to listen.'

'But is Destiny elbowing me?' I asked. 'Is it Destiny or is it just being irresponsible? I'm ditching my plans, Madame Christophe. I'm wasting money and time on a wisp of a dream, aren't I?'

'You are choosing the life you wish to pursue, are you not?'

'Do I have that choice?'

'Who else but you has it? You cannot do always what your mother expects. You cannot do always as your teacher tells you. Or a boyfriend. Or a husband. You must decide for yourself, Lisette, what is best for you. As for the money, pouf!' She pretended to blow it away in a disdainful puff. 'The money, it comes. It goes. If it helps, try to hear your father's voice inside your head. What would he have advised?'

'You just told me I shouldn't do what other people tell me!'

'But if you are going to listen to other people, listen to them all. Assemble the arguments. Then make your own decision. Of course, if you decide to stay in Paris, I can find you another arrangement. That is no problem. But I do not think this is really what you want.'

I put my hands over my face. It was too hard. As soon as I thought that, I wondered why it was hard. Was there something wrong with me? People crossed the Channel all the time. They surrendered plane tickets or paid to change them. It happened. I wanted to see England. I wanted to see Wales, where my father had decided to live and where he had died. It would be best to see it with Hugo – but I could decide to go on my own. Even if I didn't see Hugo again in Paris, even if he didn't return my texts, maybe when I got to England he'd realise we were worth a second chance. In the meantime, no one had died.

'I have to ring him,' I said, 'and explain everything.' But Madame Christophe had turned back to her magazine as if she had known all along what I was going to do.

When I called Hugo, heart pounding, clutching Babette in my free hand, a strange voice answered the phone. It was a woman's voice, speaking French. She was not Maxine.

I switched to French. I explained it was important I speak to Hugo. That was simply not possible, the voice answered. Hugo was unable to take calls. Who was she? I asked her straight out.

'I am a friend of the family,' she said. Family friends weren't supposed to sound sexy. 'And who are you?' She was amused.

I considered the question. Who was I? It was difficult to know who I was in relation to Hugo anymore. Did I have any claim on his affection or was he now comforting himself with this 'family friend'? In the end I settled for simply saying my name.

'I shall tell him you called,' she promised, but I didn't believe she would. 'He is currently out of reach.'

What did that even mean? I thanked her through gritted teeth and hung up. 'I don't care,' I lied to Babette, 'I really don't care. I'm going anyway. Madame Christophe's right – Destiny has elbowed me. *We're* going,' I amended, wondering how I was going to pack the doll.

Methodically I made the arrangements. I rang the airline and waited on hold. I explained to the bored staff that I needed to change my ticket and that, yes, I did understand the cost involved but I didn't care. I left Hugo out of the conversation – I didn't want them thinking I was the victim of another holiday romance. I told them instead about my father's wife and how we'd made contact. In the end I settled on a reduced refund. I didn't book a return flight. I could do that anytime.

I booked a rail ticket on the Eurostar. One way. It was a seat that was surrounded by empty seats. There was still a chance. Maybe there was still a chance.

When I'd done it all, I rang Maxine. As soon as she answered I said I knew I'd hurt Hugo but to please not hang up on me, and told her that I was going after all, that I had been unable to contact Hugo but wondered if someone could possibly give him my ticket information? Her tone was courteous but cool. I babbled out the train time and my seat number. 'Please, Maxine, tell him I'm going to England. I've made more time for us.'

She said she would pass this message on. I believed her. Before she hung up, she wished me good luck. 'Bonne chance,' she said and her voice sounded warm and kind. I googled the weather in London. I checked out the Victoria and Albert website and then, for good measure, I finally put my father's name in Google. It immediately came up with a dozen hits. He seemed quite well-represented in regional galleries. That made me feel better.

Then I went downstairs to tell Madame Christophe everything that I'd achieved.

She was not alone. Fabienne was seated in the client's chair in the shop. There were no cards spread out; instead there were teacups and the familiar scent of Madame Christophe's linden tea.

'Ah, Lisette.' Fabienne half rose and I obediently kissed her on both cheeks. 'You disappear, too. They all come and go, these students. I will have a whole new class soon. Such is the job. I begin again. I correct all their accents. I correct all their attitudes. I tell them about Paris, art and life.'

'You are wonderful,' Madame Christophe clucked and at the same time shot me an unmistakable prompt.

'Absolutely,' I said. 'I am very grateful.'

'When you return to Australia where they learn nothing, you will need to practise with someone very French,' Fabienne said. 'If you return to Australia. Otherwise you will sound ugly again. Now, I must go. I have seen these shoes, oh là là, they make me wish to – how do you say it in English? When your heart, it . . .' She made a funny jerky gesture with her hand.

'Skips?' I guessed wildly.

'Perfect,' Fabienne purred. 'Bon voyage, Lisette. Bonne chance!'

How did she know I'd need good luck?

'So, you rang him?' Madame Christophe turned her attention to me.

'I didn't speak to him. There was a woman. A "family friend". But I can go anyway.'

Madame Christophe removed a deck of cards from the desk drawer and began to shuffle them. 'You can,' she agreed. 'You have a train ticket?'

'I have,' I said, and felt unexpectedly proud of myself. 'I leave on Saturday.'

Madame Christophe cut the cards and showed me the

images. On one side was the Two of Cups and on the other The Fool. She laughed. 'The cards are always correct,' she said, 'see, both are true. The Two of Cups, minor arcana of the Lovers and the Fool – look how he dances, so close to the edge with his little dog.'

The Fool was not reassuring. 'What does it mean?'

'Life,' Madame Christophe said cryptically, and slapped the pack together again. 'That is all that it means, Lisette.'

'That's not very helpful.'

'Lisette, it is absolutely helpful! It is the most helpful advice the cards can give.'

'I don't even have a dog,' I said, clutching Napoléon as though he would make all the difference.

Madame Christophe rolled her eyes. 'A dog is not what you need to catch the train.'

'Do you think I'll see him again?' I asked her.

'I think you will find what is necessary to you,' Madame Christophe said. 'And, of course, he must do the same.'

Was he necessary to me? Was I necessary to him? I thought of his smile, which made two little creases around his mouth, and expressive eyes. I remembered the way his trousers always hung off his hips, rather than his waist, the fraying cuffs and collar points. I remembered us lying together in my bed, arms wrapped around each other and the heat rising. We'd been on the way to becoming necessary to each other. I just hoped we hadn't blown it.

Chapter
27

EVEN MORE RULES

Pack so that if your suitcase is checked by customs, you're not embarrassed when your oldest knickers and bra fall out on the airport floor. Who told me that? Who cares what falls on the airport floor, so long as it's legal? And I've nothing better to do. If I pack beautifully, he'll text me.

It was my last proper day in Paris. Packing made me think about how Mum had tried to help me pack when I was leaving Melbourne. I'd held her off. I'd shouted, 'I'm doing it my way! I'm not a baby.' I was sorry I'd been so mean. Would she see my actions as a betrayal? Would she think I was turning out like my father? Was that such a bad thing? I thought of Sarah and her bouncing dreads. They'd had chooks together. She had called him her soulmate. I was never going to *be* my dad or my mum. I was myself, Lisette Rose Addams, and I was packing to go to England.

Somewhere at the beginning of packing, I recognised how precision had staved off Mum's anxiety and held fear at bay. Somewhere in the middle, I admired how my clothes sat in my suitcase, the shoulder seams resolute, the edges defined. At the end, I was surprised at how little Paris had physically weighed me down. Some new boots and clothes, a small espresso maker, a fish-eye camera, catalogues from exhibitions. Babette, of course – although she wasn't really mine. I wrapped my glass woman carefully in a T-shirt. She would always remind me now of meeting Hugo. I folded my canvas backpack into the suitcase. Everything I needed for the train would fit into my daisy handbag.

After some soul-searching I threw my Vivienne Westwood homage into the bin. The girl who had needed that skirt was gone. I would leave Paris in grown-up clothes. I wasn't forsaking Vivienne, but the next homage would be well-made! I texted Mackenzie to tell her my decision.

You go, girl! she replied. *One day I bet you find an authentic Westwood at some market! I'm so excited for you! We'll have bon voyage drinks with Goldie. I'm going to miss you, Lise, my Australian friend.*

I didn't Skype Mum but I sent her an email. I told her I was going to England and that I knew it wouldn't make sense to her and that she'd worry but that Madame Christophe had encouraged me. I figured Madame Christophe would smooth things over with Mum and I knew how much Mum respected her clairvoyant. I said that it wasn't all about Hugo. I was going to Wales, to meet Sarah and see my father's world.

I confessed that I wasn't even sure that Hugo wanted to see me again. I told her how much I loved her. I told her I missed her and that I was sorry we had parted on such bad terms. I told her Vietnam sounded exciting and asked her to give my love to Ami and Vinh.

I Skyped Ami.

'I'm doing it,' I told her.

'I knew you would,' she said. Her fingernails were dark green. She waggled them at me in case I hadn't noticed.

'I threw away my kilt,' I said.

'Good. I never did think it worked. Hey – thanks for the stay-ups!' She lifted one leg up so I could see she was wearing the stockings I'd sent. 'They're fabulous. When you get to London, send me a policeman, yeah? Or a tall Irish guy. Talk me up to one of Hugo's friends.'

'I don't know whether I'm seeing him again,' I said, then I told her the whole story.

'But you're still going?'

'Yes. I mean, I'm still hoping to hear from him, obviously, but I'm going even if I don't. I want to see the Victoria and Albert.'

'So, you'll phone him when you get there?'

'If I haven't heard from him before, yes. I guess that's what I'll do.'

'You've got a place to stay?' Ami was sounding more and more like my mother.

'I've looked up some places. I'll find a hostel.' I said it as though I always set off with no fixed destination in mind.

I pretended to be nonchalant. 'It's the United Kingdom, after all, not the Gobi Desert. I like the nail polish.'

'It matches my uniform – I'm one of Vinh's minions. Hey, he's talking about taking Sally to Vietnam. He's started a Pinterest board.'

'That's so weird.'

'That he's taking Sally to Vietnam? Why is that strange? They'll have a ball.'

'I knew *that* – once Mum mentioned fabric! No, that he's got a Pinterest board!'

'Vinh moves with the times. Or that's what he thinks. He still isn't on Instagram. I have to set that up for the business.'

'I miss you,' I said.

'I miss you too, but the way I'm earning, I'll be over there before you can say Doctor Who. So long as I pass economics.'

Mackenzie texted me and we met up with Goldie at the Scottish bar we'd made our local.

'I can't believe you're doing this,' Mackenzie said, raising her glass to clink with us.

'Yes, bon voyage, Lisette.' Goldie chinked her glass. 'Love that shirt! Did you do the sales?'

'I wanted something different,' I said.

'You're different,' Mackenzie said. 'Don't you think, Goldie?'

'Am I? What do you mean?'

'You're more solid,' she said eventually, 'like, if I had painted you in that first class, I'd have chosen watercolours or pastels, you know? Back then it was as though you were in dress-up clothes, trying to be bold. You've moved from a sketch to a painting.'

'That's so American,' Goldie complained.

'It's so Canadian.' Mackenzie rolled her eyes. 'America doesn't have a monopoly on pop psychology.'

'Really? That surprises me.' Goldie laughed and clinked our glasses again. 'To friendship across the seas.'

'That's so old-fashioned,' Mackenzie said, 'but I guess you're not a brash new Canadian.'

'Exactly. Where I come from, we give bon voyage presents. Lise, these are for you.' She poured a small glass bead necklace into my cupped hand. 'I know we'll keep in touch, but I wanted to give you something you'd remember me by.'

'They are beautiful,' I said and held the necklace up so Mackenzie could see how each bead was subtly different – the blues and greens shifting shades like an ocean. Mackenzie did the clasp up for me and we all admired how they looked with my new shirt.

'I brought something, too,' Mackenzie said shyly. 'It's not as beautiful as Goldie's present but – anyway. I don't want to talk about it. I just want you to have it.' She slid a large envelope into my hand. 'I would have framed it but I was worried about the weight. It's fixed and everything, so it won't smudge. Just keep it as flat as you can.'

I opened the envelope and carefully took out something that was sandwiched between two thick pieces of card. It was a sketch portrait of me. Mackenzie must have done it in French class because my notebook was in front of me and my left hand was holding a pencil to my mouth. The sketch, hasty though it was, caught me exactly, leaning forward, slightly anxious with my too-broad mouth open and my eyes wide and steady.

I looked from Mackenzie to Goldie and back again. 'You have been – no, you *are* – the best friends. I will miss you so much. Paris would not have been half so wonderful without you.'

It was after midnight when I crawled up the five flights to my apartment. It was no longer mine, I thought, in a wash of sadness as I turned the key. It was no longer *my* apartment. I had packed and by tomorrow morning, every last reminder of me would be erased. There was still no word from Hugo – perhaps he had also erased me. I kicked the phone under my bed. Stupid, silent thing.

Chapter

28

There are two quintessential French items of clothing –
sunglasses and a scarf. They are practical and stylish.
You can hide unwashed hair in a scarf and tear-red eyes
behind dark glasses. If only I'd bought vintage sunglasses.

I walked down the stairs slowly the next morning. It was my last breakfast with Madame Christophe. I was sad, anxious and a little hungover. I gave her the scented candle I'd bought for her, along with the card I'd made.

When we said goodbye, she pressed a tissue-wrapped envelope into my hand. 'One for you and one for your mother. A little piece of Paris.'

We kissed, not twice, but three times. I hugged Napoléon again. I'd find a new collar for him in England. 'Buy some food for the train,' were her last words. 'You'll need it – if not for the journey, over there. There will not be good cheese.'

I wasn't convinced that was true. But I wasn't going to argue with Madame Christophe, so I bought the Frenchiest cheese I could – a pyramid of the goat's cheese I'd bought when I was first here. Now they smiled at me in the cheese shop. I was the Australienne.

I gave some of my last euros to the beggar with the two gleaming dogs.

'I'm going to London,' I told him.

'You should stick around Paris and find a Frenchman,' he said. 'But you can't tell a woman anything.' He raised a toast for me with his half bottle of wine.

I was early, of course. I half-expected Hugo to walk onto the platform, all his disappointment dissolving at the sight of me. For all I knew he could already be back in Yorkshire. Or he could have changed his plans entirely and be staying on in Paris. Maybe the 'family friend' had lent him money and he was buying more for the shop? I closed my eyes and imagined him loping towards me, his duffel bag banging at his side. He'd sweep me up, we'd kiss, just like the lovers in the Doisneau photograph, and our lives would be perfect.

I bought a French *Vogue* and a bottle of water at the station with my very last euros and then wished I'd kept enough for a coffee. The *Vogue* made me feel like a proper international traveller but I couldn't settle down enough to read it. I went through the customs check. I walked up and down. I sat for a while, holding my phone as though I could summon a text from Hugo through willpower alone. I opened up Madame Christophe's present. There were two silk scarves. My mother's was very chic with dark and light roses. Mine was vintage and decorated with line drawings of Paris life. It went perfectly with my new shirt. I draped it around my neck for luck. I flipped through *Vogue* again but I still couldn't read a word. I thought I might be sick. I found a toilet and stared at my reflection while my nausea settled. I applied more eyeliner. I brushed my hair. I went back to the seats.

My phone pinged and my hands shook as I checked it. It was only Mackenzie. Not *only*, I corrected myself. That wasn't fair. It was a text from my friend Mackenzie. It was a bunch of kisses and a big hug and a heart. The next ping was Goldie with an almost identical message. After that the phone was silent and even its clock didn't seem to work. Time was passing too slowly.

Then it sped through three-quarters of an hour and there was an announcement telling us the train was ready to board. I tried to swallow the fear rising in my throat but it was as impossible as swallowing stones. This was it. I was going by myself.

I yanked my suitcase along the platform behind some Americans who were each pulling a huge bag. At least I could put mine on the rack without help. Which was a good thing, because there was no one to help me. I wiped the tears away. All the recently applied eyeliner smudged on the back of my hand. A few of the passengers looked at me pityingly. Holiday romance. Broken heart. It happens. I reached my seat and sat down. Babette poked out from my handbag. I took her out and put her on my lap. I didn't care that I resembled some kind of mad girl. Babette wasn't a doll. She was an antique.

She was all that I had left of Hugo. I smudged away more tears and opened *Vogue* once more and forced myself to read.

Ironically the team from French *Vogue* had gone to London. Of course they had. There were shots of models posed beside a canal, wearing Vivienne. The photographs blurred. I rubbed my eyes. The canal was in Camden. Yeah, that figured. I flipped past the London shoot and started to read an interview with Vivienne instead. I made myself read slowly, thinking about each word and the construction of each sentence. It was strangely like folding clothes.

'Do you mind if I join you?' His voice. His dimples just showing as he looked down at me.

My mouth was too dry to speak.

'Does she have a ticket?' He gestured at Babette.

I just shook my head. I could feel tears forming in my eyes.

'I thought we'd got rid of 'im,' Babette whinged.

'I never wanted that,' I told her, my eyes not leaving Hugo's face. 'I love him.'

The tray table was in the way but I reached up, Hugo bent down and we hugged as though we'd never let go, but of course we had to breathe, so we did let go. Or almost. I kept hold of the edge of his jacket. I wanted to make sure I wasn't dreaming or imagining it all.

'I'm sorry,' Hugo said, 'I shouldn't have walked away. I was so . . . confused. And then Maude told me you'd rung my phone, which I'd made her hold on to so I didn't contact you. I didn't know what else I could say except come with me, please, and you'd made it so clear—'

'Who's Maude?' I asked. My voice was muffled in his jacket.

'Unc's old flame. The one I was staying with.'

'She sounded young.'

'Maude? She's about – I don't know? Fifty? It's hard to tell. She's well-preserved. Oh Lisette, you're here.'

'I thought you might be . . . that there might be something between you two.'

'Between us? You're kidding!'

'It was just that Edouard said something about distinguished clients. Remember?'

'Oh, that's Edouard. He's French. I'm English. Hey, I'm chuffed you were jealous!'

'You never called!'

'I was with Max's brother, in Rouen. He's a therapist, but he was useless. We got drunk together. You should have been there. They lit up the cathedral with a light show of Impressionist paintings. It was beautiful but I could only think about missing you.'

'I rang Max.'

'I know. She rang her brother.'

'You still didn't call me.'

'I should have. I wanted to, but I didn't know what to say. I just couldn't even think by then. I'd been up for about twenty-four hours. I shouldn't have drunk so much. Lucien told me to just book the ticket. Sort it out later.'

'Some therapist!'

'Actually he's a teacher. But you know – little kids, hopeless blokes. It's all the same, right? This morning I looked for a cafe with an English breakfast. Stupid thing to do – I nearly missed the train. I just managed to grab a baguette.'

'I bought cheese,' I said. 'It's in my handbag.' Had he heard me tell him I loved him? He hadn't said anything. I swallowed. I couldn't say it again. I just couldn't.

'See – we're perfect together.' Hugo took my hand.

He wasn't going to tell me he loved me? I shook my head. My mouth was dry again. I stared out of the train window.

'I'm sorry,' Hugo said. 'I've tried to tell you how sorry I am. I behaved badly. Lisette! Look at me. What have I done? What's wrong?'

I couldn't tell him. There was no way I could say anything. Each second dragged past.

'Okay,' Hugo said, 'let me tell you a story. There was once a girl who left a little glass woman on a bench in the Place des Vosges. She had sad eyes. The next time I saw her she told me my clothes needed mending, but not in those exact words. Then I ran into her again and she bargained like an expert. I don't know when exactly I fell in love with her, but each time I saw her, I was a little more smitten.' He took my hand and held it against his heart. I slipped my finger through the gap in his buttons. His skin was warm. 'I asked her to come home with me and she wouldn't. I was selfish – but I loved her. I love her.'

I found my voice. 'There are rules, you know. If you have a plane ticket you use it. You have to be sensible. If you break them – well, my father did. He broke the rules. I thought he'd broken my mother, except now I know he didn't. '

'We'll be okay,' Hugo said, settling his arm around me. 'We won't break each other, Lise. We're careful people who know how to live with fragile things.' He lifted my hand to his mouth and kissed my knuckles.

This was it, I thought as the train rushed away from Paris. What had Madame Christophe said about the tarot cards she had cut? That it was just life.

Mysterious, foolish, wonderful life.

Retro singlet

Leather jacket

Patched jeans

Hoops

Red lippie

Skull scarf

Tote bag

Clutch purse

Boots

Sunglasses

Vintage Chanel

Silk scarf

Little black
dress

Totally
impractical shoes

Je t'aime

Airport snack

Author's Note

This book would never have been written had I not been the recipient of an Australia Council for the Arts three-month residency at the Cité Internationale des Arts, a huge complex of artists' studios in the Marais. To have three months free to write, wander and *live* in Paris was extraordinary.

My love affair with France began when I first read the novels of Colette as a young adolescent. It was Colette who inspired me to take up private French lessons with Madame Campbell-Brown, then a woman in her mid-seventies, who had been a lecturer at the University of Queensland and was 'une dame formidable'. Once a week I turned up to her home in Spring Hill, Brisbane, clutching my copy of *Le Petit Prince* and an ancient French grammar book. She despaired because I had not learnt Latin, but we persevered nonetheless.

Years later I decided to brush up my French language skills and attended the Alliance Française in Melbourne. The French grammar book was far more modern but the lessons catapulted me back to Madame Campbell-Brown's old Queenslander, the jasmine blooming in two enormous pots beside the front door and the huge map of Paris that took up one wall of her study. I remembered reading novel after novel by Colette, immersed in her sensual world in an almost trance-like state.

I applied for the residency, still thinking of Colette, and was amazed and delighted, months later, to be standing in the place Colette. I spent a good amount of the time I was in Paris saying, over and over again, 'Paris! Shakespeare and Company! The Métro!'

The NYU Writers in Paris program was on, so there were weekly readings by poets and novelists at Shakespeare and Company. I'd walk across the Seine (the Seine!) and hear some wonderful work and then stroll back to my studio apartment fuelled with words.

I gave many of my own experiences to Lisette. Like her, I saw the haute couture exhibition, bought a camera (a La Sardina) to take black-and-white photographs with and attended the French classes at the Cité. I got lost countless times as I've never been good with maps. I went to the flea market at the Porte de Vanves and, yes, was cursed by a woman in the Métro with two cringing dogs. Unfortunately, Madame Christophe is entirely a fictional character, so there was no smudging ritual to lift my curse.

I can remember the exact moment I thought of Madame Christophe. The night before I had seen a small bookshop up near the rue des Rosiers and tucked in one corner of the window was an advertisement for tarot readings. The next morning, I thought – that's what I need – a clairvoyant! Enter Madame Christophe with her little dog and sharp wisdom. The novel started to slowly come together.

My husband joined me in my final two weeks in Paris and together we visited Versailles and Rouen before heading over to the UK. Hugo was created after a trip to a London flea market and his appearance changed the direction of the novel.

I am so grateful to the Australian Council for the Arts for the opportunity to have three unfettered months' writing time – and in Paris (Paris!). It was an inspiring and unforgettable summer. I am also grateful to my family who encouraged me to study French again, and who so actively supported my decision to apply for a residency.

Thanks to Sophie Splatt for her close editing and to Erica Wagner for her unwavering belief in Lisette. Thanks, too, to my daughter, Helen, who years ago asked me to write her a 'summer' book.

About the Author

First published as a poet, Catherine Bateson has twice won the CBCA Book of the Year for Younger Readers, and been awarded the Queensland Premier's Award, Younger Readers. She's written more than a dozen novels for young adults and younger readers, including *Star*, *Magenta McPhee* and *His Name in Fire*.